THE GATES OF DARK DEATH

Alan Reynolds

Fisher King Publishing

The Gates Of Dark Death

PRINT ISBN 978-1-916776-68-5
DIGITAL ISBN 978-1-916776-69-2

Published by Fisher King Publishing
www.fisherkingpublishing.co.uk

Also by Alan Reynolds

Arthur's War
Breaking The Bank
Exfil
Flying With Kites
Pendle Cottage
Smoke Screen
Taskers End
The Baker's Story
The Coat
The Favour
The Last Poppy
The Sixth Pillar
The Tinker
Trent Island
Twelve
Uncertain Times
Valley Of The Serpent

It is easy to go down into Hell; night and day, the gates of dark Death stand wide; but to climb back again, to retrace one's steps to the upper air - there's the rub, the task.

Virgil

Acknowledgements

Many hours of research went into the writing of this book, and I would like to thank all those who have written articles that helped in the creation of this story, including Ruth Goodman and her book 'How To Be A Tudor', which was a valuable source of information on life in Tudor times.

I would like to add a special thanks to Stefanie Bischof and Tanja Kayser from the City of Cologne Historical Archives for the significant information they gave me, including street maps of the city in the early 1500's. It enabled me to add richness to the narrative.

As always, a huge thanks to Rick Armstrong for his unstinting support, guidance, and friendship, also, to Samantha Richardson, Rachel Topping and all the team at Fisher King Publishing. My thanks also to Jane Wheater for editorial and proof-reading support.

Dedicated to my family, friends, and the regular readers who have supported me in my writing –

your encouragement has been inspirational.

Much love

Preface

Table showing the times of the peeling of bells
by Catholic Monasteries 1530

Bells	Equinox (March/Sept)	Midwinter	Midsummer
Matins	5:00 a.m.	6:40 a.m.	2:30 a.m.
Prime	6:00 a.m.	8:00 a.m.	3:40 a.m.
Terce	8:30 a.m.	9:40 a.m.	7:00 a.m.
Sext	12:30 p.m.	12:20 p.m.	12:20 p.m.
None	2:30 p.m.	1:40 p.m.	3:00 p.m.
Vespers	5:00 p.m.	3:00 p.m.	7:00 p.m.
(Sunset)	(6:00 p.m.)	(3:50 p.m.)	(8:20 p.m.)
Compline	7-8:00 p.m.	5-6:00 p.m.	9:30 p.m.

16th Century drawing of The Tower of London

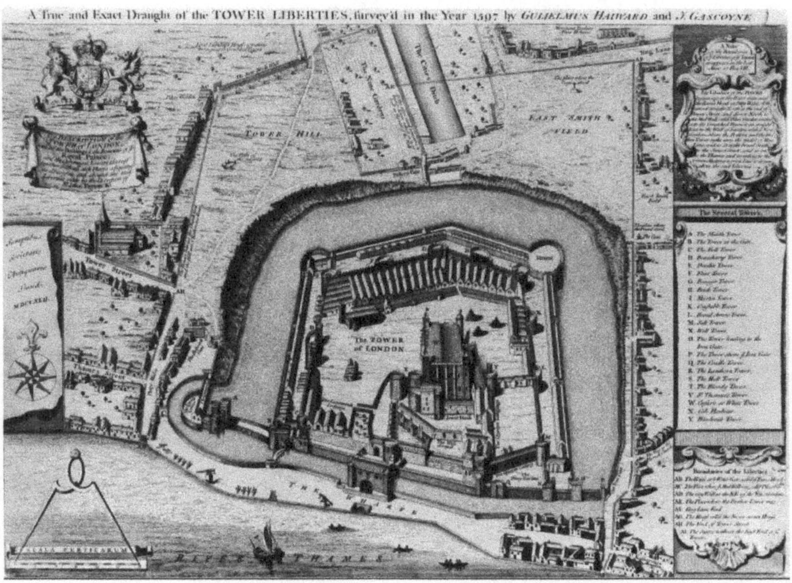

Chapter One

August 1531, the cobbles of Newgate glistened following a sharp shower. The man kept in the shadows under the overhangs of the black and white houses that predominated the area, walking with purpose. A liquid of some sort cascaded from the first floor and splashed in the gutter. The contents of someone's piss-pot.

The man ignored the distraction. Bitter smells of rotting vegetables and excrement were as common as unnoticeable. He continued his quest; his dark eyes missed nothing. Tall, lank-long hair, a scar on his right cheek, and bearded - shaving was the privilege of the gentry, and would be considered effeminate by lower classes. He was dressed modestly in worker's clothes – shirt, breeches, boots, his hat pulled down disguising his features.

He reached the busy Carter Lane market and walked unnoticed past the various stalls. Vendors, with their carts and roughly-made wooden tables, were extolling their wares to anyone who would listen. The man barged his way through the modest crowd queuing to be served, causing annoyance from those disturbed by his aggression. He turned right towards the river, a mile or so hence. He knew the area like the back of his hand and where the likely pickings were. He stopped for a moment and checked his bearings, looking this way and that. His senses were on high alert, his shoulders rose and fell in tune with his breathing, primed and ready for action.

He walked on, ten minutes or so, then stopped again - Paternoster Row, a busy thoroughfare. The weather was hot and humid; beads of sweat fell from his brow into his eyes, momentarily obscuring his vision. He wiped away the offending moisture with the back of his hand. He could see several merchants standing outside one of the many taverns discussing things that merchants discuss. The man stayed in the lee of the houses on the opposite side of the road and watched, and waited. Timing would be critical.

There was one standing on his own, some yards away from the group, seemingly engrossed in a parchment. He was the prey the man had decided. He was dressed in the finery of wealth, feathered hat, a white ruff, a jacket that hung to mid-thigh, fine breeches, and shoes.

The hunter checked his surroundings. He would make his move – now!

He walked briskly across the road. The uneven cobbles and piles of horse manure made the traverse hazardous, but his eyes were firmly fixed on the prize.

The man removed his dagger from its sheath, then, in an instant, grabbed the merchant from behind. He wrestled him into an alleyway and onto the floor, placing the knife at his throat. The merchant had been taken completely by surprise, his eyes wide with fright.

"I'll take the money-belt, if you want to see another day."

The merchant lay prostrate and acquiescent in the fetid gutter. The money belt circumvented his portly frame. In a split second, the vagabond had cut the purse from its tethers, then took off.

It was over before the victim could cry help.

The merchant gradually regained his senses and crawled to the street.

"Stop! Thief!" he yelled at the top of his voice.

On-lookers turned and fled in horror, not wishing to become involved.

The merchant looked around but could not see the culprit. The felon was already running down one of the myriad of lanes that joined the road and was soon swallowed among the labouring residents.

The victim's merchant colleagues had been busy in debate and had not seen the incident, but turned on hearing his cries. They ran to him and helped him to his feet.

"Pray, Master Burton, what's happened?" asked the first to reach him.

"A cut-purse, he's taken my money, twenty crowns or more."

"Are you hurt?" enquired another.

"Nay, by the grace of God, the caitiff had a knife to my throat."

The remaining merchants immediately set up a hue and cry, shouting first up the street, then across, then down, calling out for witnesses. One of the merchants held up a gold angel from his purse and held it high. "This gold angel for anyone handing over the culprit," he called.

The street was now deserted.

"Come, Master Burton, let us see if we can find a sergeant."

The man had stopped running; he was far enough away from the scene of the crime to feel safe. He stopped in another anonymous alleyway, and, with his back to the street, took out the purse from inside his shirt. He weighed it in his hands; it felt heavy. He slowly tipped out the coinage into his palm. He couldn't believe his luck. Twenty gold crowns, three angels, and several smaller denominations, a year's wage and more for a clerk, never mind a labourer, who would be happy with half that.

John Wolfe, although calling himself a merchant, had made a living from petty felony, and was a wanted man in at least half of the twenty-five London wards. He felt secure on home territory in the shadow of the magnificent St. Paul's Church.

He made his way to his lodgings in a row of typically black and white timber-frame houses, the spaces between the wooden frames filled with wattle and daub. It was in one of the many anonymous side passageway between Carter Lane and Knight Rider Street. He had rented a meagre room, which served his purpose.

He pushed open the door to the dwelling and headed up the stairs to the room he called home. It smelt stale; he had yet to empty his bucket. He went to his bedding and moved the straw mattress to reveal the wooden floor, then lifted one of the floorboards and examined his haul from previous excursions. He took out the three gold angels from the merchant's purse and secreted the rest in the hiding place, before returning the floorboard to its rightful position.

He felt good; the adrenaline of the chase and subsequent robbery had given him renewed energy. He needed a release.

He was at least two miles from the scene of the earlier crime, but he was taking no chances. Among his belongings he had a leather bag, an expensive item, but a necessary accoutrement, containing a change of clothing.

He took off his shirt and breeches and replaced them with a tunic, belt, and green hose, the dress of a clerk. A black floppy cap completed his wardrobe.

He left his dwelling. He was hungry; his actions had given him an appetite and his first priority was get some food. He strode along the alleyway and exited on Carter Lane, then turned right and headed for his local hostelry. He entered another archway which opened out into a small courtyard strewn with straw. Wooden tables were set with benches either side. To his right, set back in a brick-built chamber, a pig was being roasted in front of a fire on iron spit dogs. On his left, hogsheads of ale were being attended by two women wearing smocks and wimples.

The sun burst through into the courtyard, which was surrounded on all sides by wooden dwellings, their black, timber frames warped into strange shapes by years of neglect. Glass windows were the privilege of wealth, most houses had square gaps in the walls to let in light, covered by cloth curtains soaked in linseed oil to discourage the flies. Some newer dwellings had wooden shutters which were more substantial.

One of the women spotted Wolfe.

"Good den, Master John, take a seat yonder, I'll bring you ale."

Only one other person was in the open-air tavern. He was slumped over a tankard with his head resting on the table. An empty wooden plate was next to him.

The woman filled a tankard and presented it to Wolfe.

"Will you be wanting food? I can do you some pottage, or you can have some pork. It's nearly ready?" She pointed to the spit; her tone was one of forthrightness.

The woman was of stern nature, matronly, with hair protruding from facial moles.

"Aye, happen, I'll take some meat from spit … and bread, enough to fill a hungry belly."

"Wait, Master John, I'll be there directly."

She walked over to the sleeping customer and shoved him hard in the back.

"Come on you candle-waster, get ye home."

The man groaned and looked up at the formidable serving woman.

"Go on, get off with you."

He slumped back to his slumbers.

Wolfe could see the impasse and intervened, grabbing the

man by the back of his collar and pulling him off his bench. He slumped on the floor and Wolfe aimed a kick at the man's midriff. He immediately spewed vomit across the courtyard.

Wolfe picked up the sot by the breeches and manoeuvred him into a standing position.

"Now be off with you before I land another."

The man mumbled something incoherent and staggered slowly towards the exit, swaying this way, and that.

"Thanks Master John, he's been on the tickle brain methinks."

"Aye, I'm sure you're right."

Wolfe sipped his ale, reflecting on his good fortune, considering his options. He was interrupted from his meanderings by the serving woman who presented Wolfe with a large pewter plate piled with meat from the roasting pig and hunks of bread.

"A feast fit for a king, Master John," said the woman, as she presented the meal to him.

Wolfe nodded, and picked up the first hunk of meat with his fingers and started to gorge, as if he hadn't eaten for some time.

"Hungry, I see, Master John. Take your time, there's plenty more if you need it."

The woman stood watching Wolfe for a moment. "Did you hear about the whoobub earlier?"

"I can't say I did," replied Wolfe, spraying bits of meat and bread from his mouth.

"Over Newgate way, some merchant got robbed. There was a hue and cry after the thief. They're offering an angel for information."

Wolfe looked up at the woman, wondering if it was some sort of test.

"Is that so? No, I can't say I've heard." He put another

mouthful of pork in his mouth. “An angel, you say. Father’s would sell their daughters for less.”

“Aye, and ev’ry guinea hen will be pointing fingers, you mark my words.”

“True, but who would believe a common whore?”

“There’s some that might.”

She looked at his plate which was now cleared of food. Wolfe finished the last of his tankard.

“Would you like another plateful before you take your leave, Master John?”

“That will suffice, Miriam. I have somewhere to go.”

“And where might that be?”

“Heading up Spitalfields way, Catherine Wheel Yard; there’s a cockpit anon after vespers.”

“You will lose your coat, Master Wolfe; gambling is for fools, you mark my words.”

“I’ll heed your words, Miriam.”

He handed the woman a groat. “That’s for the meal.” Then handed her another.

“What’s that for?” asked Miriam.

“Not pointing fingers.”

“Nay, Master John, I would never point fingers in your direction. I can’t afford to lose the custom.” She laughed.

Wolfe got up from the bench and nodded to his host.

“Mind you take care, Master John; there are cut-purses about.”

“Pay no mind, I’m more than a match for any varlet who would try their luck.”

He turned and headed through the archway to the adjoining street. A pony trap went by, the passenger a man of wealth judging by his clothes. Out of habit, Wolfe looked at him as a potential victim, but, now, with his present financial situation, he could buy his own pony and trap; now there was a thought.

He quickened his stride. The bells sounded from a nearby monastery, St Martin's le Grand, in Fleet Street – Vespers.

He reached Spitalfields and found Catherine Wheel Yard. It was a poor area with signs of poverty everywhere. Beggars and vagrants clad in lice-filled rags, lurked in the shadows; their beady eyes watchful and wary. Wolfe kept close attention to his money-belt. He entered another yard behind a butchery. The smell of stale meat lingered in the passageway which lead to an open yard. Any morsel of discarded food would have been devoured by vermin or the homeless. Water dripped from the roof; a rat scurried down the margins.

There were benches placed around a circular 'pit' about six feet across which was covered in sawdust. About thirty men were surrounding the area all trying to get a clear view of the fighting fowls. Screaming and shouting, hoots and cries, could be heard echoing off the surrounding dwellings.

Two large, evil-looking men, with bushy beards and menacing dispositions, were acting as gate keepers, and stood across Wolfe's path.

"A groat to pass," said the first, whose left ear was missing.

Wolfe reached in his pocket, took out a coin and handed it to the ogre. He stared at the coin with suspicion, then stood to one side allowing Wolfe to pass.

Crammed in on four sides, the atmosphere was stifling in the early evening heat; the sun was setting, but the day was still inflicting its wrath on the locale.

Wolfe watched as a sorry owner removed a dead cockerel from the blood-spattered sawdust, while two more hopefuls were waiting for the next fight.

There was much raucousness as men queued to receive

their winnings from a bag-man who had brought his own bodyguard, another brute of a man.

Wolfe made his way to the front and watched as two cocks were raised by their tail feathers to the onlooking crowd. He made his choice and approached the bag-man and handed him a shilling. The bodyguard watched with interest. There were no books or paper, the bag-man would remember the faces, the amounts wagered, and on which bird. There were no odds, just an agreed amount for the winning bet. The evil-looking watchman would ensure there were no disputes.

The fight started to a tumultuous roar. Sticks were waved; hats were waved. Sweat poured off the watching throng as the excitement grew. The birds pecked and clawed each other until one of them collapsed. There was a man in a large floppy hat acting as a referee. He picked up the prostrate bird and dropped it to the ground. There was no movement, and the surviving bird was declared the winner.

Wolfe smiled as he walked to the bag-man to collect his winnings.

As dusk started to fall, so the last fight was called. The area was becoming dim and, with darkness, there lurked more dangers. Men started to drift away having had their share of excitement for the day. Some with sufficient winnings for a visit to a tavern; others, considering an explanation to their wives for the loss of coin.

Wolfe was happy; today had been a good day. His winnings were not great, but beating the bag-man was always a cause for rejoicing. He would celebrate in an alehouse on his journey back to his dwelling.

A few streets away, next to a company of candle-makers, was Wolfe's most-frequented ale-house. The nauseating smell of fat lingered in the chandler's doorway. He reached the establishment, the entry ceiling low enough to require a stoop. Inside, candles of varying sizes were set at regular intervals in iron chandeliers providing an ethereal light-source. Faces were not easily recognised. Shapes sat at bench-tables, supping from tankards. There was a low hum of discourse.

Wolfe found a table and was approached by a lithesome serving wench. "What will be your favour, sir?"

He looked at the girl, no more than nineteen, an agreeable sight in the flickering light from the table candle.

"A tankard of ale, if you will."

"Aye, sir."

The maid walked towards a row of six hogsheads of ale, chose the nearest one, took an empty pewter tankard from an adjoining shelf, and started filling it.

Wolfe who had found a better seat in a corner, away from the middle area where most clients were seated in conversation. Wolfe was not looking for male company. The girl took a moment to find him.

"Your ale, sir," replied the girl.

Her face was illuminated as she stooped near one of the candles. A freshness, suggesting she was not from the city; her bodice gaped as she bent to serve Wolfe.

"I've not seen you here before," said Wolfe as he sipped from the tankard. "What's your name?"

"Alice, sir, Alice Tankerville."

"And where are you from, Alice?"

"Mile End, sir."

"And, pray, what brings you into the city?"

"Work, sir, my mother and father were recently lost to the sweating fever."

"And money is short?"

"Aye, that it is, sir."

Wolfe felt inside his pocket and took out a coin.

"Oh, no sir, that is too much. The ale is but a farthing."

"I'll gladly pay that and more for your company." He handed her a groat.

The girl looked down demurely. "You make me fair redden with your flattery, sir."

"Not so, young Alice. I'm in need of some company tonight. What say you lay down your apron and sit with me a while?"

"Why, sir, I am working, how can I do such?"

"I will pay your master, fetch him to me."

Alice left and came back a few minutes later with a weaselly-faced man with a prominent nose. He was ringing his fingers obsequiously.

His voice matched his demeanour, more a high-pitched whine. "Wench here says you want her services."

"Aye, I'll pay you for the evening; shall we say a groat?"

Wolfe felt in his pocket and took out another coin, part of his gambling winnings and flicked it onto the table where it rattled a few seconds before settling. The landlord's hands were swift as he scooped up the coin and put it in his pocket.

"Very well, you can have her; serving wenches are of no consequence. There'll be many ready to take her place."

The man left clutching his coin with a callous grin.

"Come sit, fair Alice. Take a sup … They call me John Wolfe."

She didn't respond as Wolfe handed her the tankard. Her hands seemed too small for the handle of the jug as she held it to her lips and drank.

"Thou hast lodgings near?"

Alice wiped her mouth with the back of her wrist. "No, sir."

"But where do you sleep?"

She looked down, her face wrinkled; there was a hint of

shame in her reply. "Where ere I can, sir. Last ev'n I was in sanctuary. The priest took pity on me."

"We can't have that; you are too fine a girl to be sleeping in sanctuary. I have lodgings and room enough for you."

"But sir, I couldn't possibly."

Wolf took out some loose change. He handed her a shilling. Alice's eyes lit up, then her face changed into one of disapproval.

"I'm no harlot, sir."

"If I thought you were, we would not be talking. Harlots 'round here are naught but pox-queens."

Alice smiled, demurely. "In which case, I will gladly accept."

Just then there was movement in the doorway. Three men appeared, adorned in finery, with hats and feathers; a lower-class man, judging by his clothes, was accompanying them. Identification was impossible at a distance, but for some reason, Wolfe was on his guard.

The leading man, Wolfe could see, was a sergeant-at-arms, complete with sword. He approached the weaselly landlord and handed him a parchment. There was a conversation and money changed hands in the landlord's favour.

The three men and their stooge started going from table to table, one holding a candle stick. They eventually reached Wolfe's table. Alice had moved closer to Wolfe, as a couple might do.

The sergeant lifted his candle, illuminating Wolfe's face, and the serf was called. "What say you?"

"There might be some resemblance; it is difficult to tell. I was far away."

"So you keep saying. Now is this or isn't this the man?"

"What be the issue, sergeant?" interrupted Wolfe.

"There was a cut-purse, this morning involving a large

sum of money."

"Where was this?"

"Newgate way, this gentleman saw the whole thing."

"Well, I've not been to Newgate for a while, and this morning I was hard at labour."

"Where would that be?"

"Steelyard Warfe."

"A merchant?"

"Aye, sometimes."

"You don't dress like a merchant."

"And how should a merchant be dressed when he is not at labour?"

Before the sergeant could answer, Alice leaned forward, displaying more from her gaping chemise. The light from the candle flickered creating patterns. She looked at the sergeant, and in an indignant fashion, addressed him.

"My husband is no thief, sir. Do you think I would not know on the pittance he gives me on which to feed us."

The sergeant looked at her and down at the distraction. He turned to Wolfe.

"A woman of spirit, sir. You have my condolences. Methinks you are punished enough. We will not disturb you further."

The sergeant and the three others walked away. There appeared to be a heated discussion between the lawman and the vagrant who had been produced by the sergeant as a witness. There would be no reward coin passing in his direction, the man-at-arms exclaimed, accusing him of being unreliable.

Wolfe turned to Alice. "Your intercession was most welcome, Mistress Alice."

"It's of no consequence, sir; I can see you are a God-fearing man, and of virtue."

"Ha, you flatter me too much. What say we retire? The hour is quite late. They have sounded the compline."

"Aye, that we should, Master Wolfe."

"You can call me John."

"John it is then."

"There is a bath house next to my lodgings; what say we make use of them?"

"Aye, John. I need to get my wares. I'll be but a minute."

The pair got up from their seat and headed for the exit. Candles flickered in the draught caused by the movement of their passing.

Wolfe waited by the door for Alice to retrieve her belongings. He noticed the parchment which the sergeant had given to the landlord was now hung on the door. It was headed, *'Most heinous crime.'* Then the narrative beneath.

'Reward of one guinea for the capture of the cut-purse who stole coin in Newgate Yard.'

It went on to describe the witness account and description of the assailant.

Like most of the alehouse customers, Wolfe was unable to make sense of the narrative; reading was the privilege of the educated clerical class and above, but he quickly realised it would be reference to the robbery. Word would soon get around, especially with the amount of coin on offer as a reward. He would avoid a return to the alehouse for the time being.

Alice returned from a back room carrying a small bundle tied in a blanket under her arm, her worldly goods and chattels. The pair left the tavern and walked back towards Wolfe's dwelling.

As was the custom, John walked on the outside, nearest the cobbles, offering Alice some protection from discarded chamber pot contents. Alice was keen to learn more about her adopted 'husband'.

"You have an accent, John, you are not from round here, I think."

"No, Kolener born, but have lived in London for some years."

"I don't know Kolener."

"It is in Germany; here it is called Cologne."

"You are clearly a travelled man."

"Only to Germany, when there is coin to be made."

"You really are a merchant, then?"

"Aye, of sorts."

"And when do you plan to return to Germany?"

"Soon, methinks. Maybe the next sailing."

Given the amount of interest in the cut-purse felony, Wolfe had already decided to leave the country for a while.

The couple arrived at the bath house adjoining Wolfe's dwelling. It was in darkness.

Alice looked at the building. "There's but no one about."

"Aye, they will open if I ask. I often bathe at this hour; it is a peaceful time."

Wolfe knocked loudly on the wooden door with his fist, then again when no-one answered. Eventually, there was a shuffling noise the other side of the door and it opened. A man of advancing years peered at the visitor.

"A bath, please, Robert. I have coin enough," said Wolfe, and presented the man with two groats.

"Very well, Master John, there is still hot water to be had; fire has not burned out."

The pair were ushered inside into a sparse room with four empty circular wooden tubs about three feet tall and slightly more in diameter.

"Would you like a drink, Master John, while I top up your bath?" enquired the bath-house owner.

"A tankard of ale would be welcome, Robert."

"And you, my dear, what, pray, you?"

"I will share Master John's."

The room was dim, lit only by candles placed on holders around the wall. There was one window with a cloth covering, it flapped slightly with a passing breeze; it was a warm night with little air.

The man returned to the room with the ale. There was a small waiting area with a table and two chairs. The landlord placed the tankard on the table, then left before appearing again carrying a pail with steam coming from the surface of the water within. He struggled with the weight and used both hands to carry the container.

He approached the nearest bath and started to fill it; it would take several journeys. Meanwhile, Alice and Wolfe shared the tankard.

When the bath was of sufficient depth, the man turned to John. "Would you like a second bath filling?"

"No, one will suffice," replied Alice, before Wolfe had chance to answer. "Do you have soap?"

"Aye, but it will require more coin. It is very dear."

John went to his pocket and pulled out a halfpenny. "That will cover it, Robert."

"Aye, that it will, Master John."

The man walked back to another room and returned carrying a candle in a holder. He handed Wolfe the bar of soap. It was perfumed, and not unpleasant.

"I will leave you to your bathing. I'm away to my bed. See the'selves out."

The man left the pair and closed the door.

"Undress, John, I will bathe you as I bathed my father."

Wolfe complied, climbed in, and sat down; the water was warm and soothing. Alice immediately picked up the soap and started to lather his back.

"You have nice hair, John," said Alice as she poured water over his flowing locks.

Wolfe started to relax.

"You best stand, John. Let me clean you properly."

Again Wolfe complied and Alice continued the bathing. With attention now centred on his manhood; it started to respond. Alice became particularly attentive.

"Why John, it seems you have needs. Let me bathe and I will see to them."

"I see you are not unfamiliar with a man's body."

"Nay, I would bathe my father frequently, and sometimes he would take advantage of me. He took my maidenhead."

"Why would a father do such a thing?" said Wolfe, looking at her disapprovingly.

"Why indeed? But I loved my father dearly and would not refuse such demands. It was naught but a small imposition for what he had done for me."

"That is love indeed," said Wolfe, as Alice continued the ablutions.

"You are done now, John. Let me bathe and I will see to your needs."

As John and Alice consummated their relationship, a clap of thunder echoed around the alleyways of inner London. Lightening illuminated the room through the cloth-covered window. The curtain swayed more vigorously. Rain was now audible, splashing down the sloping roofs and into the rubbish-strewn streets.

Half an hour later, Wolfe and Alice left the bath house and turned into the alleyway to Wolfe's lodgings. Sheltered by the overhangs of the dwellings, the couple were able to keep away from the worst of the torrents, but the gutters were awash with all manner of detritus running in whichever direction led downhill.

They reached Wolfe's dwelling and entered, then climbed the stairs in front of them. They reached his modest room. John opened the door and led Alice inside. The smell of the unemptied bucket and sweat hung in the air. The noise of the rain pattering on the roof negated any conversation. There was another flash of lightening, followed quickly by a loud retort.

The room was in darkness. "Wait, I have a tinderbox. Let me light a candle," said John.

Alice was stood in the doorway.

There was a wooden table next to the door on which Wolfe kept a small tinderbox. He expertly used the fire-steel to induce a spark and the small tinder was soon alight. There were several candles next to it and Wolfe lit them in turn, bathing the room in a warm glow.

Alice looked around. "The room needs a woman's touch."

"Aye, of that I am sure," replied Wolfe.

Chapter Two

"My Lord, will you walk with me awhile? I have matters of most import I need to relate."

The corridor of Westminster Hall was draped with tapestries, giving relief to the carved wooden veneer. Sunlight streamed through the diamond-shaped casement windows, picking out dust particles in the air. The late summer temperature was making the passageway oppressive.

"Why, of course, William. What ails thee?" replied the Earl of Shrewsbury.

The Lord Steward moved alongside his younger protegee.

At forty-one, William Fitzwilliam was an experienced campaigner. He had been rewarded with the position of Treasurer of the Household following his naval activities where he had risen to the rank of admiral. Rugged features, with a Roman nose, he was dressed in a fine tunic, breeches, skull cap, and velvet hat, which covered his lengthy hair at the back. His eyes were attentive and alert. He epitomised his position of power and influence. He talked with his immediate superior with confidence rather than subservience.

"It's the King's coffers," replied the former navy man.

"Ha, I might have known. It is something I have been loathed to broach with His Majesty for fear of losing favour. He continues to be frivolous in his regard to financial matters."

"But what's to be done? We need to find money from somewhere," asked Fitzwilliam.

"His Majesty dismisses such an issue; he believes he can extract more from the monasteries."

"I'm not sure that will be soon enough. Have you spoken to the Lord Chancellor?"

"Hmm, I fear Thomas More's influence is in decline. It's Cromwell who has the King's ear, and he's consumed with the question of the Queen. Little else warrants his attention."

"Aye, I had heard such, but the question remains; we cannot continue financing His Majesty's extravagancies indefinitely."

They continued walking towards the open door which led to the grounds. The Lord Steward thought for a moment. "We need to look abroad, methinks."

"You mean raise taxes on our French lands?" enquired the Treasurer.

"It is a route worthy of consideration."

"Well said, my Lord, but on consideration, I do have a better idea."

"Pray tell, William."

"I have it on good authority, that our friends in The League have aligned themselves with the King with regard to his struggles with Rome."

"Indeed so; they, too, have issues with the Papacy."

"Aye, my Lord. It occurred to me they might look favourably on perchance a loan, or even a donation towards His Majesty's toils with His Holiness."

They left the confines of the interior and continued walking slowly along the rectangle outside, beside St Stephen's Chapel. Lord Shrewsbury was deep in thought considering the possible consequences of such an approach. He turned to his companion.

"This raises a significant question. What would they want in return … if we were to make such overtures?"

"Yes, my Lord, it is a consideration."

"A consideration, indeed. We could not commit His Majesty to any military alliance. Raising an army would be too costly and defeat the purpose."

"Would it not suffice for the King to give the League his gratitude?" asked the Treasurer.

"Ha, if only it would be so. Unfortunately not, and if we want to keep this transaction away from the King's ear, we cannot be involved in any trumpery."

"Aye, I agree, but I have put my mind to the issue and I do have a suggestion, my Lord."

The Lord Steward looked at his companion with impatience. "Then speak of it, William."

"I have the acquaintance of Georg Giese … "

"The Steelyard merchant?" interrupted Lord Shrewsbury.

"Aye, the very same; we met at a banquet most recently, a man of great influence … and integrity within Hansa; indeed he is now an Alderman's Deputy. Happen he might subscribe to an approach to the council on our behalf." Fitzwilliam was persuasive in his argument.

Lord Shrewsbury looked at his colleague with an inquisitive expression. "Do you think he would agree to such a venture?"

"One can but try, my Lord. One can but try," repeated Fitzwilliam.

"What do you suggest?"

"By your leave, my Lord, I will visit him anon and seek his thoughts."

"You wish to make such a journey?"

"Aye, my Lord; I will take a carriage. Tis but an hour hence."

His Lordship raised his eyebrows. "Very well, William, so be it, but you must take a man-at-arms. These are dangerous times."

"Aye, my Lord."

"Report to me directly when you have his mind."

The two men went their separate ways. The Lord Steward

returned to his offices; William Fitzgerald summoned a guard to arrange a carriage and escort for the three mile journey to the Steelyard wharf.

The Steelyard area of London had been the home to the Hanseatic League merchants for centuries and was one of their most important 'kontors' – the name given to the League's trading posts. The present site was gifted to the League as part of the Treaty of Utrecht in 1475. Relationships between England and the Hansa in previous years had not always been convivial. The Utrecht Treaty ended a five-year 'war' when ships of both sides were engaged in preventing trade by blockading, even boarding ships and confiscating goods.

It was a walled community, bordered on three sides by Thames Street, Cosins Lane, and All Hallows Lane, with the river providing the natural fourth boundary; guards, armed with swords, controlled the gates. Women were barred from entry. It occupied over an acre of land off the north bank of the Thames, just west of London Bridge. There, the merchants lived in a separate world from the rest of London, a mini, Germanic community. It was composed of around ninety buildings with various functions, not only storehouses for their cargo, but accommodation for the merchants, a guild hall with their own elected aldermen, multiple cloth halls, a wine-house and kitchens, as well as a wharf on the Thames. The Steelyard was governed by its own code of law, enforced not by English authorities, but by those of the merchants' home cities in Germany.

In exchange for these privileges, the merchants were required to maintain Bishopsgate, one of the original seven gates of the city, from where the road led to their interests in the Boston and Kings Lynn townships, which were also

Hanseatic League outposts and important ports for Hansa's ships to access the English northern market.

Steelyard wharf saw a substantial amount of traffic with ships regularly docking from Hanseatic ports, particularly Cologne. Imports of wheat, rye, and other grain; chandlery supplies such as cables, ropes, masts, pitch, tar-flax, hemp, linen cloth, and wax were landed. London was also the largest market for Flemish cloth. English exports, mostly finished goods, were ferried from there in the opposite direction.

It took over half an hour for the carriage to be prepared and an escort arranged. Coaches were commonly used for transport by the wealthy, with most being open to the elements. However, as the King's Treasurer, William Fitzgerald was able to use one of the three closed carriages designated for senior officers of State. He was accustomed to the wealth associated with his position. For the meeting, he dressed in his formal robes of office. The sext bells rang as the two-horse carriage departed from the Westminster complex, accompanied by two armed out-riders.

The route would take the party along the well-used dirt road that ran parallel to the river on the right, before crossing the River Fleet and entering the city via Ludgate. The cobbled streets were still puddled following the overnight storm, making the journey treacherous for the horses pulling the carriage and the accompanying guard. They passed the grand St Paul's Church which dominated the area, then headed towards the river. Within the hour, they had reached Thames Street and the north gateway, the entry into the Steelyard community. During his journey, Fitzwilliam was thinking about his idea, and was confident it would be favourably received.

They had passed the small chapel on the corner of All

Hallows Lane, not regularly used by the German residents owing to its size. The merchants and other Steelyard staff would normally congregate at All-Hallows-The-Great, a larger place of worship just outside the boundary walls.

The carriage drew to a halt. Fitzwilliam alighted and approached the entrance. He was immediately confronted by a man in a leather tunic, black hat, and a sword, sheathed at his side.

"Ho, there, your business, sir?"

"I'm here on King's business to see Master Giese."

The guard could see the carriage and the accompanying guard. He eyed the Treasurer up and down, assessing his credentials. Fitzwilliam certainly looked the part, and it was enough to allow entry.

"You will find him yonder … in Winter Hall." He pointed down the passageway.

There was a long corridor that bordered the Wine House on his right, a large building which served as a warehouse, primarily for storing wine. Above him, apartments straddled the walkway. One or two residents, on hearing the echoing footsteps, stared in curiosity as he strode along the passageway, before moving back away from the diamond-shaped windows.

On his right, he reached the Winter Hall which was where he was hoping to find Georg Giese. He walked around to the front of the building and accessed the ornate, front door; it was open. He entered and looked around. It was a large space, probably a hundred paces in length and half that in width. The decor was fine wood veneer. Iron candle chandeliers were placed around the walls at regular intervals.

There was a line of six windows over halfway up the side wall, their small diamond panes allowing a modicum of light from the surrounding alleyway. Despite the benefit of candles, the large room was gloomy.

As his eyes adjusted to the light, Fitzwilliam could see a group of men, dressed finely in business attire, some carrying parchments, clearly merchants doing business. He approached the first gathering and attracted the attention of one of them.

"Herr Giese?"

The man replied in German. Fitzwilliam shrugged his shoulders, his hands displayed outwards in incomprehension.

The man pointed. "Over there." His English was heavily accented.

The Treasurer was directed to an office in the corner. He crossed the floor, passing more groups of merchants who took little notice of the visitor, and reached the indicated room. The door was ajar and he knocked and pushed it open.

A man was seated at an impressive writing desk holding a quill pen. His head was down, concentrating on his endeavours.

Fitzwilliam gave a slight cough to attract attention. The man looked up.

"Herr Giese … William Fitzwilliam, we met last month, if you recall, at Westminster Hall, the banquet."

The room was brighter with the benefit of two windows directly behind the writing desk. The man put down his pen and stood up.

"Herr Fitzwilliam, yes, of course, I do remember."

He walked around the desk and greeted Fitzwilliam formally with a firm handshake.

Giese was an impressive character and surprisingly young at thirty-three to hold the position of Deputy Alderman. His clothing reflected his status, a vermillion shirt with extravagant sleeves, a velvet tunic over the top, breeches, and leather shoes. He was not an attractive man; he had a prominent crooked nose, his hair thick and well-groomed. His hat lay on the desk next to his seal and other items. For his comparative youth, he displayed a portly frame, another indicator of his wealth.

Fitzwilliam bowed reverently; although from a protocol perspective, it wasn't entirely appropriate.

Greetings over, Giese eyed up his visitor. "To what do I owe the pleasure of the King's Treasurer?" His English was excellent, as befitting an educated man, although slightly accented.

"It is a delicate matter on which I need to speak to you, one of utmost confidentiality."

"Verily? I am intrigued... Oh, forgive my manners, you have made a long journey, let me arrange some refreshment."

"My gratitude, but no. Time is pressing and I would like to conclude our business without delay."

"Very well, tis a fair day, what say we promenade along the riverside? We will not be disturbed and there will be no opportunity for other's ears."

"I am in your hands, Master Giese."

Giese picked up his hat and manoeuvred it carefully on his head, adjusting it until he was satisfied with its position. Fitzwilliam watched with some mirth as the long pheasant tail feather flapped around until it was correctly in place.

The gentlemen left the office and crossed the floor of the great hall. Giese acknowledged greetings from several merchants as he passed them. As they approached the impressive entrance door, the daylight made Fitzwilliam blink, and it was a few moments before his eyes adjusted to the light. Giese led the way, turning right and then left down another long open corridor containing apartment buildings on both sides. With the height of the buildings, the sun was unable to penetrate, making the area dismal. Unlike most of the streets in London, it was remarkably free of household waste and litter.

They reached an archway with living quarters above.

"That's the superintendent's quarters. All cogs that enter the wharf have to report to him before unloading, and the manifest checked," Giese explained.

Through the arch they were greeted by the sight of the river. The weather had cleared after the previous evening, and sunlight shimmered on the fast-flowing water.

The wharf was in in front of them. Not a large dock, compared with others along The Thames, like Gibson's Quay or Sommer's Quay, room for only two ships at any one time. Waiting cogs would anchor mid-stream for their turn.

Fitzwilliam watched as the ship in dock was being unloaded. The craft, a one mast, flat-bottomed cog was ideal for manoeuvring some of the shallower waters and docking areas along the North Sea coast and the Baltic where it would normally be found.

Giese noticed his companion's interest. "Just arrived from Cologne, Flemish cloth, timber, and other supplies for the King's navy," he explained.

Fitzwilliam watched as the dockers laboured with the unloading, many bare-chested in the warm August sunshine. There was a small crane, rather a winch contraption, that they were using for heavier items.

The men resembled freebooters and Fitzwilliam found them intimidating. One even had a scar on his cheek; he quickly turned away.

"Over here, in the lee of the wall; we won't be disturbed."

They walked away from the activity in the dock to the end of the wharf where the wall of the compound separated it from Cosins Lane. The river in front of them was alive with small rowing boats, ferrying paying passengers along the river. It was a much-favoured mode of transport, and was generally safer than walking around the streets.

There was no seating and the pair stood.

"So, Master Fitzwilliam, how can I be of service to the King's treasurer."

Satisfied their confidentiality was secure, Fitzwilliam rather hesitantly explained his mission.

"Master Giese, I cannot stress the sensitivity with which I am here to talk to you; it could cost lives if it were to be discovered."

"Yes, of course, you have my word on that," he responded.

"I know Hansa are supportive of the King's position regarding Rome, as I believe it is of similar mind."

"It is, indeed, Master Treasurer. You may have heard we have but recently denounced the Pope in favour of the Lutheran faith."

"Aye, it has come to our ears, hence the approach I am making today." He paused and breathed deeply, before continuing. "His Majesty's conflict with Rome of late has been a drain on his purse."

"Not to mention his many banquets and other frivolous merriment," countered Giese.

"Hmm, His Majesty enjoys a full life; it is true."

"So, what is it you are seeking from me?"

"It occurred to His Majesty's Government, by way of the Lord Steward, I should mention." He paused. "That through your good offices you could enquire of the Council whether they would consider a donation to His Majesty in his fight with Rome... It would appear to be in our mutual interests," he quickly added.

"A donation, you say?"

"It would be considered a grand gesture and attract future favours."

"Hmm, I am not so sure of the League's reaction to such a request. Not without something of substance in return. What is His Majesty's position on this request?"

Fitzwilliam looked down, sheepishly.

"Ah, I see, so King Henry is unaware of this approach?"

"His Majesty is troubled in other directions; we felt it prudent not to burden him with further trials."

"I understand. And you know we are at war with the Pope? His armies are already attacking our cities in the east. Wars are expensive."

"Aye, I am mindful of the imposition, I am putting on you."

Giese turned and looked towards the river, considering how he should respond.

There was a dilemma. The Hansa were keen to cement relationship with England to build their trade links and, possibly, provide support in the Hansa's war against the Papal States. It would be a chance to create some indebtedness, which did have merit. Nevertheless, getting the individual council members to agree to such a request would be difficult.

The Hanseatic League was never more than a loosely aligned confederation of city-states pursuing their own interests. It lacked a permanent administrative body, a treasury, and a standing military force. Each Council Member was independent and had their own autonomy. Decisions and actions of the League were the result of a consensus-based procedure. If an issue arose, the league's members were invited to participate in a central meeting or Diet, known as a *Dritteltage.* Convincing them to contribute towards Henry's treasury at the present time would be hard without a clear benefit to the donor cities.

Giese turned to Fitzwilliam. "Your request has merit,

Master Treasurer, but holding a *Dritteltage* to discuss such a matter would mean the possibility of it finding the ear of King Henry."

Fitzwilliam thought for a moment. "Would you know those cities that would be more favourable to such a proposal?"

"Ja, I think so." He thought for a moment, his brow furrowed. "I presume your need is pressing."

"The soonest would be most convenient."

"Very well. It might be possible to raise such a matter at the next meeting in private, away from the chambers, with those members who may be favourably disposed. I have the ear of them..." He paused for a moment, still considering the implications of the request." I will need to speak to my Chancellor, and, if he agrees, I will make arrangements to journey to Cologne at the earliest opportunity and report to you on my return."

"I can ask for no more, sir. His Majesty's Government will be truly grateful. I will rely on your discretion."

Earlier, John Wolfe was lay on his mattress having been awoken by the Terce bells. In mid-summer bells were rung at two-thirty and three-forty a.m.; he had slept through those. It was now around seven o'clock. Despite the window-cloth, flies buzzed everywhere.

He looked at the naked shape of Alice, lay peacefully sleeping next to him, not for any thought of coitus; she had satiated that three more times the previous evening. It was a question of what should be done about her. He could, of course, throw her back to the streets, but having her close had many benefits, not just the carnal attractions. She was clearly resourceful, and appeared educated, for a girl. The appearance of a married couple may attract less attention of the sergeants-at-arms than a singleton, although thoughts of marriage were out of the question. For the moment, it served its purpose.

She stirred. Her eyes opened, a countenance of innocence as she lay on the straw mattress. She swished away marauding flies from her face.

"Good morn, John," she said sleepily, as her eyes focused.

"How fairest thee, Alice?"

"I'll be better for use of the piss-pot."

She got up from the mattress and went to the bucket in the corner and stooped.

"Have you water for bathing, John?" she said, having finished her toilet.

Wolfe watched as she returned to the bed. "I will get some from the bathhouse."

"And perchance some bread or such; I've not eaten for some time and my belly complains."

"Aye, I'll see to it. I'll return shortly."

Wolfe dressed casually, just breeches and tunic, and left the room. His heavy feet clomped on the wooden staircase as he descended to the street. He blinked on leaving the darkness of the passageway into the daylight. The sun was bright, the sky, blue; water from the previous evening's storm still lay in puddles on the uneven cobbles. The smell of rotting vegetables and excrement hung in the air. A rat, the size of a cat, crossed his path and scurried back down the passageway where Wolfe had just come from, in pursuit of food.

A short distance away, along Carter Lane, in the lee of St Pauls Church, street vendors were setting out their goods on push-carts, as the daily market started taking shape. It was where Wolfe would regularly shop for food. Despite the early hour, there were many folk about seeking the vendors' produce. There was a good variety, a welcome change from the shortages of two years earlier when the crop had failed and many died of starvation.

Urchins with grubby faces ran about, most in bare feet, looking for food or coin that may have been dropped by an innocent pedestrian. At low tide they would scavage the riverbank searching for anything that might be of value left behind by the ebbing tide.

The first cart Wolfe passed contained the carcasses of six dead rabbits, a squirrel, a large rat, and several pigeons. All would be bought for the pot before the end of day by those who could afford it.

"Good den, Master John," greeted a familiar face. A visage, old and world-weary, but eyes that missed little. His thinning hair, lank and grey-flecked, his woollen shirt, stained and dirty.

Wolfe looked up at his inquisitor. "How fairest thou, William?"

"Aye, survived the tempest last e'en. Not seen the like in my lifetime."

"Aye, true enough."

"There were rows of circular loaves on his cart, piled in threes."

"You have Yeoman bread, William?"

"Aye, made fresh this morn. You have coin to pay for such?"

"Aye, that I have."

"Tis pleasing to see your fortune has turned."

"Aye, that it is."

"Just one will it be?"

"Aye, suffice for now."

Wolfe paid for the bread and headed back to the room via the bathhouse where he collected a pail of water.

He reached his quarters carrying the bucket in one hand, the bread in the other. Alice was dressed in her undergarments and sweeping the floor with a besom.

"I've put broom to good use; I fear it's not seen such in recent days."

"Aye that's a fact, never had the need or time for such domestic matters."

Wolfe handed her the pail. The water was cold but with the temperature in the room it would be refreshing.

"I have bread when you are ready," said Wolfe and handed her the loaf.

The remainder of the soap from the bathhouse, little more than a slither, was on the table next to the candles and had hardened overnight. Alice retrieved it, took off her clothes, and started to wash. Wolfe watched her and his carnal desires returned. This time he needed to resist his ardour.

"What be your plans for today, Alice?" asked Wolfe.

Alice looked up from the pail, her face was soap-ridden, her eyes closed to prevent stinging them.

"Here, use this," said Wolfe, passing her his shirt he had worn the previous day. It smelt stale from sweat. Alice showed no reaction.

"I have none, John; I am at your favour."

"I have been giving it much thought, Alice, and I would like you to stay here, with me."

"That would be most generous, John."

"Not so, Alice, This room is not fit for pigs. I have in mind somewhere more in keeping with what you deserve."

Alice stood there, water trickling down her body in little streams. "Pray tell, John."

"I know a man who has lodgings for rent with a bedroom and a kitchen. It has even a hearth and chimney for cooking."

"But have you coin to pay for such luxury, John?"

"Aye, that I have, but for now, I must away to my labours. I will return before Vespers with news."

"I will make this room suitable for leaving, while you're away," replied Alice and started washing her private parts.

Wolfe turned and left the room with the sight of Alice's mound of Venus firmly in his mind.

John Wolfe's place of work was the Steelyard Kontor. He had laboured on the ships there since his arrival from Cologne. To people who asked, he would say he was a merchant, for that is what he aspired to be, and now with coin, it remained an ambition.

His felonious exploits were well-away from the area. The Steelyard was where he felt safe, protected as it was from any external hue and cry.

He skirted past the Carter Street stall holders and turned into a passageway. He needed to stay away from the main thoroughfares, where the sergeants-at-arms might loiter. Instead, he would use the back alleys and lanes which threaded through this part of London.

He entered another alleyway and passed the body of a dead dog, swarming with flies. Someone would retrieve it for the pot or throw it into the Thames before the morn was out.

He skipped the puddles and eventually reached Lovat Street, known locally as Grope Lane, the home to many prostitutes. He would need to run the gauntlet of their offerings. One bared her chest to him as he walked by.

"Want to touch, deary? A farthing to you, kind sir."

Wolfe ignored the beseeching and arrived on Thames Street and the entrance to the Steelyard. It would be an hour after the Terce bells that had awoken him earlier. The morning was still bright, but a touch cooler after the night's storm. Puddles still lay in between the broken cobbles.

Alice, meanwhile, was now dressed, having completed her ablutions, and was continuing to clean the room. She moved the mattress and swept out the stray strands of cain-coloured straw that had become loose from its binding. The area beneath was strewn with them. She swept them into a small pile, then noticed something odd. There was a piece of floorboard, about the length of her foot, that was out of line with the other planks and slightly raised.

She examined the wooden panel more closely. It was warped, and, as she tried to replace it in its rightful position, it sprung upwards. She removed it completely and looked inside. There was a cloth bag.

She retrieved it from its hiding place and tipped some of the contents into her hand. She couldn't believe her eyes. Crowns, Angels, half-crowns, shillings, groats and smaller coins. She gasped; she'd not witnessed such wealth before. It was a King's ransom. In fact, Kings would have been released from capture for less.

Her first instinct was to take the bag and run. She could go anywhere; abroad even. But something was stopping her. She considered the consequences for a moment. As well as making a fearsome enemy, who would no doubt kill her if she were discovered, her new acquaintance was strong, virile, and she felt safe with him. Where else might she find such a man?

She took out a shilling piece and two groats from the purse, which she thought would not be missed, then replaced the bag in its hiding place. She positioned the wooden slat then stamped down on it with her heel. It snapped back in place and was not noticeable. She dragged the straw mattress to where it was laid before. A mouse scurried across the floor, disturbed from its search for food. Alice jumped momentarily in alarm,

Motivated by her recent fortune, she decided to get some air and buy some food for when Wolfe returned. She might even purchase some booties to replace the slips of leather that adorned her feet which gave sparce protection from the jagged stones littering the pavement. She deserved a treat she convinced herself; she had coin enough.

The sun was now higher in the sky, the area, rich with life; the teeming, fetid flotsam of human society that inhabited the alleys and passageways of London with survival as the single goal.

Wolfe had reached the wharf and joined other longshoremen waiting to unload the latest cog to reach the berth.

With its own administration, imports from the Hanseatic League were managed and checked at the Steelyard. This was done by a superintendent before the goods were discharged. Once cleared, the cargo would be unloaded and then positioned on the quayside before being transported by porters to the different warehouses in the Steelyard to await wider distribution.

Non-Hanseatic League traffic, using the myriad of wharves along the river, were required to obtain a certificate of the vessel's cargo at The Custom's House Quay, where the duty was calculated and paid.

There were over thirty men engaged in the unloading the Cologne cog, and, once the manifest had been checked and the duty agreed, the dockside sprang to life.

Recognising the arduous nature of the job, two barrels of water with ladles were provided next to the winch/crane, to keep the dockers hydrated. They would be drained before the day was out.

There was little in the way of fraternisation, partly because of language barriers - over half were German speakers, but mostly, the men just wanted to complete their work and get paid for their labours.

It was after midday when Wolfe noticed two men walking towards the dock from one of the passageways. They were dressed in the finery of wealth and standing. They seemed to be in deep conversation. One of them caught Wolfe's gaze; he quickly turned away. He wondered the nature of their discourse.

Chapter Three

The Reformation Parliament was still in its infancy. It had been set up at the instigation of the King in his fight with Rome, and would eventually pass laws transferring all religious authority from the Pope to the English Crown, giving the King control over the wealth and buildings of the old Church and settle official religious doctrine. It would become the cornerstone of democracy for centuries.

It was late afternoon as the Treasurer of the Household returned to Westminster Hall. He entered the main chamber and sought out his mentor and master, the Earl of Shrewsbury.

George Talbot, the 4th Earl of Shrewsbury, was a much-favoured Lord in the King's Court. He was Godfather to the previous King's daughter, Margaret, and continued good patronage with Henry V111. He had fought bravely in battle, earning him rewards and positions of power. He was a supporter of the King and a signatory on the letter to the Pope urging him to grant the King a divorce from Catherine of Aragon. He was now elderly, in his sixties.

He dressed the part of a man of wealth, silk shirt, doublet and hose, a white ruff, and extravagant hat complete with feather. As well as a portly-belly, his age gave him pronounced eyebrows, a round, ruddy face with sparkling eyes. He was known for his stentorian voice which would boom out across the debating chamber; he would always be heard.

Fitzwilliam saw him in conversation with another member of the Parliament and hastened to his side. His Lordship saw the Treasurer anxiously awaiting his audience and excused himself from his present discourse. There was a courteous removal of hat and bow by the discharged knight of the shires.

"Pray, Master Fitzwilliam, you have news?"

"Aye, my Lord, Master Giese appears amenable to our request."

"Verily? But that is good news, indeed." His face broadened into a smile, indicating a sense of satisfaction.

Fitzwilliam's expression did not, though, reflect the joy of his Lordship's demeanour.

"He did indicate, however, that not all the States might be suitably disposed."

His Lordship's visage turned to one of disappointment. "Pray, what does this mean? Will they help us or not?"

"Master Giese has agreed to discuss it with the Steelyard Chancellor; then, if he is of a mind, return to Cologne at the earliest opportunity to discuss our proposal at their next council meeting. I stressed the urgency of our need … " The Treasurer paused, noticing an expression of concern from His Lordship. He leaned closer, secretively, close enough to catch the fetid breath of the Earl. "He has a mind to raise the matter discreetly with those members who he thought would be predisposed to such a request. A formal approach at Council would likely reach the King's ear."

"Then questions would be asked," reflected the Lord Steward.

"Indeed."

His Lordship stroked his chin in a sagely fashion. "Then we can do no more but wait."

The cog had been unloaded and the men congregated in groups around the water barrels satiating their thirst. Wolfe was bare-chested, his torso glistened with sweat. He picked up his third successive ladle and drank it down in one gulp. He wiped his beard with the back of his hand. With no ship due for docking until the morning; he had completed his work for the day and would collect his earnings from the superintendent.

With the clement weather, the traffic on the river was endless; watermen in ferries were faring well with custom. In the near distance, London Bridge with its pontoons and housed superstructure stood as a symbol of the city's wealth. It was possible, if squinting, to see the pike-staffs on which the severed heads of those who had crossed the King were slowly rotting in the sunshine. A message to others, if any were needed, at the price of treason.

Wolfe had an errand to attend.

He was now properly-dressed. He left the Steelyard by the Thames Street gate and headed into the lanes to return to his dwelling. He had been thinking about Alice. Setting up home with someone had never crossed his mind before, but maybe the time was right, and, as he had surmised earlier, might also prove to be useful cover.

Wolfe had an occasional drinking companion with whom he had shared many a tankard; someone who owned several properties, and he knew where to find him. He headed for the Paul's Head Tavern, an ale-house in the shadow of the great church which dominated the area. It meant just a short detour from his usual journey back to his dwelling, but with the hue and cry still in operation, fraught with danger. Wolfe was on alert.

The half-mile journey through the back alleys was uneventful, just the usual beggars and harlots, and the pervasive smell of rotting vegetables. He reached the ale-house and stooped through its low entrance. The warped framework would ensure its door could never be closed again.

It was busy, late afternoon, and full of men who had

completed their labours for the day. There was a mixed clientele, mostly doublet-clad businessmen, uncomfortably hot in their layers of cloth, but also the occasional varlet spending his ill-gotten gains on his only pleasure in life.

He could hear raucous giggling and mayhem in an adjoining room as he looked around the many wooden bench-tables.

His eyes scanned the darkened room and fixed on a man, older than he, with long wavy hair, still wearing a patterned pourpoint from his days in the military. He was in his usual place, on his own with his head seemingly in his thoughts.

"Master Thornton?"

The man jumped, as if woken suddenly from slumbers, then made recognition.

"Why, John Wolfe, prithee, find yourself a tankard and sit thiself down. I'll be glad of your company."

Wolfe attracted the attention of a serving wench, and collected a pewter tankard filled with beer, then returned to the man.

"Tis early for your custom, John. What brings you here at this time?"

"Aye, work has finished till the morn. I wanted to seek you out to discuss a matter of dwelling."

"Of dwelling, you say?"

"Aye, you are a man of property, and I am seeking such."

The man furrowed his bow in suspicion. "You have coin to pay for such a transaction."

"Aye, I have in mind a modest house with windows and a fire for cooking."

"But, prithee, why would you want such a dwelling?"

"It is time to see the fruits of my labours, for I have suffered enough on the altar of poverty."

"Aye, tis a good cause indeed, but how come this change

of fortune?"

"I had some luck last e'en with the cocks."

Thornton looked at Wolfe, incredulously. "You've been at the cockpit? I'm surprised you still have a shirt on your back."

"Aye, the good Lord was on my side."

The landlord took a swig of his ale and paused before replying. The background hum of conversation seemed to increase in volume.

"Very well, John, you are an amiable fellow and good company, I will look favourably at your request. I do have such a place in Bishopsgate that would serve you well."

"Can we go there, directly?"

"Aye, we can, but prithee, what's your haste? Tarry a while and enjoy your tankard."

Wolfe looked around, on edge. News of the previous day's robbery would be about, and he was anxious not to stay in a tavern for any length of time for fear of being recognised.

"Aye very well."

"Good, let's finish this and take another. My thirst needs satisfying; it's been a fire of a day."

"True enough."

Wolfe looked over his shoulder. The alehouse continued to attract custom and there was barely room to move. The raucousness in the adjacent room seemed to be getting louder.

With just one window, there was little natural light and the tavern was gloomy. Facial recognition would be unlikely, but nevertheless, Wolfe would be happier on the move.

There was a woman's shriek from next door, not one of danger, a playful one. His companion noticed Wolfe react to the scream.

"Ha, pay no heed, John, mariners off the cog at Queen

Hythe, spending their coin on a couple of drabs, methinks."

Wolfe took another gulp of ale.

"There was a whoobub in here, not half an hour since," continued Thornton, making conversation.

Wolfe looked up from his tankard.

"Aye?"

"Aye, two sergeants-at-arms searching for some cut-purse who robbed a merchant yesterday over Newgate way. Came in with some varlet who claims he witnessed the deed."

Wolfe's blood ran cold. He leaned closer. "Aye? What happened?"

"Ha, they took some caitiff away for questioning. You could hear his screams of innocence in Spitalfields, methinks. They're off'rin a crown for apprehending the miscreant. There's been talk of little else around the yard."

"A crown?"

"Aye,"

The stakes had been raised.

The none bell sounded from the Monastery on St Andrew Hill, less than a quarter of a mile away. Mid-afternoon, Wolfe needed to be away.

With even more customers having entered the ale-house, the room was becoming oppressive. Sweat trickled down the face of Wolfe's companion and absorbed into his beard. The irritation warranted a wipe of the arm.

The noise from the adjoining room had lessened and been replaced by grunts and groans.

Thornton could detect Wolfe's nervousness.

"Art thou feeling unwell, John? You seem not of yourself."

"Nay, nay, just anxious to conclude our business; I have much to do."

"Very well, we will tarry no longer. You have coin, you

said?"

"Aye, you have my word."

"Your word is good enough for me, John. Let's be away and take some air. This place is fair suffocating."

The pair left their table and made their way to the exit. With so many men in conversation in the room, their departure caused little notice.

Outside, Wolfe squinted as the sunlight reflected from the adjacent, white-walled buildings. The tower of the grand church of St Paul's was visible over the roofs of the houses across the road as if standing guard over the community, arms outstretched, protecting all those within its reach.

For Wolfe, the great building offered little protection. Sanctuary would not normally be given to those committing a felony.

Staying in the lee of the houses, Wolfe would remain a shadowy figure, and the journey to Bishopsgate, less than a mile away, was made without incident.

Wolfe followed Thornton down an alleyway which opened into a small courtyard with houses on four sides. They were clearly of better quality, black beams, a timber frame filled in with wattle and daub, black wooden entrance doors, and wooden-shuttered windows.

The landlord approached the nearest house on the right-hand side and walked up to the front door. He produced a key from his purse on his money-belt and opened it.

He led Wolfe inside. It was a small room and smelt musty from being shut up; dust was everywhere and particles were visible in the sunrays from the open shutters. There was a floor covering of rushes, a bulky, oak dining table in the corner with a bench on either side, an open fireplace with an iron hanging point for kettle or pot. A window was positioned on each side of the entrance door which gave some natural light.

Thornton walked through the room to a door which led to the first floor via a bare wooden staircase. Their footsteps echoed as they ascended.

In front of them was the bedroom with a large bed supporting a mattress stuffed with flock. There were two pails. One was half a size larger.

"That's piss-pot," he pointed to the smaller one. "T'other's for water; care not to confuse the two." He laughed.

They returned to the ground floor.

Wolfe turned to Thornton. "This is satisfactory for my needs."

"How long will you require this dwelling?"

"For as long as I'm in London, methinks."

"Then I will need coin for three months lodgings. If you need it for longer we can discuss that."

"Aye, that suits."

John went to his money belt and took out some coins. "Will that see to it?"

"Aye, John, that it will. I'll take my leave."

Thornton handed Wolfe the key and left. As he walked back to the tavern, clutching the coin, he wondered about Wolfe and his new-found wealth, but made no connection with the cut-purse incident.

Back in Wolfe's hovel, Alice was waiting for his return. She was unsure whether to confess the discovery of his secret hoard. She examined her new booties, coif, and chemise, her first new clothes since leaving home, and considered her good fortune. Could she have taken more? It was unlikely that Wolfe would have missed it, given the amount of coin in the bag. It was a consideration, but for now, she was content.

It was an hour to vespers as she heard the rattle of the door. The noise made her jump; she was unsure of the reception.

The smell of ale preceded Wolfe's form as he entered the room. She was seated on the mattress and stood up to greet him.

"Welcome home, John. How are you?"

He ignored the question. There were many who knew of his dwelling.

"Get your things together; we need to be away before vespers or we'll need a light-boy to lead us the way."

"Aye, John, everything is prepared. I have a pie for you. Why don't you eat? You must have an appetite after your labours."

"Aye, I have, but happen it can wait. I have a new dwelling for us, not a mile thence. We should leave now. Have you your chattels at hand?"

"Aye, John, I will collect them directly."

Her demeanour was one of subservience; she had no knowledge of his temper, but had no intention of discovery.

She picked up her bag of clothes and belongings, which lay next to her on the mattress.

"Meet me in the street; I will be down directly. I have one or two matters to attend."

Alice guessed he would be retrieving his booty out of her sight. She headed for the door carrying her bag in one hand and the pie in the other; grease oozed from the pastry and ran down her fingers.

Her new booties made a clomping noise as she descended the staircase. She felt anxious, concerned about his reaction if he should discover her trumpery. She decided if challenged she would confess and place herself at his mercy.

She stood outside the dwelling and waited, watching the comings and goings of the early-evening passers-by.

Wolfe heard Alice's steps lessen in volume as she descended the stairs. It was all-clear. He pulled back the bed and was surprised to see the underneath bereft of straw which usually littered the place left by the mattress; it helped disguise his hiding place. He concluded that it was Alice and her fastidious cleaning but was not unduly concerned.

He went to the floorboard and tried to prise it open, but it was firmly held. He took out his dagger and entered it into the slight gap between the joists and pushed down. The piece of wood sprung from its security and flew across the room. Wolfe put his hand in the hole and retrieved his bag of coin. He weighed it in his hands as if checking it was all intact, then placed it inside his tunic, causing it to bulge outward.

He collected the errant plank which was some five feet away and returned it to its rightful place. It was not flush and he jabbed it with his heel until it was wedged down, then replaced the mattress.

His leather bag was in the corner, containing his change of clothes and the rest of his worldly belongings, then left the room without a backward glance. He was not sorry to leave the hovel; someone else would soon claim it once word had got round that it was empty.

He descended the stairs, heavy of foot.

Alice was waiting in the dimming light; the bells of vespers sounded from the nearby monastery, the oncoming of eventide.

"Is all well, John?"

"Aye."

He looked up and down the street and across the road into the passageway opposite. He could see nothing of concern.

Alice could see Wolfe's anxiousness. "Do not worry, John, there are no watchmen about. I have been vigilant for such."

Alice linked her arm in his as a promenading couple might do. The pie was still in her left hand it was difficult to tell if it would be still edible. John was content. A watchman would not be looking for a couple.

"Come, John, I am anxious to see our new home."

Just then, Wolfe stopped; he could hear the sound of a solitary bell. "What goes hence?"

It came into view from an adjoining street; a large wagon being dragged along by a mangy horse. Two men were walking slowly beside it, one was holding its reins leading it forward, the other was ringing the bell.

"It's the plague-cart, John."

"Aye, it seems the curse of death is everywhere."

They watched from a distance as the wagon continued on its way with half a dozen bodies piled on it."

It took no more than twenty minutes with a good stride for them to reach the small courtyard.

Alice looked at the surrounding properties.

"Why, John, this is a handsome house indeed," she said, as he led her to the new dwelling.

He opened the door and they entered; Alice's eyes widened.

"We will soon have this place fit for a king."

Back in the Steelyard, Georg Giese was in the quarters of the Chancellor, Hermann Hillebrandt Wedigh, his direct superior, and effectively in overall charge of the kontor's administration. It wasn't a large office, but contained an impressive writing desk, complete with ink and quill, a bench in front, and a fine chair in which the head of the Steelyard was seated. Sunlight streamed down through the large window behind him.

Wedigh was an impressive but humourless character, with a distinctive light-brown beard and moustache. He had piercing blue eyes, one of which was slightly larger than the other. He hailed from a wealthy Cologne family, and dressed accordingly in a black cloak with a velvet collar and velvet at the wrist, beneath, a white, silk shirt. A flat black cap was on his head, of the type worn by all the Steelyard merchants. On his left hand he wore a signet ring on his index finger with family crest – a black chevron surrounded by three green willow leaves. They spoke in German.

"Sir, I need your council on a matter of great import and utmost secrecy."

The Chancellor looked at him inquisitively.

Giese continued. "It has implications for our relationship with the English crown."

"The King?" He viewed Giese with a degree of concern. "Then, pray tell, Master Georg."

He looked around; the Chancellor's office was stuffy and dust particles hung in the air. There was no-one within earshot.

"Sir, I must insist on your discretion. In these difficult times, lives are at stake."

"Of course You have my word."

Giese took a deep breath.

"I've been approached by the King's Treasurer, no less, seeking the League's support, financially, for His Majesty's exchequer."

"What kind of support? A loan? Extended credit?" Giese looked down, recognising the absurdity of the request. He replied awkwardly.

"He is seeking a, how can I put it? A 'donation' towards the costs of the King's continuing divorce proceedings and his battle with Rome. I said I would approach those cities who might be sympathetic to such an idea."

The Chancellor looked at Giese with some incredulity.

"Donation! Donation! Well, the cheek of it! Do they not appreciate the League's present predicament? We are fighting for our very lives. Russia and the Teutonic Knights have abandoned us; our cities are under siege in Pomerania surrounded by French and Savoy troops." The Chancellor was getting angry, his face reddened. "And for what? So the philandering King can continue his dalliances? You'll be the laughingstock of the League, and your career will suffer, you mark my words. No one will take you seriously … and you won't get your money; I can assure you of that."

Giese was beginning to regret his involvement. "But, sir, I could not rightly refuse to make enquiries; it would be viewed as an insult to The King, and possibly damage the relationship between Hansa and Britain, particularly if we need their help against the French. The English do have an excellent navy."

The Chancellor thought for a moment, then backtracked.

"Yes, yes, my boy, I can see your point. This requires a great deal of thought … You say you want to return to Cologne?"

"Yes, sir."

"When does the next cog leave?"

"There's a cog in dock, due to sail for Cologne tomorrow, high tide."

"How long will you need to complete this task?"

"I was intending to speak with certain members when they attend the next *Dritteltage*, then return."

The Chancellor was deep in thought, then a broad smile lit up his face.

"No, no, don't do that; I have an idea … " He curled his moustache in his fingers. "Go and make arrangements for your journey to Cologne then return here." His demeanour was one of drama. "I'll explain what I have in mind."

John Wolfe was deep in thought. He hadn't realised the hue and cry for his cut-purse activities would continue for this length of time. With every day that went by, there was a chance of being discovered. He made a decision.

He and Alice were seated opposite each other at their table having consumed the pie that Alice had bought. Night was closing in and Wolfe had lit some candles brought with them from the hovel.

"What ails thee, John? I can see you are troubled."

Wolfe didn't reply immediately and Alice made no attempt to nudge him into a response.

Eventually, he looked her in the eyes. "I need to leave London for a while."

"Leave London?"

"Aye."

"But why? We've just moved in here." Wolfe kept staring ahead. "I think I know," continued Alice, and walked around the other side of the bench.

She placed her arm around his shoulder. "I have to confess something to which I am not sure what you're reaction will be, but please remember you can trust me."

Wolfe looked at her; his expression changed to one of inquisitiveness.

"While I was cleaning; I found your secret hiding place … " She waited for his reaction, but there was little, just a raised eyebrow. "It was an accident, John, I swear. I was just sweeping the floor and the floorboard lifted."

Wolfe remained silent; Alice didn't know if it was a good thing or not. She continued.

"I know you have wealth, and I will not ask how you came by such a sum, but your secret is safe with me; I will take it to the grave."

Wolfe raised his hand and at first Alice was expecting it to land on her person. She flinched, waiting for the blow, but he stopped and rested his hand on the table.

"Whatever trouble you are in, John, I will protect you," she reassured.

Wolfe was trying to take this in; he had never experienced this degree of loyalty before, and was unsure how much credence he should give to it.

She placed her hands either side of his face and looked him directly in the eyes. "You don't need to leave, John." Alice's voice was confident; her expression, one of concern.

"Aye, I do. Just for a short time; until the hue and cry has died down."

"I heard they had caught a caitiff for such crime."

"Aye, so I heard."

"Then they will not be looking for anyone."

Wolfe was thinking.

Alice continued. "I have an idea." She hesitated. "What if we become a married couple? Not in church, but by appearance. I will change my name to Wolfe. That could protect you."

Wolfe couldn't take it in. "You would do that for me?"

"Aye, and more besides, John Wolfe."

There was a silence, broken only by the sound of a single bell as the plague cart passed by outside.

"I'll not betray you, please believe me, John."

Wolfe was taking in this revelation. It was true, Alice could easily have given Wolfe up to the watchman and collected a substantial reward. She could even have taken his money and run. There was much to trust.

"Aye, very well, but I must leave for a short time, until the hue and cry has died down; you can arrange the house while I'm away. I will give you coin for such."

"How long will you be away?"

"I have in mind joining a cog as a seaman. I will sign for the next sailing from the Steelyard."

Chapter Four

August 28th, 1531, a cog, bearing the flag of the Hanseatic League, eased gently out of its berth at the Steelyard Wharfe into the centre of the River Thames, destination, Cologne. The sext bells emanated from a nearby church, indicating post midday. It was overcast, but warm, and, with a favourable wind and tide, the augers for the voyage were good.

The craft, a one mast, flat-bottomed ship was ideal for accessing some of the shallower waters and docking areas along the North Sea coast and the Baltic where it would normally be found. It was however notoriously difficult to manoeuvre and relied heavily on wind direction.

On board were a crew of around thirty and a number of passengers, mostly merchants, returning to Germany. It was also loaded with a cargo of English ink and finished cloth from London workshops. It was settled low in the water.

Georg Giese, dressed in the finery of a wealthy merchant, stood next to the captain at the stern, as the boat edged towards the centre of the river. Captain Harvey was an experienced seaman and expertly manoeuvred the boat into position via the tiller. Above them, London Bridge, with its houses and shops, stretched out before them. On the bridge, a team of men were labouring with the mechanism that would raise the drawbridge, allowing the cog to pass through.

Giese could see people going about their business on the busy Thames crossing, some just stood watching in curiosity as the ship passed below them. Then the gruesome sight of tarred severed heads displayed on spikes appeared, representing a long row of treacherous intent. He turned away his gaze.

On the other side of the bridge there was a bustle about

the Thames, where larger vessels that couldn't negotiate the arches were berthed. Hulks and carracks from Spain and the Mediterranean, smaller Picards unloading fish, and numerous watermen in their wherries, moving passengers and cargo along the river.

Among the cog's crew, John Wolfe was busy helping to manage the sail, as the current and wind propelled the cog downstream toward the river mouth, several hours away.

The previous evening, Wolfe was lay in bed. It was a hot and sticky night; sweat glistened on his chest.

He listened as the matins bells tolled their time, two-thirty a.m. Alice lay beside him; her naked form illuminated by the moonlight that radiated through the window. Flies, the normal nighttime irritant, were mercifully absent, unable to penetrate the glass barrier. The candles, which hours earlier had provided the room with a warm glow, were now exhausted, just the charred remains of the wick where a living flame had burned.

Outside, a dog barked; disturbed by movement, almost certainly a rat. Wolfe was used to these sounds; they had become ambient to him.

The flock mattress was soft and comfortable. After so many years sleeping on straw; it seemed strange, but that wasn't the reason for his insomnia; he was torn. His concern at being apprehended by the watchmen loomed large in his mind. He was content with his decision to get away; London, at the moment, was just too dangerous.

His dilemma, though, was money; it always came down to that.

His money belt would need to contain no more coin than a humble dockworker would carry. If he were found with more in his possession in the event of a search, questions would be asked. He could hide a gold crown or guinea elsewhere on his person; he had done it before, but what about the remaining haul?

He sat up in bed then got out and walked to the piss-pot to relieve himself.

"You seem ill-at-ease, John."

The voice made him jump.

He turned around, he could make out her profile in the dim light, Alice was looking at him, leaning on her elbow.

"Aye, perchance I prefer a harder bedding."

"Come back to bed; I will help you sleep."

He climbed back into bed and Alice wrapped her arms around him.

"I've been long in thought," said John, lay on his back, staring at the ceiling, Alice's head under his chin.

"Aye … you're still worried about the watchmen, I fancy."

"Aye, that's true."

"Do not worry, John, I will always protect you."

"And for that I am grateful, but the soonest I leave London the better. It will ease my mind."

"Then you must do what you think is right … Where will you go?"

"There is a cog sailing tomorrow for Cologne. I will sign on for that."

"When will you come back?"

"One voyage, I will not be long away, just a few weeks."

"Then while you are gone, I will make the house fit for my husband."

"Husband?"

"Aye. I too have been deep in thought. I will take your name; if you are of a similar mind."

Wolfe thought for a moment. "Aye … aye."

"In which case, husband, we can't have you in need of a harlot while you are absent from me."

Her hand moved down Wolfe's body and grasped his sleeping member.

The terce bells tolled; it was Wolfe's morning wakeup call. He got dressed and started to collect together the things he would need for his journey. He was still troubled. He had never before had to consider anyone else in his decisions. He had always been an independent, some would say ruthless, individual. He trusted no-one; it had helped him survive. Yet here he was, trusting his very life to a relative stranger.

Alice woke, disturbed by the movement in the room.

"Why did you not wake me, John? I should be finding food for your journey."

"Aye, there's plenty of time; I'll be there before the sext bells."

Alice dressed.

"I'll fetch some breakfast; I'm sure you have things you need to attend to. Do you have coin?"

Wolfe's money belt was under the bed. He leaned down and retrieved it.

"Here," he said, handing Alice, some change. "That should be sufficient. Buy some meat if you can find a butchery."

Alice put on her wimple and left the room.

Wolfe knew this would be the opportunity for him to secrete the remainder of his robbery money. There were no shortages of places. He went to the corner of the bedroom and removed his purse from its temporary hiding place and searched for something more secure. He had an idea.

He pulled back the bed from the wall. It was bare brick and in need of repair. As with his previous dwelling, the floorboards were uneven and it was straightforward to raise one to reveal the ceiling of the room below. He took out two crowns and the small change. He counted out the remainder, seventeen crowns, which would enable him to live well for a considerable time. He would replenish his money belt and ensure Alice had sufficient money to last until he returned.

Westminster Hall, an hour after the terce bells had sounded, William Fitzwilliam, Treasurer to the Crown, was seeking his Lordship, The Earl of Shrewsbury.

Fitzwilliam had spent the evening at his London quarters away from Cowdray House, his country seat, as he was due to attend a Privy Council meeting today. Sleep had been elusive.

"My Lord," said Fitzwilliam, seeing him walking down the corridor ahead of him. Lord Shrewsbury turned and recognised the caller.

"William … Fair thee well, this fine morning?" he responded warmly.

Fitzwilliam ignored the greeting. "Can I take a few minutes of your time, my Lord?"

"Why, of course. Walk with me; we will take the air."

They continued down the corridor and left the confines of the building into the rectangle.

"What news of His Majesty?" asked Fitzwilliam, making conversation.

"I have not seen him in a month or more. Most of his time these days seems to be spent in Greenwich."

"Ah, yes, he's making changes, I hear."

"Hmm, yes, another pointless drain on the treasury."

"Quite so, My Lord, quite so."

"But you have not sought me out to discuss the King's construction projects. So, what is it that needs my attention?"

"Hmm, yes, well, I have been giving more thought to the subject of the King's coffers."

"Ah, yes."

"On reflection, methinks we have exceeded our authority."

"We … William?" Fitzwilliam reacted to the question.

"Why, yes."

"Hmm, this is your venture, William, which I have supported tacitly. I did counsel caution against such an enterprise. Have you news?" added His Lordship.

Fitzwilliam was starting to feel isolated.

"No, My Lord, I sought your counsel on whether it would be prudent to seek Cromwell for his blessing."

"To what end? The deed is done. I'm not sure how he would react at being presented by such a decision which has already been taken. What if he reacts against such an endeavour?"

Fitzwilliam's expression was one of despair; he had not expected this response, or his Lordship appearing to distance himself from the initiative.

"Come, William, don't look so downcast; if Hansa responds favourably, it will be a real feather in your cap. If not, then no-one will be any the wiser."

Fitzwilliam thought for a moment; His Lordship was right. For the moment, he would let matters take their course.

Elsewhere, the hunt for the cut-purse continued unabated, fuelled by the substantial reward being offered by the victim. Notices appeared on the doors of taverns for those who could read, detailing the reward on offer. Such was the quest for coin, fingers were pointing this way and that. Potential perpetrators arrested, then released as a suitable alibi had been established, much to the frustration of the men-at-arms.

With Wolfe safely on his way to Cologne, Alice decided

to walk the twenty minutes to the market stalls in Carter Street in search of food and other items she needed to furnish the house, a cooking pot and bath were top of her shopping list. Wolfe had left sufficient coin to cover the costs. She was dressed simply in kirtle and apron, a white wimple covering her long hair.

The sext bells had rung and the marketplace was bustling, mostly women with their baskets, queuing at the wooden stalls or push-carts. There were very few men; those who were fit and of working age were at their labours, leaving just old men and beggars.

As Alice wandered around the vendors, a group of men, led by a sergeant-at-arms, were roughly pushing and shoving their way through the throng gathered around the stalls. She watched as a pregnant woman was thrown to the ground. Alice rushed to help her to her feet.

“Take care, sirs, can’t you see this woman is with child.”

Alice’s protestations were met with a slap from a gloved hand which felled her. She lay on the floor, covered in horse droppings. Her lip, which had taken the full force of the strike, was swollen. She dabbed away the blood; her anger rose.

“Curse on you, you varlet. May the malady of France shrivel your pistol,” she yelled at her assailant.

The man was taken aback by the vehemence of Alice’s words, and went to strike her again but was prevented by another of the group.

“Leave it, Master Wainwright, she’s nought but a common strumpet. We have more important tasks to complete.”

The perpetrator pushed away the constraining arm of his fellow man-at-arms, cursed, and gave Alice a withering look, then skulked away with the rest of the unit. Alice watched as the men continued walking through the crowds, paying particular attention to any younger men who were present. It appeared that yet another eye-witness was helping the watchmen with their enquiries hoping to be rewarded.

The pregnant woman went to Alice's aid and helped her to her feet.

"Please accept mine most humble gratitude for your kindness," said the woman as Alice struggled to rise up.

She checked her lip again and wiped the blood from her mouth with the back of her hand.

"They are naught but animals, pay no heed."

Alice had yet to make any purchases but was concerned for her new-found friend.

"Let me escort you back to your dwelling."

The woman looked down. "I fear I have no dwelling, my lady."

"Ha, you are mistaken, I am no lady. So, where do you sleep?"

"Anywhere there is shelter."

"But what about your husband?"

"The plague took him not two months since. Without coin for rent, I was forced to leave, and in my condition, I have no way of earning a living."

Alice stood for a moment and looked at the piteous waif before her, no more than sixteen-years-old, her lank blonde hair protruding from her wimple. The girl's soiled dress was hardly able to contain her swelling belly.

"I need to collect a few chattels and some food; you can accompany me. My husband is at sea and I have room; you can stay with me … verily I would welcome the company."

"But I cannot repay you."

"That's not necessary: I don't need payment. What is your name?"

"Margaret, ma'am."

"I am Alice; you must call me Alice."

Alice took her hand. "Come, Margaret, I need to make some purchases; you can help me carry them."

The pair walked through the crowded marketplace, Alice buying the items she needed. Her swollen lip was irritating her and the bitter taste of iron lingered on her tongue, but she ignored the inconvenience; she had suffered worse. It would serve as a reminder.

After completing her purchases, Alice led her companion back to the dwelling carrying the new bath, which was too cumbersome for Margaret to manage.

Alice opened the door and led Margaret inside.

"Oh, but this is grand," she said, looking around.

"We are still making it home, but since my husband has returned to sea he has left me to attend to what needs to be done."

"Then I can help," said Margaret.

Three days into the journey, and the cog was making steady progress towards its destination, winds had been light to moderate. The coast of the Lowlands could be seen approaching in the distance as a dark outline on the horizon.

Captain Harvey was well-acquainted with the waters and, having crossed the North Sea many times before, the sight of land and familiar landmarks would guide them along the coast in search of the estuary that would take them down the River Rhine and their final destination.

He looked at the sky; he knew the signs. It was dusk, but the fair weather that had blessed the journey so far was at an end. Clouds had rolled in from the west; conditions had deteriorated considerably in just half an hour.

The force of the wind caused the single sail to flap violently, as if complaining at the strain being placed on it.

The noise as it wrapped against the mast echoed around the boat deck. The cog picked up pace, driven by the increased wind velocity, and it was taking all the skill and strength of the crew to control it. John Wolfe was in the thick of things, directing fellow crewmen to the ropes.

The waves had increased in size with white tops breaking over themselves, making the boat toss alarmingly. Many passengers were on deck having succumbed to motion sickness. The captain looked on with concern.

"Break sail," he hollered. "Rigging-men aloft."

With the wind speed approaching the capacity of the sail, this was a usual precaution in strong winds and the crew knew the drill. There was a danger of the mast being snapped off; the captain was taking no chances.

The crew set to their task. A rope rigging stretched from the deck to the top of the mast some fifty feet above them, and without hesitation, two men scrambled upward. The boat was swaying violently making the exercise extremely hazardous.

The crewmen reached the top of the mast; the huge, hemp-based canvas billowed below them, complaining bitterly at the strain. They managed to release the shackles that held the sail beam to the top of the mast, allowing the men below to begin lowering it.

The two sailors started to descend. The first man made it to the deck, but the second had become entangled in the rigging. He was frantically trying to free himself. With an almighty effort he tugged himself free, but the momentum coincided with a large wave that pitched the cog ten degrees. The motion was enough to force the seaman to lose his grip of the rigging and drop some thirty feet into the sea.

Wolfe was on deck helping to pull in the sail and saw what had happened. Several men were watching the water, then spotted the seaman break surface. Without thinking, Wolfe climbed up onto the side of the cog and dived into the waves. It was like being stabbed by a thousand needles as the cold hit him, but he shrugged it off. He could see the stricken sailor and started swimming hard towards him. In less than a minute, Wolfe had reached and secured the man; he then turned to head back to the boat.

Unfortunately, the tide and wind was taking the cog further away. Undaunted, Wolfe continued to swim hard. Men were on deck shouting encouragement. One was holding a rope which he threw towards Wolfe; it fell short. He reeled it in and tried again. This time it straddled Wolfe who managed to grab hold.

There were shouts of heave, heave, as several crewmen pulled Wolfe and the drowning sailor towards the boat. It seemed to take forever, but within minutes, they were hauled on deck.

Wolfe lay for a moment trying to recover, his body overflowing with adrenalin. He spat seawater from his mouth, then inhaled deeply trying to catch his breath. The cold returned; he started shaking violently. Meanwhile, attention was being given to the sailor who had fallen. He was unconscious, but breathing.

Captain Harvey handed the tiller to his deputy, then joined the crewmen who were crowding around Wolfe.

"Give them some air, give them some air," ordered the captain,

The group parted, allowing the captain to clearly see the state of his men.

Wolfe sat up and put his head in his hands, slowly recovering from his ordeal. The other sailor was beginning to regain consciousness, mumbling incoherently.

Wolfe struggled to his feet, still shivering uncontrollably.

The captain approached him. “What’s your name, seaman?”

“Wolfe, sir, John Wolfe.”

“You’re a brave man, John Wolfe. Go below; we need to find you some dry clothes.”

With the sail down, the cog was being taken by the tide, but was now stable. The passengers had been confined to below decks to enable the crew to work. The accommodation on board was sparse, the travellers who had paid for the journey, had been housed together towards the stern, allowing space for the cargo. Comfort was not a great priority; they had been provided with straw mattresses or, if they had one, a blanket. Crewmen were even less accommodated, and had to make do with loose straw; most would just sleep on deck.

Wolfe followed the captain to his quarters below the stern castle. It was a modest room with a desk; sea charts were open on top. There was a small bed in the corner and a table and two chairs.

As the pair entered his quarters, there was another man seated at the table, his head in his hands, and appeared to be groaning.

“Master Giese, this is John Wolfe; he’s just showed remarkable bravery in saving one of the crew. He needs a change of clothes.”

Giese looked up. “Please excuse my appearance, Master Wolfe, I admit I have been trying to sleep. I have recently been struck down with sickness of the sea. I heard the commotion.”

There was a bucket in the corner which had been used, confirming Giese’s condition.

The captain intervened. “Pay no heed, Master Giese, I will find some clothes for this man and leave you to your slumbers.”

There was a small trunk in the corner and the captain went to it and opened it. He pulled out a pair of breeches and a tunic.

"Here, these would suffice, I believe," said the Captain, handing the garments to Wolfe.

After a few minutes Wolfe had changed into the fresh clothes. His body temperature was starting to recover.

"Verily, I am with gratitude, Captain," said Wolfe, viewing the garments.

"Before you return to your duties, your courage deserves some recognition."

Captain Harvey opened his desk and pulled out a small purse. He rummaged inside and pulled out a coin, then handed it to Wolfe.

Wolfe nodded in acknowledgement, then left the cabin. More retching sounds could be heard, as he made his way above deck.

The captain was surveying the scene as dawn broke. The storm had subsided and the sail re-set, billowing contentedly in the stiff breeze.

The coast of the Low Countries was much closer now. Giese had joined the captain on deck.

"Ah, Master Giese, how are you feeling this morn?"

"Much improved, Captain, much improved."

"Good, good. We are making favourable time. That is the coastline of Holland, one of the Seventeen Provinces." He pointed at the dark shape not more than ten miles away. "We should be in the estuary by this afternoon, then conditions will be much easier."

"I'm pleased to hear it."

As they entered the Rhine delta, more cogs came into view. Most were coastal vessels, serving the ports of Bruges and Antwerp.

The remainder of the journey passed without incident, and two days later, early evening, the cog moved slowly into the harbour in Cologne.

Cologne was an important, arguably the most important city, in the Hanseatic League. The main conurbation lay south of the river and was contained within an impressive stone wall with the Rhine providing the northern barrier. It had some fine architecture, not least its many churches which dominated the skyline.

The English trade remained a major asset in Cologne's long-distance commerce, and England continued to flourish as the primary market for wine traded from Cologne. The city's merchants succeeded in largely monopolising the distribution of English tin, as well as the trade in weaponry, (swords, armour, spears).

The harbour was busy as Captain Harvey guided the cog to its berth. Georg Giese was alongside as the crew secured the boat and started to unload the cargo.

"Captain Harvey, I have a matter of great secrecy I need to discuss with you. Can we go to your cabin?"

"Why, of course, Master Giese."

Having checked everything was in order on deck, the captain returned to his cabin accompanied by Giese.

"How can I help the Deputy Alderman?" asked the captain.

"What I'm about to tell you, must not go beyond this cabin."

"Very well, you have my word."

"I am embarking on business regarding King Henry's financial situation."

The captain looked at Giese with expectancy.

"I will be putting together a significant amount of coin to

be transported back to London as soon as it can be arranged, and I want you to deliver it. You will, of course, be suitably recompensed."

It was part of Giese's plan to outline the nature of his return journey; ship's captains were renowned for their gossip once in an ale house.

"Aye, I'd be pleased to."

"How soon before you are ready to return?"

"There is cargo to arrange, two, maybe three weeks."

"Excellent, excellent. I will give you more information when I can. How do I reach you?"

"I will be staying onboard," replied the captain.

Originally from Danzig, another important Hansa port, Giese had moved with his family to Germany when he was twelve, following his father's appointment as Chancellor of the Cologne district of the Hanseatic League. Giese would stay at his parent's house while he waited for the return journey. He, too, had some arrangements to make.

Giese's father, Heidrick, was a prominent figure in the Hanseatic League, having served as Chancellor for five years before retiring. His counsel on important matters was still sought. Georg needed to discuss his mission with him.

He was welcomed with open arms as he presented himself at the door of the family home, a large mansion close to the city wall.

His mother, Greta, hugged him fondly. They spoke in German.

After catching up with his news and enjoying his mother's cooking, Georg revealed his plan to his father over a glass of brandy, while his mother cleared the kitchen.

Heidrick listened, then summarised. "So, your intention is to present the English with an empty chest and claim the contents to have been stolen?"

"It was Hermann's idea."

"And one with a degree of danger, not just to you personally, but to Hansa's reputation."

"But it is the only solution; I could not rightly refuse such a request from the King's Treasurer."

"But why would the King's Treasurer make such a request? It must be clear to anyone that the League would not countenance donating money in this way while we are waging war with Rome."

"Aye, but not if it were to court favour and support from the English. They do have the best navy in Christendom," countered Georg.

"And King Henry is behind this request?"

George looked down. "In truth, I am not sure how much knowledge the King has of this transaction; I understand he is distracted with other matters, but his Treasurer is responsible for His Majesty's financial affairs."

"And you have met this man, in person?"

"Aye, father, William Fitzwilliam, a man of influence … and integrity," Georg added quickly.

"Hmm … And if this subterfuge is discovered? What then?"

"I have been very careful, father."

"But there will be an investigation."

"Yes, which we can control."

"Well, it is not something that I can endorse, but I know you well enough that you will go ahead. I will try to protect you should it go wrong."

Chapter Five

John Wolfe left his lodgings. It had been two weeks since he landed in Cologne, and he decided to find a suitable tavern to pass the time. Although being born in Cologne - his parents had moved to London when he was fourteen, his recollection of the city was hazy. He also had to readjust to speaking German again, having not used it for some twenty years. Both his parents were now dead and he had no family in the city of which he was aware.

He had chosen a more expensive boarding house than he might have done in the past, one with a real bed and a bathhouse in an outbuilding, and, with coin in his pocket – his seaman's wages, plus the 'bonus' the captain had given him for saving his fellow crewman, he was feeling good.

It was a grey evening; nights were drawing in and leaves were starting to turn colour. He headed towards the dock area where there were numerous ale-houses.

With so much time on his hands, boredom had settled in. He had visited the docks on several occasions to see when the cog would be returning to London, but there was no news. There was a rumour that the boat was waiting for a special consignment, but no-one seemed to know what the nature of the shipment was.

Wolfe had spent most of his free time drinking with some of his fellow crewmen, most of whom were in more modest accommodation, or more often, sharing a floor space. They were generally raucous affairs with fights a regular occurrence. No-one would attempt to challenge John Wolfe. His reputation had preceded him and, in any confrontation, possible opponents would always back down.

Tonight, he had decided to try a tavern on the dockside,

one he had not visited before. The usual array of harlots catcalled as he walked by, but he wasn't tempted; they would be riddled with the pox.

As he reached the alehouse, he looked across at the wide river, grey and swift-flowing. Several cogs were tied at their moorings in preparation for sail. He could see the London-bound ship bobbing rhythmically in the current, mast lowered. It would be a few more days before it would retrace its journey.

He entered the tavern and looked around. It was nothing special, a reasonable size with probably thirty or forty drinkers. The noise of conversation buzzed, in several languages; someone in the corner was trying to sing, but there were little takers to join in. The singer eventually collapsed on the table with his head in his hands.

A serving wench approached. Wolfe ordered a tankard and then spotted a familiar face seated at a table in the corner on his own. It was Captain Harvey.

Wolfe collected his ale and approached his acquaintance.

"Captain Harvey, would you care for some company this e'en?"

The captain looked up at Wolfe, his eyes were glazed, clearly the worse for drink.

"John Wolfe, if I'm not mistaken. Aye, sit yourself down." He spoke in English.

Wolfe pulled up a chair and sat opposite the captain.

They exchanged pleasantries and it was Wolfe who posed the question. "What news on the sailing, Captain?"

Harvey leaned forward and looked around to ensure no-one was listening.

"I have heard just this afternoon that we will be leaving in two days' time. I will need all crewmen to report for loading duties tomorrow. I have a note of their lodgings. If you want to earn yourself a groat, you can collect them for me."

"Ha, they will be in a tavern or two, you mark my words," countered Wolfe.

"Well, as many as you can. Once word gets out they will turn up."

"Aye, true enough … " Wolfe paused. "There's a rumour that we will be carrying a special consignment."

The captain took another swig of ale.

"Aye, is that so? Not sure where you heard that. It's not something I can discuss." His words were slurring.

"You can trust me, Captain; I shall not breath a word."

The captain leaned forward. "All I know is that it is the King's business."

"King's business?"

"Aye, a special consignment for the King."

"Coin … or gold, perchance?"

"The content has not been shared with me. There, I have said too much."

"I'll not speak of it, Captain, you have my word."

Wolfe and the captain continued their deliberations until well after dark, but, despite more ale, the captain was not forthcoming about the mysterious consignment he was entrusted with to return to London.

Charged with rounding up the crew members, Wolfe decided to return to his lodgings before midnight, leaving the captain asleep at the table, unable to stand up.

Once outside, he sniffed the invigorating cool air; it was pitch black. Wolfe waited for his eyes to adjust to the dark. The night was quiet as he walked along the quayside back towards his accommodation, even the harlots had gone home. There was no illumination apart from the occasional 'light-boy', employed to guide a customer to their destination by a pitch-torch, thus avoiding the many trip-point obstacles that were everywhere. The candle-glow from alehouses provided some comfort and would guide Wolfe back to his lodgings.

He was about to turn left, heading away from the river when he suddenly heard a groaning noise. Wolfe squinted his eyes to get a better view. He could see the masts of maybe twenty cogs at their moorings on the river. The noise of rope clicking against wood as the breeze caused the riggings to flap against the masts echoed in the night air.

There it was again, a low groan.

There was a small cog tied to a capstan directly opposite. The noise appeared to be coming from the wharf alongside.

There was little ambient light; clouds hid any moon. Wolfe decided to investigate, walking slowly towards the groans. He could see the cog moving gently at its mooring against the skyline, its mast swaying in the breeze.

Wolfe almost stumbled on the prostrate form of a man holding onto the capstan and trying to haul himself to his feet.

He had heard Wolfe approach and spoke in German. "Please help me; I fear I have been robbed."

Wolfe reached the stricken man. On closer examination, Wolfe could tell he was a man of wealth, the feel of the cloth of his tunic and robe, thick and expensive. His feathered hat was lay on the ground; there appeared to be blood coming from the back of his head.

"Sit down and catch your breath, sir," said Wolfe, helping him onto the capstan. "Tell me what happened."

His speech was slurred as if drunk. "This is my boat. I was making my way back to my house … Someone attacked me; I didn't see them."

"Them?"

"Yes, at least two. It was dark. I was hit about the head. I fear I have been robbed."

"Where do you live, sir?"

"It is an hour-less stride from here."

"Come, I will help you, but you will need to guide me."

"That is most kind, sir. I shall forever be in your debt."

Wolfe lifted the man from his seating position and held him under the arm. Together, they shuffled into the city, making progress by the light of taverns as they passed. There was an irony here; in different circumstances, Wolfe would be targeting such a man for possible gain.

Wolfe had no idea where he was. On the east side, he thought, heading away from the river, into an area of wealth and affluence.

It was over three quarters of an hour of shuffling pace before they eventually arrived at a large house, set back from the road, fronted by lawns. A path led to the entrance door. There was light coming from inside. The man spoke in German.

"It is here, please, come inside and let me reward you for your kindness."

"It is not necessary."

"Please, I insist."

The man knocked on the door, an urgent knock. A lady of mature years quickly answered it.

"Mathias! Where have you been? We have been so worried, the boat docked hours ago."

Wolfe helped him inside. It was a grand hall, lit by many candelabras around the room.

"I was knocked to the ground and robbed; this gentleman helped me, but for his intervention, I most probably would have died."

"Oh, sir, we are in your debt. Please come in, let me get you some refreshment."

Wolfe helped the man through another door into magnificent living quarters. A blazing fire warmed the room which was filled with fine furnishings. A serving wench appeared.

"Emilinda, please get this man some of our finest ale."

The girl left the room.

The man sat down in front of the fire. "Are you hurt, Matthias?" asked the woman.

"I was knocked unconscious; they hit me about the head."

She went behind him and started rummaging through the man's matted long hair. "Yes, you are bleeding. Where is your hat?"

"In the river, by now, I warrant."

"Wait, dear, I will get something to bathe your wounds." She looked at Wolfe who was standing, observing the events. "Herr … I'm sorry, I don't know your name."

"It's Wolfe, ma'am, John Wolfe."

"Herr Wolfe, please take a seat."

The serving wench appeared with a pewter tankard filled with foaming ale and handed it to Wolfe.

He took a sip. "Mmm … that is a fine ale, so it is."

"That is one of our best... I'm sorry we have not been properly introduced. Mathias Koch, brewer. The woman is my wife, Heldin. I hope you are enjoying a small sample."

"Aye, Herr Koche, tis a fine ale indeed."

Wolfe could see the man more clearly. He was younger than at first glance, dressed warmly in the garments favoured by wealthy merchants. There was blood on the back of his collar.

The brewer continued. "I have just returned from a delivery of casks to Dusseldorf. We landed at dusk; my crew were paid and I was on my way home when I was attacked. It seems they were after my purse."

"I hope you have not suffered a great loss."

"Several silver Thaler, I fear. But I am alive, thanks to you. Where are you from? Your tone is accented."

"London, sir."

Wolfe took another sip of ale. The serving wench returned carrying a plate of bread and cheese, followed by Heldin carrying a wooden bowl filled with warm water.

Heldin spoke. "I don't suppose you have had anything to eat, Herr Wolfe. Please help yourself, Emilinda will get more, if you are hungry. We have plenty."

"Aye, I shall be grateful."

Wolfe took the plate and started eating.

"Where are you staying, Herr Wolfe?" asked Mathias.

"In lodgings near the dock. I am due to sail in two days."

"You work on the cogs?"

"Aye."

"And you are from London?"

"Aye."

"Your German is very good."

"I was born in Cologne and moved to London as a young man," responded Wolfe.

Heldin started bathing the back of her husband's head and dabbing it with a cloth.

Mathias looked at Wolfe. "Well, you must stay here tonight; I insist; we have the room. You can't be wandering the streets at this hour."

"Do not concern yourself, Herr Koch, I can look after myself."

"I have no doubt, but they hide in shadows, two or three; you will be no match."

Wolfe took another mouthful of bread and cheese. The brewer was right, and he had no idea of his route back to his lodgings. In the darkness it would be difficult to pick out landmarks.

"Aye, very well, Herr Koch, I will accept your kind offer."

"Excellent, excellent. You must join me in another tankard before you retire."

So, for the next hour, Wolfe, Mathias, and Heldin, sat around the fireside and exchanged stories. Wolfe learned more about the family. There was a seventeen-year-old daughter, Inga, who was away at a convent school. They had had four other children; all had died early in life.

The Koch brewery was an old established firm in Cologne; Mathias was the fourth generation. As well as having the monopoly of beer production in the city, they shipped casks all along the Rhine by cog. It was a profitable exercise and, by any measure, the Koch family were very wealthy.

Mathias eventually excused himself, overcome by shock and the effects of concussion. He stood up.

"If you ever decide to move back to Cologne, Herr Wolfe, there will always be a job for you here."

"That is something to consider, Herr Koch," replied Wolfe.

"Emilinda will show you to your quarters."

The serving maid was summoned, and, holding a candlestick, led Wolfe up a set of stairs and along a landing.

"I have prepared this room for you, Herr Wolfe; I hope it will be to your satisfaction."

"I'm sure it will be, Fraulein Emilinda."

Like the rest of the house, the room was palatial and well-furnished with fine paintings on the wall and exquisite floor covering, with a large bed opposite the window.

"Will there be anything else, Herr Wolfe?"

She was waif-like, no more than sixteen. She lowered her eyes, suggesting other delights were possibly available, but with a full stomach of ale, Wolfe made no further demands.

Church bells sounded as dawn broke, waking Wolfe from a deep slumber. Dreams had haunted him, men with swords.

He got out of bed and used the piss-pot; then splashed his face with water to refresh himself.

His clothes felt clammy as he put them on.

Feeling more alert, Wolfe went downstairs and was greeted by Emilinda.

"I am making breakfast, Herr Wolfe, please go through to the dining room."

Wolfe was shown into another room where Mathias was seated at a table.

"Ah, Herr Wolfe, I hope you slept well."

"Aye, sir, most comfortable. I trust you are not experiencing any enduring consequences from your injury."

"A sore head, no more. I will report the robbery to the watchmen, but it will be to no avail, I fear."

"Aye, sir."

Breakfast took an hour, but then Wolfe excused himself, he had work to do,

Earlier the previous day, back in London, Alice was cleaning, being aided by the new lodger, Margaret.

They had become good friends since they met, and Margaret had provided much-needed company for Alice while Wolfe was away.

The sext bells had rung, it was early afternoon, when there was a banging and commotion at the door. "Open in the name of the King," came a cry.

Alice went to investigate.

The door flew open and a burley sergeant-at-arms stood there, blocking the light. He was accompanied by five other men, all armed with swords.

Before Alice could comply, they barged in. She

recognised the sergeant straightaway; it was the same man that had knocked her down in the marketplace.

He suddenly grabbed her by the throat and lifted her off the floor.

"Where is John Wolfe?"

"Put me down, put me down, you varlet, my husband is at sea," Alice screamed.

He dropped her to the floor and Alice started rubbing her throat.

"We have reason to believe he was involved in a robbery in Spitalfields this last month."

"No, no, that can't be right; I told you; he's been at sea … for several weeks … By my troth."

He looked at her, not convinced and shouted to his soldiers. "Search the house."

The five soldiers went through the dwelling, ransacking everything, paying particular attention to the mattresses which were torn to shreds.

After twenty minutes of fruitless searching, the soldiers returned to the sergeant. "Nothing, sir," said the leading soldier.

Alice was now sat up; her chemise had become undone and her skirt rumpled below her, risen above her knee. She clutched her top to protect her modesty.

"I told you my husband is at sea; he couldn't have been involved in any robbery."

The sergeant considered this for a few moments, then stooped down to Alice. She could smell his fetid breath.

He grabbed her head and turned it to the right, then to the left. Then looked down at the flesh on show.

He took out a dagger and ran it down her throat to her hands that were clutching her bodice.

"You're a fine looking woman, Mistress Wolfe, your

husband is indeed a lucky man. I expect you provide much comfort for him... I have a proposal."

Alice gasped.

The sergeant shouted at his men to wait outside. They turned and exited the cottage.

Margaret was still in the corner, shaking with fear.

The sergeant sheathed his dagger. "Now, I can forget this visit; verily, I can ensure this call never happens again."

He grasped the top of her bodice and wrenched it open.

"It doesn't seem fair that one man should have this much pleasure to himself." He ripped her bodice further. "As I was saying, I can forget your husband's name in this matter. What say you?"

"You want favours from me?"

"Aye, I am sure your husband would understand, given the circumstances. It could even save him from the hangman."

Alice thought for a moment. Resisting would be fruitless and, if it meant protecting Wolfe, she would comply.

She pulled the top of her bodice together and slowly stood up. "Very well, follow me."

"No, Mistress Alice, you can't," cried Margaret.

"Worry not, Margaret. All will be well."

Alice led the sergeant to the bedroom, and looked in horror at the devastation as she entered the room.

"What is this, sir? Is this how you treat innocent folk who go about their daily business, God-fearing? Who will pay for all this damage?"

He looked at her. "I will see you are suitably recompensed."

"Aye, you will indeed … Let's get this done."

Alice lay on the floor among the bits of mattress, raised her skirt, and waited for the inevitable.

It was over in less than a minute, and the sergeant-at-arms collapsed sweating on top of her. She pushed him off and straightened herself.

She looked down at the man with disdain. “I trust you are a man of your word, Sergeant?”

He raised himself. “We will have to see; the informant was very certain.”

“Then your informant was mistaken. They would say anything for coin; been on the tickle brain, I warrant.”

He stood up and pulled up his hose, then looked at her.

“We could make this a regular arrangement, if you are willing, just to ensure your husband is not troubled by the magistrate. I will see you are suitably recompensed.”

“My husband is due back shortly. I fear he would not think fondly of such an arrangement.”

“Well, let’s hope the informant withdraws his statement.”

The sergeant-at-arms turned and left the room, clearly not entirely content. Alice immediately started washing herself in the bucket. Margaret entered the room and could see Alice in her ablutions.

“Oh Mistress Alice, are you hurt? Men, they are naught but animals.”

“No, no, I’m well enough. Here, help me clean this room. We will need to buy more bedding, I fear.”

Back in Cologne, with two days before the sailing, Georg Giese had purchased a large seaman’s chest from a riverside chandlery. He had also hired five men-at-arms to accompany the trunk to the cog and onto London. The rumour of a special consignment had been shared among the ship’s crew, and spread among the numerous taverns that populated the dock.

Giese was aware that rumours were abound; he did nothing to allay them.

Meanwhile, Wolfe had left the hospitality of the brewer

laden with food for the journey, given to him by the brewer's wife. He had managed to round up most of the crew. Word would soon get around the ale houses that the sailing was imminent; then he headed to the quay.

As Wolfe reached the dockside, the wharf, that was home to the London-bound cog, was busy as the boat was being prepared for its journey. It was a blustery day, and the vessel bobbed up and down at its moorings. Captain Harvey was on deck, supervising the activity and saw Wolfe walking up the gangplank.

"Ah Wolfe." He rummaged in his tunic, pulled out his purse, and handed Wolfe a coin.

"The groat, I promised."

Wolfe accepted it with a nod of appreciation. "What news of the special consignment?"

"Master Giese spoke to me this morning; he will be arriving later today. He's bringing five men-at-arms with him for the journey." Wolfe looked quizzically. "They'll be standing guard on the voyage," the captain confirmed.

Wolfe was thinking. "Hmm, so it must be important."

"Aye," replied the captain. "Take over the loading; I need to return to my cabin."

"Aye, captain," Wolfe acknowledged, then left the cog to supervise the dockside activities.

Mid-afternoon, the none bells had rung from several churches across Cologne. A horse and cart approached the cog from along the waterfront flanked by two soldiers each side and one following behind. All were suited in armour and carrying a sword.

Georg Giese, dressed in his formal merchant's clothing and fine hat, was seated next to the coachman as it pulled up alongside the cog.

All loading duties stopped as the crewmen stared at the arrival.

Giese stepped down and ordered the chest to be unloaded. Wolfe was on deck and watched as two soldiers climbed onto the cart and started lifting the container down to two other soldiers. The consignment did not seem to be particularly heavy, but it took two to carry it.

Giese supervised the loading, leading the soldiers up the gang plank, two carrying the chest by side-handles, three following behind.

Down in the lower deck, the chest was secured by chains to the side and floor of the boat among some of the cargo that was being loaded. Giese personally supervised the containment.

Captain Harvey came down from the upper deck and approached Giese.

"Is everything to your satisfaction, Master Giese?"

"Aye, Captain Harvey, my men will stay overnight and for the duration of the voyage; ensure you have enough provisions."

"Aye, Master Giese."

Giese turned and alighted the carriage next to the coachman.

"I will return on the morrow," he called down.

"We sail on the morning tide," reminded the captain, and watched as the carriage pulled away.

The following day, John Wolfe vacated his accommodation and walked to the wharf carrying his leather bag containing his worldly goods and the food he had received from the brewer's wife. It was a grey drizzly morning. He reached the cog and stowed his belongings below deck, then took up his duties. There was much talk among the crew concerning the special consignment which was in the hold being guarded by two men at arms. The two remaining soldiers were relaxing awaiting their turn for duty.

Giese's carriage returned as the terse bells were sounding. He was again accompanied by men-at-arms. Two men were assigned to carry his luggage onboard. He was greeted warmly by the captain.

"Master Giese, please make yourself comfortable in my cabin."

"Aye … I take it my consignment has not been disturbed."

"Nay, Master Giese, your men have ensured its security."

Giese was not of good cheer, realising he was facing a possible week of seasickness and went below deck to check on the trunk. It was still chained and sealed. He nodded in satisfaction, then made his way to the captain's cabin.

With all the cargo and provisions stowed, the vessel slowly eased out of the dock into the full flow of the Rhine. With the current flowing seaward taking the cog along with it, the journey time to the estuary and the North Sea would be quicker than the inbound journey.

As well as the crew and Giese's soldiers, there were six passengers making the trip, Hansa merchants returning to the Steelyard; accommodation would again be basic.

The voyage back to London was uneventful, the wind was favourable, the sea choppy, but insufficient to cause too much discomfort to those on board.

Captain Harvey was in charge of the tiller for most of the journey, catching only a few hours' sleep, whilst handing over steering duties to his second-in-command. Speculation on board continued to grow regarding the contents of the special cargo.

Whilst on shore, John Wolfe had made friends with one of the crew, Thomas Drake, and they had shared many an evening in various alehouses together. Two days into the journey, and they were seated on deck below the forecastle taking food.

"What say you to the cargo? Seems soldiers have not left it since we set sail," said Drake.

"I have no thought on the matter. I heard it was King's business," replied Wolfe.

"But you must have some curiosity. There's a rumour it's gold crowns; someone said they saw it."

"Sounds like alehouse talk, pay no heed. Best say naught; it could cost you your head."

Drake looked at Wolfe with concern. "Aye, you could be right."

Three days later, the cog was making its way slowly up the Thames. The tide was with them and they made good progress towards their destination,

They passed the many wharves of the city; the Thames was again alive with traffic, boats of all kinds. The cog slowed while the span of London Bridge was raised to allow it to pass through and dock at the Steelyard.

It took over an hour to berth and secure the cog. The merchant passengers left the boat and made their way to their quarters a short walk away, while the crew started to unload cargo. Georg Giese was on deck watching the activity.

With the ship secure, Captain Harvey returned to his quarters preparing to pay the men for their service, The soldiers were still guarding the chest.

After a couple of minutes, Giese followed him below deck. The captain was seated at his desk. The merchant addressed him. “I have an errand to run, Captain. My men will stay here until my return.”

The captain looked up; he was holding a bag of coin. “Fear not, sir, your cargo will not be disturbed. I will be staying aboard tonight,” he announced.

Georg Giese left the cog, dressed in his formal merchant’s clothing. He straightened his hat before traversing the gangplank.

Stepping onto dry land after a lengthy spell at sea, caused his legs to buckle temporarily. He slowly recovered, holding on to a nearby wall, and staggered further into the Steelyard like a drunkard. Luckily, no one was about to witness this ungainly stride. He reached his destination, Winter Hall, the quarters of the Chancellor, Hermann Hillebrandt Wedigh. He needed to brief him.

Giese entered the building, which was still busy, despite it approaching vespers, late afternoon. Merchants were busy completing business. He reached the Chancellor’s office and knocked on the door. He was called in.

Wedigh was seated behind his writing desk and looked up. He had a quill in his hand and a parchment on his desk; he had been writing. The wet ink glistened. The Chancellor smiled warmly genuinely pleased to see his deputy.

He got up and greeted Giese with an embrace.

“Master Georg, my dear boy, you have been much in my thoughts. Please take a seat and recount your news. Have you fulfilled the plan?”

Giese outlined his journey and explained that the chest was safely on board the cog.

“That is most excellent news … And no-one suspects anything?”

“No, sir, it has been carried out with complete secrecy.

There are rumours, of course, which I have done nothing to dispel, about the content of the chest … ”

“Good, good,” said the Chancellor, cutting off the conversation.

“What should I say to the Treasurer? I was hoping for your wisdom before I go to Westminster and seek him out.”

“No, don’t go to the Hall; let me compose a letter and we will send a messenger.”

Chapter Six

Giese watched on as the Chancellor produced a blank parchment from his desk and started composing a message to be delivered to William Fitzwilliam, Treasurer to the King, at Westminster Hall.

Preferring not to be too specific, it merely stated that a consignment had arrived for him from Cologne and was awaiting collection at the Steelyard Wharf. He would leave security arrangements in the Treasurer's hands.

The parchment was sealed with wax. The Chancellor left his office and scanned the available merchants in the hall. He noticed a youthful-looking clerk and summoned him. The young man approached.

"Ah, Hans, I want you to deliver this to William Fitzwilliam, Treasurer to the King, at Westminster Hall, in person. It is not to be given to anyone else. I expect you to guard it with your life. You may take a horse." instructed Wedigh.

The messenger acknowledged.

The Chancellor handed over the document, then returned to his quarters.

"Well, Master Georg, now we wait. Would you care for some refreshment?"

The messenger was smartly dressed as all Steelyard merchants, and made his way to the stables and chose a suitable mount. Then, he left the compound through the Thames Street exit gate and headed east.

The Vespers bells tolled as he passed the huge church of St Pauls, visible over the tops of the houses.

Westminster Hall was almost three miles away from

the Steelyard compound. The messenger headed towards Blackfriars and across the River Fleet via the Pilgrim Street bridge, a fortified crossing.

The road followed the Thames as it meandered south in a ninety-degree turn. Small craft and ferrymen could be seen going about their work.

The messenger continued his journey at a steady canter, and arrived at the impressive seat of Parliament before dusk. He led his mount by the reins and tied it alongside several other horses outside the quadrangle, then made his way inside.

The main hall was bustling with activity as administrators went about their business. It was gloomy, illuminated only by dozens of large candelabra in alcoves set in the walls. The messenger approached one of the clerks and made enquiries regarding the whereabouts of the Treasurer. He was directed to the Lord Steward's offices, where he was in conference with Lord Shrewsbury.

The messenger reached the door and knocked. It was Fitzwilliam that answered; Lord Shrewsbury was seated behind his writing desk.

The messenger announced himself in a strong German accent. "I have a message from Herr Giese from the Steelyard for The Lord Treasurer, sir."

"I am Treasurer to His Majesty," replied Fitzwilliam.

The merchant bowed and the parchment was handed over. He remained standing, as Fitzwilliam went around the other side of the writing desk and joined Lord Shrewsbury. Together they opened the letter.

Fitzwilliam looked at his mentor and smiled. "This is excellent news, my Lord."

Fitzwilliam looked up at the merchant. "Can you take a message in return?"

"Ja, my Lord."

"Very well, find some refreshment and return in half an hour. I will have a reply."

The messenger left the room,

"What should we do, my Lord?" asked Fitzwilliam.

The Earl read the message again. "It doesn't say how much, just a consignment. Hmm, well, I don't want to collect the goods tonight. It will be dark within the hour, and gold is far too dangerous to transport at night. I will tell them we will arrive tomorrow morn. We will need some men-at-arms. You have done well, William."

"Aye, my Lord; I will see to it."

The messenger returned at the allotted time, and was presented with a sealed linen letter to deliver to Georg Giese.

John Wolfe had completed his duties on the cog and had been recompensed for his labours. Captain Harvey offered him further work, but Wolfe refused to commit for the moment.

He was in good spirits as he walked through the streets back to the house carrying his leather bag over his shoulder. He was, however, still watchful, keeping in the shadows of the houses. He had no idea whether the hue and cry was still active.

He reached the dwelling without incident and opened the door. Alice was seated at the table and looked up. Her expression a mixture of surprise and pleasure. Wolfe entered and placed his travel bag on the floor beside him. The fire was burning in the alcove, and, with no chimney, it created a smoke haze across the room.

"John, you have returned. Thank God you are safe!"

Alice got up and went to greet him with a warm embrace.

Wolfe looked around the room.

"You have it looking homely."

"Aye, tis true... I have had some help."

"Help?"

"Aye, I have taken in a lodger to keep me company. I didn't think you would have any cause to disagree. She is with child."

"Where is this woman?" said Wolfe with a hint of disapproval.

"She is resting; she has not been so well these past days. But come, you must recount your journey and I will prepare a bath for you."

Wolfe gave Alice the briefest details of his travels while she set up the wooden bath in the middle of the room and started to boil some water on the pot over the fire.

Within a few minutes, the bath was ready and Wolfe undressed and got in.

"I have purchased some soap. I thought you would not mind, John."

"Nay, it is of no concern."

Alice was scrubbing Wolfe's hair and back, the water running down his body was a grey/brown colour from the dirt that had accumulated.

Waiting for the right moment, Alice anxiously broached the topic of the watchmen.

"I have something I need to confess, John, and I am uncertain of your response."

She stopped her washing.

"Three days since, a watchmen and five soldiers called, looking for you. They said someone had identified you as the cut-purse. The sergeant beat me about the head."

Wolfe turned to make eye contact; his face etched with anger.

"What did you tell them?"

"Happen, she prefers her own company."

"But she was not well. We must find her and bring her back."

Wolfe showed less concern than Alice. "She has left; it was her choice. We have more pressing matters to attend."

Alice was deep in thought. "I'll fetch your breakfast."

Georg Giese was anxiously awaiting the arrival of the party from Westminster Hall. He and the Chancellor had been in his quarters since daybreak.

Giese had been to the cog and checked on the chest; it was still sealed and in its position. All the remaining cargo had been unloaded. Captain Harvey, and three of his crew, who had no onshore lodgings, were the only presence on board.

It was mid-morning in the Steelyard when a guard arrived at the Chancellor's office from the Thames Street Gate to say that soldiers were waiting.

Giese left Wedigh's quarters and went to greet the party.

Arriving at the gate, he was approached by William Fitzwilliam on horseback, dressed in the formal attire of his position of Treasurer to the King, accompanied by nine mounted soldiers, and a wagon pulled by two horses. Lord Shrewsbury had decided not to make the journey.

"Good den, Master Giese," said Fitzwilliam, then proceeded to dismount and secure his horse.

"And to you, My Lord Treasurer," replied Giese.

After the formal greeting, Fitzwilliam followed Giese through the narrow passageways to the dock accompanied by three of the soldiers on foot. Their footsteps echoed around the walls, attracting an audience of merchants watching from vantage points. There was much speculation among them as to why men-at-arms were there.

They arrived at the wharf, there was a hazy sun peering through a cloudy sky, and a brisk wind made it chilly.

The cog was tied to the capstan on the dock and bobbing up and down in the fast flowing River Thames.

"My men will carry the cargo," said Fitzwilliam.

He ordered three of his guards to join him. They followed Giese on board the cog and below the deck.

The chest was still securely chained to the floor; Giese released the shackles with a key.

"You have the key to the chest, Master Giese?" asked Fitzwilliam.

"There is no key, my Lord. The chest is sealed. You care to open it now?"

Fitzwilliam thought for a moment. "No, Master Giese, we will keep it sealed until we reach Westminster. It will be safer."

"I have drawn a receipt in the sum of three hundred and sixty-six gold crowns, if you care to add your mark. I will see it is returned to the Chancellor in Cologne."

He produced a piece of linen paper from inside his tunic.

"Three hundred … ?" Fitzwilliam's eyes widened.

"And sixty-six," added Giese.

"This is most generous, Master Giese. His Majesty will be eternally grateful."

"I hope he will be able to extend his gratitude by more tangible means," replied Giese, and smiled.

He handed over the document, and Fitzwilliam put it inside his tunic. "I will return this once we have secured the goods."

Fitzwilliam ordered the three men to carry the chest.

There were handles on each side, and two men took the strain while one followed behind. The chest was transported off the cog, through the archway, passed the Winters Hall, and along the corridor to the exit gate of the compound where the rest of the guard were waiting. Giese and Fitzwilliam watched as the chest was loaded onto the wagon. There were more expressions of gratitude, before the party retraced their journey back to Westminster with Fitzwilliam at the head.

Elsewhere, breakfast had finished and Alice was anxious. "I want to look for Margaret. She has nowhere to go and is not a well girl."

Wolfe was still consumed with rage at the watchman's treatment of Alice. It was not a rage that would require a rant. It was a quiet, controlled rage; he knew exactly what he would do to exact his revenge. Nothing else would stand in his way.

"Aye, but first we need to find the watchman. I have an idea."

Wolfe related his plan to Alice "Aye, if you think it best," replied Alice, more in acquiescence than enthusiasm.

After a few minutes, they left together. Alice was wearing a white bodice, chemise, a full skirt, and wimple. It was the dress of a merchant's wife and would turn heads in the marketplace. They walked towards the stalls on Carter Lane. Alice had seen the watchman in the vicinity many times and would be the logical place to start.

Twenty minutes later, Alice and Wolfe were among the throng which had gathered to buy food and other materials. Suddenly, Alice spotted him.

"There, over yonder, that's him! Look at him strutting along like a peacock, the caitiff."

Wolfe turned and could see the man. "Aye, let's watch and see where he goes."

The sergeant was on his own, sword by his side. He stopped for a moment and looked around surreptitiously, as if checking no one was watching him, then entered a tavern, one popular with stall-holders and market goers.

Wolfe turned to Alice. "Very well, you know what to do. I will return to the house and wait unseen. Do whatever you need to do."

Wolfe left Alice and headed back. She checked around for other men-at-arms but could see none.

She felt a calm presence, totally at ease with her task. Alice entered the alehouse and peered through the gloomy interior. It was busy with traders and the occasional merchant. Alice spotted the sergeant on his own, staring into his tankard. She walked across the room and approached him.

"Is this seat taken, sir?" she asked, pointing at the vacant bench opposite the sergeant.

He looked up, his face at first angry at being disturbed, but then softened on seeing the enquirer.

"Why, Mistress Wolfe, I do declare, this is an unexpected pleasure. And looking so pleasing on the eye."

Alice ignored the compliment; she despised the man, and sat on the vacant bench. "I have been making purchases at the market. It is thirsty work."

"Then allow me to buy you a tankard of ale," replied the sergeant.

"As it pleases you," she replied, coyly.

The sergeant left his seat and returned with a wooden tankard. Alice acknowledged and took a sip.

"Is your husband still at sea?"

"Aye, sir, he is, and I have to admit to feeling lonely. I miss the touch of a good man" She looked at him with alluring eyes, and took a sip of her ale.

"Did you pay heed to my offer?"

"Aye, sir, indeed I did, and it would please me to accept. You mentioned suitable recompense."

"Aye, I will make it worth your while."

"But mark my words, I am not a common harlot, sir. I do not give away my favours to anyone, nor cheaply."

"Aye, it had not crossed my mind."

With little discourse, Alice finished her ale. "You remember my dwelling?"

"Aye, that I do."

"Then we will go there now. We will not be disturbed."

The sergeant tipped back the last of his ale and stood up.

It was a twenty minute walk back to the dwelling, completed in silence; Alice had no intention of starting a conversation with the man she despised. They arrived at the house and she led the sergeant inside. She turned and looked at him.

"You mentioned coin, sir."

"Aye," replied the sergeant, and reached inside his tunic.

He produced his purse and pulled out a groat.

"Is that all I am worth, sir? Tis a harlot's price."

He looked at her disapprovingly, then took out a shilling. Alice's eyes indicated satisfaction. Without acknowledgement, Alice took the coin and put it in a drawer then led the sergeant to the stairs. The pair's footsteps echoed around the short staircase as they ascended to the bedroom.

They entered, and Alice removed her wimple and started undoing her bodice ties. The sergeant removed his scabbard, then grabbed her. He ripped open her bodice in a sexual frenzy.

The sergeant had not detected the movement behind him. Without warning, a cudgel, heavy yew, carved into a rounded head, landed on the back of his skull. The sergeant dropped like a stone. Alice looked at the prone figure.

"Have you killed him, John?"

He knelt down and listened to the chest of the prostate sergeant-at-arms.

"Aye, it would seem so."

Alice fumbled about the man's clothing and found his purse.

"Happen I deserve this," she said, rattling the contents in her hands.

"Aye, that you do."

The pair looked at the stricken sergeant.

"What's to be done?" asked Alice.

"Happen he's for The Flitte."

"But someone will see."

"We'll wait until dark, but we'll need some sackcloth."

"I'll visit Mistress Rowe, the milliner. She will have some."

The River Fleet, a tributary of the Thames, at this time was little more than an open sewer, and took most of the human waste from the west side of the city. It was renowned for its smell.

It had been two hours since the compline bells had rung. Outside, it was pitch black. The room was bathed in the light from candles. Wolfe had removed and bundled up the clothes of the sergeant, then wrapped the body securely in sack cloth. It was as stiff as a board.

"What about his sword?" asked Alice.

"Happen I'll keep it," said Wolfe.

"Will you be able to carry him all the way to the bridge, John?"

"Aye, fifteen minutes good stride, should see me there."

"I should come with you. You should not do this on your own."

He looked at her, weighing up the suggestion. “Aye, very well, you can carry his clothes … here, help me lift him.”

Between them, they managed to manoeuvre the stricken sergeant to an upright position, allowing Wolfe to stoop and manhandle the body over his shoulder like a bag of kindle.

“Open the door; let’s get this done,” said Wolfe. Alice complied.

The river was less than half a mile away; the smell would often permeate the house if the wind was in the right direction.

Alice closed the door and followed Wolfe, keeping in the shadows.

The journey was fraught with danger. With walls blocking access to the river from the Thames to the Pilgrim Street crossing, they would need to proceed to Ludgate Hill and the Fleet Bridge, a much further distance.

They headed north past Blackfriars Church, using the back streets. There was no natural illumination, just the occasional light from a candle in a window. The sergeant was heavy and it was taking all Wolfe’s strength to carry the body. Alice walked alongside, keeping alert for any patrolling watchmen. They avoided the watchtower on Pilgrim Street, cutting through more alleyways, and reached Bowler Row which in daylight would be a busy thoroughfare.

Turning left onto Ludgate Hill, they were less than two-hundred yards from the bridge when Alice spotted a group of figures on the other side of the street, being led by a light-boy carrying a flaming tar-torch.

“Quick, John, a light-boy!” shout-whispered Alice.

They dodged into the shadows and waited for them to pass, then continued to the bridge. The smell was nauseating as they peered down into the slow-moving sludge.

Wolfe wasted no time, and just tipped the body into the fetid water some twenty feet below. Alice had been carrying the sergeant's clothes and threw them over the side as far as she could.

"Right, that's done; let's head home," said Wolfe.

Earlier, William Fitzwilliam led the small procession back to Westminster Hall on a fine black stallion. The wagon containing the chest was flanked by two outriders each side, with three following behind; the pace was slow, not more than a gentle trot. Bystanders stared as they passed.

It took them almost an hour to reach the gates of the seat of Parliament, then, through the archway and into the quadrangle, where the men dismounted and tethered the horses.

"Wait here," ordered Fitzwilliam.

He entered the building in search of Lord Shrewsbury; he was in his chambers. The Treasurer knocked, then entered.

"My Lord, the consignment has arrived," he announced with some excitement.

Lord Shrewsbury was reading some documents. He looked up.

"Very well. I suggest we take it to the vaults and secure it. We will need to make arrangements to transport the contents to the Tower. I will join you there directly."

Below the administrative offices of Westminster Hall, there were cellars, a secure area, ideal for storing the chest until the contents could be carried to the Tower of London where King Henry's gold and coin were kept.

Fitzwilliam returned to the wagon.

"Bring the chest to the cellars," he ordered.

Two guards removed the chest from the wagon and walked through to the entrance to the vaults. A steep stone stairway led downwards, and the soldiers made the descent. They were led by another guard, carrying a lighted torch. It was pitch black.

"Here," ordered Fitzwilliam, and the party moved through a door into a room which could have been used as a dungeon in the past.

"Wait here, Lord Shrewsbury will join us shortly."

Candles were lit, bringing some better illumination to the room.

It was over fifteen minutes before the Lord Steward arrived, preceded by a servant carrying a lighted torch.

"So this is it?" said Lord Shrewsbury, as he stared at the chest.

"Aye, my Lord, shall we open it?"

"Aye." He turned to the guards and ordered everyone out, except one guard who was holding the torch.

"Let me have your sword," ordered Fitzwilliam, and the guard complied.

The Treasurer examined the chest. The metal clasps at the side which secured the chest had been fused together by sealing wax.

Fitzwilliam hit it a sturdy blow with the sword and bits of hardened wax flew off. He repeated the exercise several times before the clasps were free of restraints.

"Give me a hand, soldier," barked Fitzwilliam, and between them they managed to prise open the trunk. The top folded over to one side.

"Pass the torch."

Fitzwilliam shone the flames over the innards of the chest. For a moment, he was lost for words.

"But … What trumpery is this?" he announced, in a state of shock.

Lord Shrewsbury peered inside.

"But it's empty."

"Aye... We have been robbed," said Fitzwilliam.

"But by who, and how. I thought the consignment had been guarded."

"Aye, every moment. It must have happened aboard the cog."

"Or in Cologne," proffered his Lordship.

"I need to speak to Giese."

"Aye, Master Fitzwilliam, make haste; we need to find out what has happened."

The Treasurer left the cellar and returned to the horses with two of his guards. He was seething at the duplicity, putting the blame firmly on the Hansa end of the transaction.

Fitzwilliam and his two men-at-arms arrived at the gate of the Steelyard an hour later and demanded to see Georg Giese. The Hansa guard was sent to find the Deputy Alderman.

Giese and the Chancellor were waiting in the Chancellor's office; they knew it would only be a matter of time before the chest would be opened and the absence of coin discovered.

The guard arrived, out of breath, and relayed the message.

"Bring them here," ordered Giese.

Fitzwilliam arrived at the Chancellor's quarters. Giese and Wedigh were seated behind the Chancellor's desk. A chair had been placed in front.

There was a knock on the door. The gate-guard appeared.

"Your visitor," he announced, and Fitzwilliam stormed in, followed by his two men-at-arms.

"What is the meaning of this?" he demanded.

Giese looked at Wedigh.

"Master Fitzwilliam … I'm sorry you have me at a disadvantage," replied Giese.

"The chest … it was empty."

Giese looked at the Chancellor with a grave expression.

"Empty! Empty … !? But how can that be so? It was intact when it left here. You saw the seal with your own eyes. Did you not ensure it was left unattended?"

"Aye, aye, I broke the seal with my own hands."

"Then we have a, how shall we say? A dilemma."

"The chest must have been opened on the voyage … or in Cologne. It could not have happened in Westminster; the chest has not left my eyes," exclaimed Fitzwilliam.

Giese looked at Wedigh, his expression one of grave concern.

He turned to Fitzwilliam. "Hmm, in which case, we need to start an investigation. I am sure there will be an explanation."

"An investigation!? An investigation!?"

"Aye, if there has been a robbery, then the perpetrator must be found and punished."

"But what about the money? Three hundred gold crowns?"

"And sixty-six," corrected Giese.

"Aye."

"Then we will recover it and return it to you, as rightful owner."

Fitzwilliam had nowhere to go with his protestations. He was crestfallen that his idea to boost the coffers of the King had been thwarted, and was considering the implications.

Chapter Seven

Fitzwilliam was in turmoil; he needed to speak to Lord Shrewsbury again. He argued with himself that the plan was sound; however, he had acted on his own initiative, albeit with the tacit agreement of the Earl. Despite his power and influence, entering into a pact with the Hanseatic League was outside his authority. Parliament would have made such a decision.

As soon as he reached Westminster Hall, he headed for the Lord Steward's chambers to update him.

"Ah, Master Fitzwilliam, what news from the Steelyard?"

The Treasurer was sweating, after his journey, but mostly from anxiety. He was about to answer when the chandler knocked on the door and entered to light the candles in the chambers. He was carrying a lantern with a burning flame inside.

"Forgive the intrusion, my Lord, time is pressing, and the light is fading."

"Get on with it, Master Smith, and be quick about it," barked the Lord Steward.

The pair waited impatiently while the chandler replenished the previous day's candles from a hessian bag and lit new ones.

The room was soon bathed in the light of four large candles in specially crafted wall-mounts.

The man turned to the pair and bowed; then left the room.

"You were saying?"

"Aye, it seems a mystery, my Lord. They accused us of taking the gold."

"Accused us! Why the very cheek of it, the arrogance!" replied his Lordship, angrily.

"Well, not in so many words, my Lord, but they were asking if we had kept the chest under guard."

"What did you say?"

"I told them the chest had not left my sight … The theft must have taken place on board the boat, or even in Cologne."

"Well, that makes more sense. What are they planning to do about it?"

"They said they will start an investigation."

The Earl rubbed his beard in a sagely manner, deep in thought.

"You realise, if this investigation is dicovered, it could reach the ears of Cromwell."

"Aye, it had crossed my mind, my Lord."

"This is a mess, Master Fitzwilliam. We should never have got involved. I did warn you."

"Aye, you did, my Lord. I take full responsibility."

"Aye, that you will. I want nothing more to do with it. You best go."

The Earl looked at Fitzwilliam with a stern expression, clearly an indication to leave.

"Very well, my Lord."

He bowed, and left the room, trying to work out what he should do.

Following the disposal of the sergeant, Wolfe and Alice returned to the house with little thought of their actions.

The following morning, Alice confronted Wolfe. "I need to find Margaret. This morning I will go searching for her."

"Aye, if tha must. Happen, I'll return to the Steelyard and earn some coin."

Alice and Wolfe left the dwelling together and walked to the Carter Street market stalls where they parted company. Alice wanted to visit the churches to see if a priest or nun had taken her in. Wolfe, meanwhile, used the passages and alleyways to reach the Steelyard to report for duty.

The cog from Cologne was still in dock and there was plenty of activity as men were loading items ready for a return journey. Wolfe reported to the dock supervisor and was allocated duties.

Meanwhile, in the Winter Hall offices, Georg Giese and Herman Wedigh were in conversation.

"I've been considering the investigation, sir," announced the Deputy Alderman.

"Aye, I've had similar thoughts," replied the Chancellor.

"We need to show the Treasurer we are sincere in our enquiries and pursue the, ahem, culprits robustly."

"Aye, that's true. What do you suggest?"

"I want to question the captain, today," said Giese.

"Very well, see to it. Use one of the offices in the Teutonic Hall; you will not be disturbed."

"Aye, I will go directly … " Giese paused for a moment. "You realise that once we start asking questions, word will out that the coin has gone missing."

"Aye, but that is of no consequence; it will add substance to our story."

Later, Giese was in a room in the Teutonic Hall, the building was slightly smaller than the Winter Hall and used for trading. It was situated on the north-west corner of the Steelyard adjoining Cosins Lane, the other side of the compound wall.

Giese had set up the room with a table and two stools. A man-at-arms was stood at the door. Captain Harvey had been sent for, and arrived promptly, uncertain of the summons. He knocked on the door; the man-at-arms opened it.

"Come in, Captain Harvey, please close the door," said Giese, on seeing the visitor. "Take a seat."

He pointed to the stool opposite. The man-at-arms stood with his back to the door.

The captain was concerned at seeing the formal setting; it seemed more like an interrogation.

"You wanted to see me, Master Giese?"

"Aye, it's concerning the consignment you recently transported from Cologne."

"Aye."

"Have you knowledge of its contents?"

"Nay, no one told me. I was to keep it under guard at all times."

"And did you?"

"Aye, sir, you knows that."

"There were no occasions when the chest was unguarded?"

"Nay, sir, you have my word."

"What about the men on board? Were they all trustworthy?"

"Aye, that they were."

"Are you certain?"

"I think so."

"You think so?"

"Aye."

The captain was finding the interrogation intimidating.

"Why this questioning, Master Giese? You were stood with me most of the voyage. You even had my cabin," he stated with indignation.

Giese lowered his eyes. "Aye, true enough." He paused. "It seems we have a thief in our midst."

"A thief? You mean … ?"

"Aye, the chest was empty when it was opened."

"But how can that be? The chest was sealed and guarded."

"That's what I've been trying to find out."

"But it couldn't have happened onboard; it must have been before we loaded in Cologne."

"That is one possibility, but what if the guards were working together?"

"But, how, Master Giese? The chest was sealed."

"It would have been simple enough to break the seal and reseal it."

"But who would carry such tools?"

"What you say makes sense, but who knows what trickery when coin is concerned."

"Coin?"

"Aye, the chest contained gold coin."

The captain thought for a moment. "Let me ponder on it for a while, Master Giese."

"Aye, if you will, but be quick, it is a matter of grave concern, and utmost haste. We cannot let the perpetrators escape."

"Aye, happen I'll make my own enquiries."

The captain left the office, and left Giese smiling. The news of the missing coin would soon get around and add more kudos to the story.

Alice, meanwhile, had continued her search for Margaret. So far, it had been fruitless. She had visited countless churches, even the odd tavern, but there was no sign of her. She had been walking for several hours and her feet were sore. She had traversed the city and reached Bishopsgate, the easternmost gate. Within its shadow was the Church of St Helens, a Benedictine priory. It was an impressive building, dating back to the early thirteenth century.

She approached the door and knocked. It opened slowly and a nun of mature years appeared. "Yes, my child."

"I'm looking for a girl who might be lost, her name is Margaret."

"Margaret?"

"Aye, I had taken her in; she was with child, but left yesterday without a word."

"You better come in."

Alice was ushered into the main hall. Several nuns were busy with chores.

"Through here," said the nun, in hushed tones.

Alice followed her down a long corridor with windows down the left-hand side providing some natural light. For some reason she felt uncomfortable in such hallowed surroundings. They reached a door.

The nun opened it and entered with Alice following. There was a strange smell, not pleasant.

Two straw mattresses, one each side of the room, were being attended by more nuns. There were wooden pales of water and a piss-pot. The nun turned to Alice.

"Is this the girl?" She pointed to the bed on the right.

It was occupied by someone sleeping in a white smock. The attending nun moved to one side to allow Alice to get closer.

"Oh goodness! Why, it is … How is she? How did she get here?" asked Alice, anxiously.

"Sister Angela found her yesterday, sleeping outside the priory walls …" The nun looked down. "She was bleeding … from … there."

"Oh dear Lord."

"Yes, we pray for her; she is very weak. You said she was with child?"

"Aye, four months, or more."

"It seems she is no longer."

Alice looked at the girl. "She is barely sixteen. I curse

the man who did this to her. He should be removed from his privates." The nun stifled a smile. "What's to be done?"

"We will take care of her … if she is not taken into God's hands."

Alice took her purse from under her skirts and took out a crown.

"She will need food and clothing. Please see she is well looked after. I will return tomorrow."

Alice handed over the coin.

"That is most generous of you, Mistress … ?"

"Wolfe, Alice Wolfe."

"You will be in our prayers."

Alice had a long walk back to the dwelling. After three quarters of an hour, she reached Carter Street, and saw the tavern where she had met the sergeant-at-arms. The market-stall holders were clearing up and putting their unsold items away for another day.

She was thirsty, and entered the inn. It was over an hour since the none bells had struck. It was a dreary day and, inside the alehouse, it was dark, illuminated only by the light from several candles.

She turned one or two heads as she walked to the serving area. Although it was not unusual to see women in the tavern; it was predominantly a male domain. The alehouse was, in fact, owned by a woman, Mistress Fry, who had inherited the business from her late husband.

Alice approached the indomitable woman who was attending to several customers.

"Good den, Mistress Fry, a tankard, if you will be so kind," said Alice, on her turn.

As she was waiting for her ale, two men-at-arms entered the tavern. Their swords clanked as they walked towards the serving area and stood next to her.

Alice froze. She quickly turned her back to them.

"Have you heard anything from the sergeant?" Alice heard one say.

"Nay, happen he's disappeared. No-one has seen hide nor hair of him," the other replied.

The landlady returned with Alice's drink, and she handed over a groat.

"Yes, sirs?"

The men-at-arms ordered their ale and continued their discussion. Alice sipped her ale not attempting to move.

"He'll not be missed; that Sergeant Wainwright, made my life hell, he did."

"Aye, mine too. The women will be safer with him off the street, an'all. Maybe he'll turn up in the Flitte; no-one will mourn his passing."

"Aye, good riddance. I'll not attend his funeral."

"Aye, if they find him."

The landlady returned with the men's drinks and they left the serving area and found a bench.

Alice drank her ale in one go and left, hurriedly. She had much to discuss with Wolfe.

Alice arrived at the dwelling. She removed several kindling sticks from the container next to the hearth and proceeded to build a fire; light was fading and the room was cold. With night approaching, the vespers bells rang across the city.

It was half an hour before Wolfe arrived. Alice had lit candles and, with the fire now providing some heat, the room looked homely, if smoky.

Wolfe took off his hat; there was no emotional greeting.

"Did you find your friend?" he asked, as he took off his

boots.

"Aye, in a Priory near Bishopsgate." Her expression was one of sadness.

"Bishopsgate? What was she doing all the way over there?"

"Happen she walked. She's not in a good way; she's lost her child. The sisters are looking after her."

"Aye? Maybe it's for the best … Have you prepared food? I need something to eat."

"Aye, I'll find something. I thought you might have taken food at a tavern."

"Nay, I'll not enter a tavern for a few days. I've signed up to go back to Cologne with the cog."

Alice stopped what she was doing and turned to him.

"Nay, John, it's not necessary. There's no hue and cry for the sergeant."

She shared the conversation she had overheard in the tavern.

"It seems he was not well-liked."

Wolfe paused for a moment. "The sergeant's death is of no consequence. He was no more than a cockroach."

"Then you have no need to leave."

"Happen I'll be best served at sea for a time."

Alice looked down. "As you wish … When will you go?"

"There's a cog leaving in two days."

"How long will you be away?"

"About three weeks, I would think."

"But you will return?"

"Aye, I'll return."

In the Chancellor's quarters in the Steelyard's Winter hall, Georg Giese was in conference with Herman Wedigh. It was a convivial, end-of-day meeting; candles were lit and a flagon of wine was positioned on the table. Each were drinking from goblets.

"So, how is the investigation going, Master Giese?"

"Well, sir, I interrogated the captain today, who, of course, protested that he was somehow implicated."

"Good, good, so rumour will soon scurry round the yard like rats."

"Indeed, sir."

"So what is your next plan?"

"I should return to Cologne. It would be right that my investigation would continue there."

"Aye, there is some merit in your thoughts. When do you propose to return?"

"On the next cog; in two days, I believe."

In Westminster Hall, Lord Shrewsbury was in his chambers considering the latest turn of events. The more he thought about the situation, the more it worried him. He made a decision, and sent a note requesting a meeting with Thomas Cromwell which was duly granted.

By the autumn of 1531, Cromwell had taken control of the supervision of the king's legal and parliamentary affairs, and had joined the inner circle of the council. He was undoubtedly one of the most powerful men in England.

His main London residence was at Austin Friars, a tenement building in the grounds of the Priory, situated close to Bishopsgate. It was a substantial property, with fourteen rooms arranged in three three-storey wings with an attached garden.

Lord Shrewsbury, as befitting his status, had access to a horse and coach, which would be his mode of transport for the journey.

He set off after the none bells had rung, mid-afternoon.

He wanted to return before nightfall.

It would not be a comfortable journey, the streets of London were pitted and covered in stones, excrement, and other obstacles, making the inside of the carriage shake. At little more than walking pace, the coach pulled up in Broad Street in under an hour.

He exited the coach with the help from the driver, and, dodging the mess littering the cobbled road, walked down the alleyway off Throgmorton Street to the entrance of the property. The carriage would wait his return.

He was dressed in his formal attire, complete with an extravagant hat, and knocked on the large wooden door.

It was answered by an assistant, who ushered the Earl through the grand entrance hall, with its wood-veneered walls and tapestries, into an ante room and offered refreshments; he felt ill-at-ease and declined.

Ten minutes later, Thomas Cromwell appeared at the door of an adjacent room.

"My Lord Shrewsbury … To what do I owe the pleasure of the Lord Steward's company? Come through."

He was wearing a brown velvet gown with red sleeves, and a dark cap. He was by no means a handsome man with his prominent nose.

"Come in, be seated."

The Earl followed Cromwell into a wood-panelled work room. In front was a large, oak desk covered with numerous papers. He waited for Cromwell to be seated before sitting opposite. His power and status made for an imposing figure, and the Earl, even with his own status, felt a degree of intimidation.

"So?" enquired Cromwell, with no unnecessary elaboration.

"Sir, I will be brief, I know my Lord is consumed with

matters of State. I wanted to acquaint you with a situation that happened a few weeks ago."

"A situation?"

"Aye, my Lord... Ahem, His Majesty's Treasurer, Master Fitzwilliam, was approached by a small delegation from the Hanseatic League."

"Ha, and what did they want, the duplicitous sots."

"They wanted to make a donation."

"A donation?"

"Aye, my Lord."

"And why would they want to do that?"

"Hmm. I questioned the motives at the time, but, according to the Lord Treasurer, they said there were no conditions. They wanted to support His Majesty's struggle against Rome with whom, of course, they are still at war."

"And this was not prompted in any way?"

The Earl looked down before answering. "Er … nay, my Lord."

Cromwell looked at the Earl in disapproval.

"And you believed them?"

The Lord Steward was feeling uncomfortable at the scrutiny, hoping his embellishment of the story would hold.

"Aye, knowing the difficulties the League are having with Rome, it would seem reasonable for them to want England to look favourable on them."

"But there must have been some expectations; I have not known the League do anything without benefit for themselves, foxships to a man."

"I think they were hoping for tacit support in some way, but they were firm that there were no expectations of repayment in kind."

"And how much were they offering?"

"Gold crowns, some three hundred or more."

“Three hundred!? Why would they part with such a sum?”

“For the reasons I’ve explained, my Lord.”

Cromwell stroked his chin sagely, far from convinced.

“Hmm … You mentioned a situation.”

“Aye, my Lord. We took delivery of a chest from them, supposedly containing the donation … It was taken to Westminster Hall under guard. When it was open, it was empty.”

“Empty? Empty … ?”

“Aye, my Lord, It appears the consignment was stolen.”

“Stolen?”

“Aye, somewhere between Cologne and here.”

“Hmm, let me give you a piece of advice, my Lord Shrewsbury. In my opinion, the members of the League are as slippery as a box of eels. In my dealings with them, they have always been less than honourable.”

“Aye, my Lord.”

“Tell me, why was this not mentioned to me at the time?”

“We knew how busy you were, my Lord; you would not welcome any unnecessary distractions. I did mention it to The Lord Treasurer, but I think Fitzwilliam was hoping to gain favour in securing coin for His Majesty.”

“Hmm.” Cromwell was thinking. He looked up at Shrewsbury; his eyes narrowed. “So to summarise, The Lord Treasurer was approached by the Hanseatic League, who offered a substantial donation to His Majesty’s exchequer, without requiring anything in return, which then mysteriously goes missing... I find the whole thing one of ridicule.”

“Aye, my Lord; it would seem thus, but that is the truth of the matter. They are carrying out an investigation.”

“Who are?”

"The League, my Lord."

"To what end?"

"To find the perpetrators of the robbery."

"Hmm, well I don't trust them one jot. There's some trickery involved here; you mark my words."

"As you say, my Lord, but I wanted to share this news with you."

"Very well … You must keep me informed."

He looked at the Earl; his eyes still scrutinising his guest. The Earl fidgeted in his seat, feeling very uncomfortable.

"Aye, my Lord."

"Now I must continue with my work. You can go."

Shrewsbury rose from the seat and bowed, reverentially, "My Lord."

He turned and left the room, and breathed a huge sigh of relief.

The following day, Alice left the dwelling to walk to Bishopsgate to visit her friend Maragret in the nunnery.

It took almost an hour to reach the Church where she had found Margaret the previous day. She reached the door of the priory and knocked.

It was the same nun. "Oh, my child, have you returned to see Margaret?"

"Aye, sister."

"You best come in."

The nun moved to one side and led Alice into the hall, then turned and faced Alice with a sorrowful expression.

"I am afraid Margaret is in God's hands now. She left us around midnight; she was weak of spirit. Would you like to pray for her soul?"

Alice was lost for words. "Aye, I would."

The nun led Alice into a small chapel which adjoined the

main hall. It was deathly quiet. Along the front pews several nuns were in silent prayer. The nun approached the alter and dropped to one knee, then found an empty pew. Alice followed.

"My Lord Jesus, please give this child strength in her moment of need. Amen."

"Amen," repeated Alice.

"I will leave you to your prayers," said the nun, and returned to the hall.

Alice spent a few minutes in contemplation then went to rejoin the nun.

"What will you do with Margaret?" asked Alice.

"She will be buried here in our graveyard. Father Benedict is visiting this afternoon to conduct the service; you will be welcome to join us."

"Nay sister, I cannot, I have matters to attend, but I am thankful for your kindness." Alice took out her purse and presented the nun with a guinea. "Can you see she has a suitable coffin."

"Yes, my child, I will see to it."

Alice turned and made her way out of the Priory, her head full of anger. If she could find the man who so defiled her friend, she would kill him.

Meanwhile, Wolfe decided to return to the Steelyard where he would be safe from any possible hue and cry and earn some coin. His money from the robbery of the merchant was diminishing and would need to be replenished soon. He would give this some thought.

He reached the Thames Street gate of the kontor, and, being a familiar face, was ushered through by the duty guard. Wolfe's forehead was specked with beads of sweat from his exertions. He made his way through the compound to the wharf. Other dockers were already carrying items on board the cog, others were using the makeshift crane for heavier items.

Captain Harvey was supervising the activity, checking the manifest as the goods for transportation were being loaded. He saw Wolfe approach and stopped.

"Master Wolfe, I hear you will be joining us tomorrow back to Cologne."

"Aye, sir, I signed with the superintendent yesterday."

"Before you start work, I need to speak to you on a delicate matter. Let's go to my cabin."

The captain walked up the gangplank and down to his quarters below deck. Wolfe followed. The pair stood facing each other.

"Master Wolfe, you were on the journey with the special consignment."

"Aye, that I were, captain."

"During the voyage, did you notice anyone taking a special interest in the chest we were carrying?"

Wolfe thought for a moment. "Nay, I can't say I did. There was a guard on duty the whole time ... You have a reason for your enquiry?"

"Nay, nay. That will be all, carry on."

Wolfe left the captain's cabin still wondering the reason for the question.

William Fitzwilliam had decided to stay in London rather than return to his country estate in Sussex. The latest turn of events concerned him. He saw the incident as an affront. He was angry at the suggestion that the gold had been stolen while under his protection. He needed to return to the Steelyard for an update on the investigation.

He left Westminster Hall on horseback in his robes of

office accompanied by two men-at-arms, and, on arrival at the Thames Street entrance some fifty minutes later, was greeted by the duty guard.

"Herr Giese," demanded Fitzwilliam, unable to hide his anger and frustration.

He was recognised by the guard straightaway. "Follow me, sir."

Fitzwilliam dismounted and tethered his horse outside the gate. He was armed with a sword which he always carried when venturing outside Westminster. It was a gift from the King. He was led through the portal to the Winter Hall. His bodyguards remained outside the kontor, and would wait to accompany The Lord Treasurer on the journey back to Westminster.

The pair entered the grand building, which was busy with merchants plying their trade. Fitzwilliam was asked to wait outside the Chancellor's office while the guard announced his arrival. Georg Giese was with the Chancellor; he looked at Wedigh and raised his eyebrows.

Fitzwilliam was ushered in and stood in front of the large desk. He removed his hat but without the customary greeting charade. He was in no mood for frivolousness. Giese was seated next to the Chancelor and acknowledged the arrival. He spoke before Fitzwilliam could open an encounter.

"My Lord Treasurer, it is fortuitous you have arrived at this moment, we were just in discussion concerning the unfortunate situation we find ourselves in,"

"You have news?" asked Fitzwilliam. He was stood with one hand on his sword, not with any intended use, more a defence in a possible confrontational situation. There was an edge to his voice.

Giese was calm and measured. "Oh, nay, nay, not as to the caitiff… but we have agreed that I will return to Cologne and conduct my investigations there. I have offered a substantial reward, and I expect progress to be swift."

The Treasurer's ire lessened and he relaxed. "Verily, tis welcome you are pursuing this grave felony with fortitude. When do you intend to leave?"

"On the morrow; there is a cog leaving at high tide."

"Would it assist if I were to sail with you?"

"Nay, nay, Master Fitzwilliam, you have enough to do here in London. The investigations are in good hands, and I am confident we will find the thief very soon."

"What about the gold? What's going to happen?"

"If we can find the caitiff, we will undoubtedly find the gold … Would you care for some refreshment? You must be thirsty after your journey."

There was a pause as the Treasurer took in the news. "Aye, some water would be welcome."

Chapter Eight

Wolfe returned to the dwelling before dark; with his pending voyage, he had much to do. Alice was waiting for him as he opened the door, and was clearly upset.

"What ails thee?" he asked, setting down his bag in the corner.

"I went to the priory this morning to be told Margaret had died."

"Aye? Happen it were for the best."

Wolfe sat down at the table, while listening to Alice's story.

"Nay, nay, she were shy of sixteen. If I could find the man who did this to her, I would kill him."

"Aye, but we don't know anything about her."

"Aye, she said she came from Putney."

"And what do you intend to do?"

"Happen I might go there and make enquiries."

"It's best part of a day's journey."

"It's of no consequence; Margaret made the journey."

"Aye, and now she's dead."

There was a steeliness about Alice which had grown since she had met Wolfe; he recognised her determination.

"You must do as you see fit."

Alice sighed, then got up from the table and went to the fire where a cooking pot was hanging over the flames. Smoke was making the room unpleasant; Wolf started coughing.

"Happen, I'll visit a tavern anon."

"Aye, I'll keep you company, if you have a mind."

"Aye."

The compline bells rang as Wolfe and Alice left the

dwelling and walked to the alehouse. Out of the house, away from the smoke, the air was clearer, but replaced by the pervasive smell from the nearby river. The vestiges of daylight had given way to darkness.

They reached the tavern on Carter Street and went inside. It was lit by candlelight; Mistress Fry was serving from firkins of ale as the pair walked into the gloomy room. Wolfe looked around; there were maybe twenty people, mostly men, drinking, some in groups, others content in their own company.

The serving area was empty, and Wolfe ordered ale for the pair. The landlady returned with two pewter tankards and handed them over. Wolfe paid; Mistress Fry pocketed the coin.

"I see they've found that sergeant that went missing," she said, making conversation.

Alice looked at Wolfe. "Aye, when would that be?"

"Some wherryman found him in the Thames. Reckon he'd been in the Flitte by the smell of him; bloated like a whale he was, according to one of the watchmen. They were in here earlier, asking questions. Mind you, no one would say naught; he were not a well-liked man." She looked at Alice. "You seemed to have taken a liking to him, I recall."

"Nay, nay, I can't say that I knew him," responded Alice, and took a sip of her ale.

"Don't worry, your secret's safe enough. Whoever was responsible has rid this world of the devil himself."

The pair were still in the serving area; Mistress Fry was attending to other customers. Armed with this information, they quickly finished their drinks and went to leave.

"Leaving so soon? Pray stay, and have another as my guest," said Mistress Fry, looking across at the departing couple.

"Best not," said Wolfe, and he strode out of the tavern followed closely by Alice.

As they walked back to the dwelling. Wolfe was deep in thought; he turned to Alice. "You need to take care while I'm gone; happen there'll be a hue and cry now body's been found."

Alice appeared unfazed. "Aye, I'll be watchful, pay no heed."

The following day, Wolfe was up early, awoken by the prime bells, it was still dark. He managed to light a candle. Alice, disturbed by his movement, turned over. "Would you like some breakfast afore you go?"

"Aye, I've a bit to do."

Alice got out of bed and went downstairs to light a fire.

Half an hour later, Wolfe was eating the bread and cheese that Alice had prepared for him.

Before leaving, Wolfe went back upstairs and accessed the hiding place where he had secreted his booty from his original theft. There were just a few crowns left which he would need to have with him; he would give Alice sufficient to keep her in food until he returned.

"You best have this," said Wolfe, as he retuned downstairs, dressed for his journey and carrying his long-serving leather bag.

Alice looked at the two crowns. "Aye, I'll look after it."

"You can use it as you see fit. I have coin enough."

Alice looked at him. "Mind you take care, John Wolfe; I'll be waiting for your return."

There were no expressions of affection; Wolfe turned around and headed out of the door. A quick stride down the alleyways and passages would see him at the Steelyard in under twenty minutes.

It was also day of departure for Georg Giese, and he was discussing his pending journey with the Chancellor. They spoke in German.

"What plans do you have for your journey, Master Giese?"

"Carry out an investigation, sir, as we discussed. Perchance, we may find a possible git on whom we can point the blame."

"Aye, that would indeed be a satisfactory outcome, and give credence to our endeavours, but remember, if our trumpery is discovered, it will have grave consequences for Hansa, and you of course."

"Aye, sir, I am aware of the consequences and will act accordingly."

"When do you leave?"

"Around midday, the tide will be favourable, according to Captain Harvey."

"Ah, yes, Captain Harvey. Is he someone you can trust?"

"Aye, sir. He is in a delicate position; we discussed the possibility of the treasure being stolen whilst on his vessel."

"Ha, and how did he respond?"

"He took it as a personal insult, I believe. But I left the thought with him."

"So he will be, how should we say, malleable, if need be?"

"Aye, sir, there's no doubting that."

"Excellent, excellent. Well, God speed, Master Giese, may the Almighty keep you safe."

"Aye, amen to that, sir."

Giese left the Chancellor's office and returned to his quarters to collect the things he would need for his journey.

Wolfe arrived at the Steelyard, and reported direct to the

cog. With only hours until sailing, there was a great deal of activity surrounding the vessel. He approached the gang-plank; Captain Harvey was on deck supervising the loading of the cargo. Late October, it was a dreary day with a strong wind and threat of rain. The cog appeared to be complaining at being tethered to the dock, pitching violently in the strong tide.

"Master Wolfe, I need you to help with the loading, Stow your baggage, and report to the sergeant."

"Sergeant?"

"Aye, we have cargo to protect, and I have arranged for a small detachment of men-at-arms. The sergeant is managing the loading. It is possible there was possibly a thief on our last voyage."

"A thief? Nay, how is that possible?"

"It seems an important cargo we were carrying was stolen."

"What cargo?"

"I am not at liberty to say, but tis a fact, and I trust you will let me know if you hear or see anything."

Wolfe was in deep thought. "Aye, Captain, that I will."

Wolfe went in search of the sergeant to report for loading duty, still considering the captain's revelation. He couldn't work out how anyone could steal any of the regular cargo. It was checked on board and off again against the manifest. Then he remembered the captain mentioning the chest they were carrying in the lower deck. There was a guard, armed with a sword, close by for the whole of the journey. Nothing made any sense.

He was soon wrapped up in his labours and, for the moment, forgot the conversation.

The sext bells rang out across London denoting a little

after midday. The weather hadn't improved and the expected rain was now falling as a steady drizzle. A merchant approached the cog, dressed in the finery of his rank, and followed by a man in worker's clothes pulling a handcart.

He reached the gangplank to the cog, and was immediately greeted by the captain.

"Master Giese, welcome aboard."

The captain signalled to two sailors who hurried off the boat to retrieve Giese's luggage and carry it on board.

"Take it to my cabin," ordered the captain.

With Giese settled below deck, the gangplank was retracted and two men on the dock removed the ropes from the capstans. The cog was free and started to move away from the shore.

The voyage along the Thames Estuary was uneventful; the rain of the previous day had been replaced by late autumn sunshine. The brisk wind meant progress was steady and the captain was anticipating a shortened journey.

Giese, meanwhile, was below deck, still finding his sea legs and spending much of the time bent over a bucket. He decided to get some fresh air and left the captain's quarters. Conditions below deck were poor; it's where the buckets were housed, although most toilet needs were done over the side of the boat. It was also where the movement of the ship induced sea-sickness.

As he reached the door, he stopped for a moment, and hid behind one of the pillars. He could see one of the crew acting suspiciously checking out the cargo. He watched as the unidentified seaman appeared to be examining the various packages stored in neat order reaching the ceiling. It was dark and the man was merely a shadow.

The cog was not carrying anything that would be considered of value to a puggard, an opportunist thief. Giese watched as the man seemed to examine each stack of produce, mostly finished goods returning to the continent for sale. They would be stored in the Hansa warehouse in Cologne before being distributed more widely through the merchants' network.

After a few minutes, the man appeared to have finished his examination and returned to the upper deck where the rest of the crew were at work.

Giese couldn't identify the mystery seaman. He ascended the stairs to the top deck and made his way to the bridge where the captain was steering the boat.

"Captain, where are the men-at-arms?" he asked, as he approached the large wheel being manoeuvred by Harvey.

"Over yonder," said the captain, and pointed in the direction of the prow.

"Why isn't the cargo being guarded?"

"From what? We are in the middle of the sea."

"Who knows the mind of a knave, but I have just witnessed someone acting suspiciously among the cargo."

"Who was it?" asked the captain with an expression of concern.

"It was dark; I was unable to see clearly, but someone with ill-intent, I don't doubt."

Wolfe was beginning to regret his foray below deck. Although he was sure he hadn't been seen, his venture had proved fruitless, no sign of any rich pickings. He quickly mingled with the crew on deck and continued his rope duties.

It was three days since Wolfe had left.

Alice was at home. Boredom was becoming a factor, and

she was yearning for company. To pass the time, she had started spinning, something in which her mother was skilled, and had inherited her spindles and pins after she had died. Metal pins were particularly expensive, usually imported from France and were much in demand. Alice had carried hers in her bag and they went everywhere with her. With sufficient coin she had bought some wool from the market.

It was mid-morning and she was in the middle of her work, when there was an aggressive knock on the door, one that demanded an immediate response. She got up from her spinning and answered it. It was a man wearing a patterned pourpoint. He seemed surprised at the person in front of him.

"Where's John Wolfe?"

Alice looked at the man. "Happen he's at sea."

The man barged into the room.

"When will he return?"

"Not for a month or so. What do you want with him?"

"He owes me rent."

"Rent?"

"Aye, this is my house."

Alice looked surprised.

"Nay, sir, that can't be right; it's John's house."

"Not so, mistress, it belongs to me and the rent is due … Who are you?"

"I'm his wife."

"Wife? I didn't know he were married; I will need more coin if you want to stay."

"And how much might that be?"

"More than you can afford, I fancy."

"I have coin," replied Alice with some indignance.

"Aye?" replied the man, dismissively.

"Aye, what's your name?" asked Alice.

"Henry Thornton."

"And how long have you known John, Master Thornton."

"A while … Have you coin for rent or not?"

She went to her purse and took out one of the crowns. "That should cover it, sir."

"I think not, Mistress Wolfe. I need more for two."

Alice looked at him. "Nay, that's more than sufficient."

"Not for three months," replied the landlord. Thornton looked Alice up and down. "Maybe we can come to some arrangement, perchance. You're a handsome woman."

"What sort of arrangement?"

"The kind only a woman can provide."

"You're asking for favours for rent?"

"I'm sure John would welcome such a gesture."

"Who knows John's mind? Happens he has quite a temper. I am not sure what he will say when I tell him."

Thornton became flustered, thinking through the possible ramifications. He knew Wolfe had a reputation for violence.

"Nay, nay, you should say naught. I'll take thy coin for now and see John when he returns."

"Aye? It would be best. Now, be gone with you, and let me continue my spinning."

Thornton turned and slunk out.

After finishing her spinning for the day, Alice decided to get some fresh air and food. She left the house and went to the market. It was a cool day, and she dressed accordingly. After completing her purchases, she went to the alehouse.

She entered the tavern; it was its usual bustle with shoppers and stall-holders. Candles were lit to improve the visibility but it was still gloomy. Mistress Fry was again in attendance, managing a firkin.

"Mistress Wolfe, good den," said the landlady, seeing Alice approach.

"Good den, Mistress Fry. A tankard if you will."

Alice received her drink and moved to a table. The room was noisy with conversation, but Alice was in reflective mode, thinking about her friend Margaret and the injustices of the world. The possibility of some redemption was fading with the realisation that there was little chance of identifying the perpetrator.

Her thoughts had distracted her. Two men-at-arms were talking to Mistress Fry; money changed hands, and she nodded in Alice's direction.

"Mistress Wolfe, or should that be Tankerville?" The greeting made Alice jump.

The two men were next to her; one had drawn his sword.

"Aye," replied Alice, trying to retain her composure.

She recognised the man with the drawn sword. He was part of the group that had come to search the house with the sergeant.

"You need to come with us."

"Why, sir, for what purpose?"

The two men roughly extracted Alice from her seat and marched her to the door. Fellow drinkers watched the show in curiosity; one or two drank down their ale and left.

"Leave me alone; I've done naught!" she exclaimed.

"That's for the constable to decide," said the man-at-arms.

Alice was frog-marched over a mile, past the grand church of St Paul's, over the brook which led to the Flite, and along the Old Bailey, until they reached Newgate. During the journey, Alice was jeered by passersby, taking her for a common criminal.

She was bundled into the building, still complaining about her innocence of whatever crime they suspected her of committing.

Newgate Prison was an impressive building, situated above the large, portcullis gate, which acted as a formidable barrier in the surrounding wall. Following its refurbishment in the mid-fifteenth century, the building could hold up to three hundred prisoners. The renovations included a new central hall for meals, a new chapel, and the creation of additional chambers and basement cells, albeit with no light or ventilation. There were three main wards: the Master's side, for those could afford to pay for their own food and accommodations; the Common side, for those who were too poor; and a Press Yard, for special prisoners.

It was customary for local Justices of the Peace to appoint constables to administer the initial stages of the judicial system.

Alice was led up to the official's room, where questioning and an initial assessment would take place.

The room was austere, with just a table and two benches. A man dressed as a professional class, similar to merchants, was seated on one of the benches facing the door. His face matched the room - dour; the gloominess of the surrounds prevented any detailed facial expression. The two men-at-arms were stood either side of Alice. She was shaking with nerves but trying to not to show it.

"Who is this?" barked the constable.

"Alice Tankerville, my Lord, but answers to the name of Wolfe, these days," said the first man-at-arms.

"Why is she here?" asked the official, impatiently.

"We believe she was involved in the death of our sergeant, my Lord."

The constable looked at Alice. "That is a very serious crime, and what say you, Mistress Wolfe?"

"I have no thought as to why I have been dragged here like a common varlet."

The constable turned to the man-at-arms. "What gives you mind that this woman was responsible?"

"She was seen with the sergeant, my Lord, just before he went missing. We have witnesses."

"And what gives you cause to say she was involved with the sergeant's death? I heard he drowned."

"Aye, so he did, my Lord."

"So, I say again, why is this woman here?"

"Seems she had cause."

"What cause?"

The first man-at arms looked down; the second replied. "Happen, the sergeant had a fondness for Mistress Wolfe."

"That's not a crime; she's a handsome woman."

"Aye, my Lord, rumour has it the feelings weren't returned."

"What say you, Mistress Wolfe?"

"Aye, he were company enough, but he had more a fondness for ale."

The constable looked at the men-at-arms. "Is this right?"

"Aye, sir, he enjoyed a drink or two; it were no secret," said the first.

"So, again. Why is this woman here? You have no evidence at all … Well?"

Both men-at-arms looked down again, unable to respond, intimidated by the presence of the constable. He looked at both of them.

"Reports I've seen suggest your sergeant fell into the river in a state of distemper. I see no reason to challenge that assumption."

The constable turned to Alice. "You are free to go, Mistress Wolfe."

There followed a heated discussion between the men-at-arms and the constable.

Alice turned trying not to show any emotion, but inside she was fraught with a mixture of fear and relief. The men-at-arms were far from happy with the summary justice.

"You should be in Newgate," whispered the first man-at-arms as she left the room.

Alice ignored the remark and hastened down the stairs back to the street. There would, no doubt, be gossip, but she would deal with that. For the moment she had a long walk ahead of her.

Two days later, the cog was nearing its final destination heading down the Rhine. The journey had been uneventful to the extent of boredom. Georg Giese was still none-the-wiser to the identity of the mystery man was who he had seen behaving suspiciously among the cargo. Suffice it to say, there was going to be a careful scrutiny of the goods being unloaded. He was in his usual place next to the captain.

The captain had given over the wheel to one of the crew and was talking to Giese.

"What course, pray, will your investigation take?"

Giese looked at the captain. "I will enlist the support of the Hansa's militiamen to help with the questioning, but I have a mind the culprit might be close at hand."

"Close at hand, Master Giese? You mean a crewman?"

"Aye, why else would someone be searching the cargo?"

"That would be a logical conclusion, Master Giese. I can make enquiries and see if anyone knows anything."

"That would be of great assistance, captain, and let it be known that we are offering a reward of ten crowns for information that leads to the arrest of the lifter that stole the coin."

"Ten crowns? Indeed, that will be a test of anyone's loyalty."

The following morning, the cog docked at the Hanseatic League wharf in Cologne. Having secured a berth for the return, Georg Giese left the boat, eager for the comfort of his own bed.

It would be a month before the next sailing to London, the last before the seasonal storms made the journey too dangerous.

Giese summoned a horse and trap to take him to his family's mansion. On arrival, he was warmly greeted by his parents; his mother hugged him, while his father was keen to hear the news of his audacious plan to fool the English authorities.

Having settled in, his father, Heidrick, invited Georg into the sitting room for a discussion. They spoke in German.

"So, my son, tell me all. I have to admit to being concerned at your strategy; it has many flaws."

"True, Papa, but it seems the English have accepted the story that the coin has been stolen. I am here to carry out an investigation."

"An investigation, you say?"

"Aye, we've even offered ten crowns by way of reward."

"But to what purpose? There was no robbery."

"But we need to make sure it seems so. A reward would be appropriate."

"Aye, but there will be no evidence to gain a conviction."

"Who knows? English Law is fickle, especially if a jury is involved."

"I hope you know what you are doing, son."

"Do not worry, Papa, I intend to spend some time here before returning to London."

"Have you considered what you will do if other council members of the League get to hear about your plan? Word is bound to get around."

"I will just say it was a misunderstanding."

"Hmm, I hope they believe you; it's a dangerous game you are playing."

Giese spoke animatedly. "As I see it, I have served the League well, dealing with a delicate situation and protecting the reputation of Hansa."

"By trickery?"

"Not trickery, Papa. The English were foolish enough to think the League would donate coin to swell the coffers of Henry and his dalliances, for naught in return. How were we to react?"

His father watched his son with pride. "My son, I believe you have acted with the best of intentions towards the League and if anyone should question your motives, I will say as such. History will serve you well, Georg."

Lord Shrewsbury had spent some time at his castle in Sheffield, a week's journey. On arrival back in London, he called William Fitzwilliam for an update.

Shrewsbury spoke. "I have not mentioned it before, but I thought it prudent to discuss the missing crowns with Lord Cromwell."

Fitzwilliam immediately looked concerned. "Oh, and how was it received?"

"Hmm, Cromwell doubts the earnestness of Hansa. Foxships to a man, he believes."

"I don't doubt Giese. I believe he is a man of integrity."

"History may prove otherwise." He paused and looked at Fitzwilliam with a serious expression. "I've had a note this morning from Cromwell wanting to know if there's any more news about the investigation."

The Lord Treasurer looked down. "Not as yet, my Lord; methinks Giese will not return for some time. According to the Steelyard, it will be a month before the next cog returns from Cologne."

Shrewsbury looked at him.

"What, pray, should I tell Master Cromwell?"

"Tell him we will let him know when we have more information."

"Is there anything we can do here?"

"I don't see what more we can do. The robbery was not here in London; of that I am certain. The chest did not leave our sight. It would have been impossible for anyone to have stolen the contents."

"I wonder what contents there were; we only have their word that coin was therein."

Fitzwilliam was thinking. "I can only report what I was told, my Lord."

"Hmm, that's the truth of it."

John Wolfe was also now in Cologne.

He had registered to work on the return journey, and was seeking lodgings for the duration of his stay. Leaving the docks, he headed into town, and called at a boarding-house he had used before. It was a substantial, stone-built property on three floors. Fortunately, they had a room for rent. It was comfortable enough and sufficed his needs, just a bed and two buckets. He was not intending on staying in his room for any length of time. He had other ideas.

Chapter Nine

After almost a week at sea, Wolfe spent the remainder of the day in his room considering what to do about his financial situation. With the money he had earned from his crewman's job, he had sufficient coin to last him until he returned to England, but wanted more to enhance his position in the world.

It was starting to get dark; he had drifted in and out of sleep, but was awoken by a peel of bells indicating the approach of night time. He decided to find an alehouse to get some food. There was a tavern a short distance away which he knew well. Some of his fellow crew members were also regulars and he would enjoy some company.

He changed into his only spare shirt and breeches and left the boarding house. Ten minutes later, he walked into the tavern, a frequent haunt by sailors. It was a low, heavy wooden doorway, and he had to duck to enter. Inside, it would be difficult to discern any difference between this alehouse and those in London. Illumination was by locally-made candlelight, thick and long-lasting that gave a glow-light. The flames cast moving shadows every time someone entered the establishment caused by the draught.

There was a buzz of conversation in many different languages, predominantly German, but English and French voices could also be heard amid a mixing pot of cultures.

Most of the clientele were sailors from the various cogs docked along the quayside. He found the proprietor who was busy attending to two customers. One of them turned around and recognised Wolfe. He spoke in English.

"John, my friend, pray tarry a while and sup with us."

Wolfe recognised one of the crewmen. "Aye, Thomas,

that I will. I'll take a jack with you."

The landlord dispensed the measures, and Wolfe's friend led him to a table in the corner where another man was seated, dressed in seaman's attire.

"You remember Patrick, John?"

There was no recognition from either party. "Nay, we've not been acquainted, methinks."

"Ah, it must have been on another voyage … This is Patrick, from Ireland," clarified Thomas.

"You're a long way from home, Patrick," greeted Wolfe.

"Aye, that I am; tis true enough."

Despite the dim lighting, Wolfe could make out the rugged features of his new acquaintance, blue piercing eyes, full beard, dark hair protruding from his cap.

"And whereabouts in Ireland do you hale from?"

"Maynooth, County Kildare, sure I worked on his Lordship's estate … Lord Kildare."

"I don't know the man."

"Lord Kildare? A very poweful man, so he is."

"Aye, there are many such, and what did you do there?"

"Attended the stables, so I did."

"So, you're a man of horses; pray why are you at sea?"

The man looked down. "Aye, there were some problems, some thieving, which I was accused of, and I was told to leave. I swore my innocence but no one would listen."

Patrick looked up directly at Wolfe. Wolfe couldn't maintain eye contact and took a long swig of his ale.

"What about you?" asked the Irishman.

"Work at the Steelyard."

"London?"

"Aye."

"Maybe I should seek work there."

"Aye, you could try."

"I'm hungered, let's get some victuals," said Thomas.

The three men went to another part of the dingy tavern where food was being served, then returned to their bench to continue their discourse.

"Have you heard anything about the robbery?" asked Wolfe.

"On the last voyage?" asked Thomas.

"Aye, I heard they're offering ten crowns for information," said Wolfe.

"Aye, I heard that too," commented Thomas.

Patrick looked up from his ale and wiped the froth off his beard with the back of his hand. "Is that right? To be sure, men would sell their daughters for less."

"Aye. Seems it was the chest we were carrying. Happen it were empty when it were opened. That's what I heard," said Thomas.

"I'd be interested to know how they did that, and make off with coin," said Wolfe.

"Aye, true enough," replied Thomas. "There's rumour that the King stole it to swell his coffers."

"Nay, it will be that Cromwell, more like. Wants another house," said Wolfe.

The story of the lost crowns was taking all manner of fanciful turns. The Irishman had lost interest and was in his own world.

Thomas changed the subject. "There's work to be had on the cog on the morrow; captain wants decks cleaned. Patrick was saying about earning some coin. What say you, John?"

"Aye, why not? Naught else in mind."

The group continued their conversation while they finished their food.

It was late when the three decided to leave to get some

sleep. The compline bells, the last of the day, had sounded long ago. Outside the tavern, they went their separate ways. All three were worse for drink.

Wolfe was finding it difficult to coordinate and stumbled towards his lodgings. The side of the road was rutted and presented a danger to those unsteady of foot. It was dark, very dark, with no street illumination and no moon. His eyes had adjusted to whatever illumination was present but only enough to make out shapes. He knew the route well enough, even without light to guide him, and he made good time.

He was close to the boarding house, and turned the final corner. Without warning, he was suddenly confronted by a man stepping out in front of him, no more than a shape. Another grabbed him from behind and held him tightly while the other started rummaging through Wolfe's doublet looking for a purse.

Wolfe's survival instincts kicked in, and in a moment he swung his left elbow with all his strength at the man behind him, connecting with his stomach. The man let go and was doubled up, clutching his midriff. In a fraction of a second, Wolfe had unsheathed his dagger which he always kept under his tunic. He turned blindly and slashed at his assailant hitting him several times in the neck and face in a frenzied attack. The second assailant was struck with fear, seeing his companion drop to the rough ground holding his wound with blood spurting out onto the cobbles around him. He turned and ran off before Wolfe could catch him.

Wolfe's looked down at the victim, now on the floor with blood oozing in a puddle. His shoulders rose and fell; his breathing heavy from the effort and stress caused by the attack.

He bent down and checked the man's tunic; he found two purses which he extracted and weighed in his hands.

Checking there was no further purses, he looked at the stricken man, now in his death throws.

"You'll think twice about trying to steal from me," Wolfe said with a sneer.

As the reality of what had just transpired began to sink in, Wolfe's thoughts turned to the boarding house. He couldn't afford to linger here, not with the possibility of more attackers lurking nearby. Taking a deep breath, he steeled himself and started towards the familiar safety of the temporary dwelling, every sense on high alert.

Wolfe reached his lodgings and pushed open the door. There was a single candle in the window which gave some illumination to the entrance, but the stairway ahead was dark. He shuffled up the stairs one at a time and reached his room. The candle he had lit earlier was still burning on the table next to the door, but would not last for much longer. There was a spare next to it and he tipped it on end so the wick was touching the lit candle.

With two candles burning, the room was marginally brighter. Wolfe washed the blood off his hands in the water bucket before relieving himself in the other. He was still on a high from his escape in the shadows; sleep would be illusive.

The following morning, Wolfe had managed some sleep but was awoken by the prime bells; it was still dark, but dawn was approaching. He had a dreadful thirst, but with no water in the room, he would need to enquire of the landlord, or wait until he got to the cog. He had used the water bucket to wash the blood from his hands. He tried getting up but fell back down and groaned.

There was little illumination in the room. The candle had been stubbed out and would need re-lighting. Wolfe decided to wait until daybreak, and promptly fell back to sleep.

He was awoken by the terce bells two hours later. The room was bathed in a gloomy hue from the cloth-covered window. There was no glass and the room was cold.

The two purses he had taken were beside him; he had not examined them yet, but they seemed heavy. He got out of bed and relieved himself; he was now desperately thirsty. He took the water bucket and left his room in search of a refill.

Downstairs, a serving wench was going about her duties. Wolfe took out a groat from his pocket.

"A fill, mistress," he demanded, and handed her the bucket.

She took the coin and bucket without comment, and headed for the kitchen. Moments later she returned with a full bucket which Wolfe drank down in one go. He handed the bucket back to the wench.

"Happen, I have a beast of a thirst, mistress. Another, if you would care." He gave her another groat.

"Aye, sir." She took the coin and, with a curtsy, returned to the kitchen.

Having quenched his thirst and returned. Wolfe was in reflective mood, thinking about the events of the previous evening. The two purses he had taken from his attacker were filled with several crowns and smaller coins, almost certainly stolen from rich victims. People would be looking for the perpetrators. Like London, in Cologne there was no police force as such, but a localised militia which maintained law and order. The body of his assailant would have been discovered by now. Wolfe would tread carefully; there was a witness.

In 1531, Cologne was the largest city in Germany. It resembled London in many ways, a river port, surrounded by a substantial defensive wall. There were numerous churches including the grand cathedral which dominated the skyline, still under construction after nearly four hundred years.

With his prominence in the city, Georg Giese had a pony and trap at his demand. He needed to visit one of the Hansa buildings.

The Hanseatic League's presence in Cologne was not in a Kontor trading-post like London with its own walled enclave; instead, the merchants and craftsmen were organised into twenty-two 'gaffs', with each gaff having its own meeting place. However, there was a central point of sale where passing merchants were required to store their goods, in the so-called *Stapelhaus*. It was the main hub of commerce and where Giese would head.

Giese had two reasons for the visit; as an important and well-known figure, he needed to maintain his profile, but also wanted to find out if there were any rumours concerning missing crowns. His father had encouraged him on this course as a matter of prudence.

It was a cloudy and cool day and Giese was dressed accordingly with a fine velvet cloak encasing his normal attire.

The League did have dedicated wharves along the Rhine and, with exclusive rights to trade with London, there was regular traffic. The recent arrival, on which Giese had travelled, had been unloaded; a few crewmen were on deck checking ropes and other equipment ready for the next sailing.

Giese had decided to take a detour and pay a visit to speak to the captain. His carriage pulled up alongside the moored cog. The coachman jumped down from his seat and opened the door for Giese to alight. The Deputy Alderman left his transport and walked up the gangplank.

Wolfe and his two drinking companions were on deck;

they had returned to the cog to assist with the maintenance and earn more coin. There was lively chatter among the skeleton crew; three had visited a whorehouse and were recounting their stories.

Giese took little notice of the workers, and was greeted by Captain Harvey. They were stood out of earshot from the seamen and spoke in English.

"Good den, Master Giese, what brings you to my boat this day?"

"I was passing and wanted to ask if you had any further thoughts on our lifter."

"Nay, Master Giese, I can't say I have. What news on the investigation?"

"I am on my way to the League as we speak to start questioning. There are people who were responsible for sealing the chest, although I cannot believe any of them would be responsible; they have been with the League for many years, but we must start somewhere."

"You did not supervise the sealing yourself, Master Giese?" The captain spoke with a hint of surprise in his voice.

"Not so, I had many tasks to attend to, having arranged the shipment."

Giese's gaze was unconsciously drawn to the figure of John Wolfe who was on the other side of the boat checking some rigging. Giese focussed.

"Who is that man?" asked Giese.

The captain followed Giese's gaze. "The one checking the rigging?" he clarified.

"Aye."

"You remember; it's John Wolfe. He saved the crewman who went overboard in the storm."

"Aye, aye, of course, John Wolfe, a brave man."

"Aye, and a good worker. Methinks another six of him and we would cut our journey to London by a day. Why do you ask?"

"Oh, naught, he seemed familiar; that's all. It was probably the rescue."

He was certain it was the same man he had seen below deck among the cargo, but, for the moment, decided to keep his council. He had an idea.

After another few minutes discussing the return journey, Giese left the cog and rejoined his carriage. The captain watched as it pulled away, turned left towards the gate, and disappeared from view.

The none bells echoed around the city; mid-afternoon. The ringing of bells to denote the passage of time was a common practice among the Catholic Monasteries in Europe.

Wolfe and his fellow crewmen were keen to get some food and quench their thirst. He had said nothing to his colleagues about the attempted robbery the previous evening; the less people that knew about it, the better. There was an alehouse that sold food close by the wharf, and, have though having received their coin for the day's work, they headed in that direction.

It was similar to the many alehouses close to the river - dark, dingy, and cold. The three entered and found themselves a seat among the sparse clientele. Wolfe looked around, anxiously. Although unlikely, the thought of discovery was still in his mind.

German was the predominate language and, as the only native speaker, Wolfe ordered the drinks and food, then returned to his companions.

"You seems ill at ease, John," said Thomas.

Before he could answer, Wolfe's worse fear came to

fruition as a group of six *Landsknecht* - German militia, walked in. They were easily identifiable, sporting full beards, and flamboyantly dressed in breeches, stockings, and feathered hats. They were armed with swords, a fearsome sight. They stood at the entrance to the alehouse and started looking around.

Several drinkers on seeing them, left their seats and made to leave but were prevented from doing so at sword point.

A scruffy-looking man, about twenty years of age, was pushed forward from the group of soldiers. His face was bruised and there were bloodstains down his shirt and tunic.

Thomas eyed the soldiers. "I wonder who they're looking for."

"It'll be some cutpurse, methinks," proffered the Irishman.

A hush descended on the alehouse as the militiamen walked further into the dismal room, dragging the unfortunate young man with them. He was protesting at his treatment. The leading militiaman who seemed to be in charge, was shouting at him in German.

"What's he saying, John?" asked Thomas.

Something put Wolfe on alert; he had an uneasy feeling. He paused before answering. "Seems he witnessed a robbery last night."

"Well, we have naught to fear. Happen we were too drunk to lift a purse or two." Thomas laughed.

The group reached Wolfe and his two companions, and the first militiaman held up a candle housed in a glass container. The light shone in the three faces in turn. He spoke in German to the ruffian who suddenly pointed at Wolfe.

The militiaman turned and looked at Wolfe. He raised the lantern higher, illuminating Wolfe's full face. He sought confirmation from the scoundrel. "Ja, ja, ja," he shouted animatedly, still pointing at Wolfe.

The two closest militiamen drew their swords. Before he could move, Wolfe was grabbed and pulled up from his seat. Thomas and Patrick got up and started protesting. They were forced to sit back down by swords at their throat. Wolfe was marched towards the door, bitterly protesting his innocence.

Outside the alehouse, it had started raining, adding more gloom to the late afternoon. Two militiamen bound Wolfe's wrists behind his back with thick twine, then frogmarched him through the streets. The third man-at-arms followed behind with his sword drawn They reached the *Frankenturm* wall and followed the impressive structure until they eventually came to a large building. Wolfe recognised it straightaway. It had a fearsome reputation. The Frankenturm had four prison rooms which faced the Rhine where culprits were incarcerated. It was known for its brutality.

Wolfe was led up a flight of stone steps and into a room where a man in clerk's clothes was writing at a desk. He looked up at the arrivals.

"Sir, I have a culprit for questioning," said the militiaman.

"Who is this?" asked the magistrate.

"We believe he was responsible for a murder last evening. We have a witness."

He turned and looked up at Wolfe who was being restrained by two militiamen.

"What is your name?"

"John Wolfe."

"How say you to these charges?"

"I don't know anything about a murder or why I've been brought here. The scoundrel is mistaken."

The first militiaman interjected. "He was quite certain, my Lord."

“Where is he?”

“Outside, sir.”

“Bring him in.”

“The young man was pushed into the room by two other militiamen.

“So, what is your name? asked the magistrate.

“Hans Burghart, sir.”

The Magistrate eyed up the witness. He resembled a street urchin; his hair and face were flecked with mud and there was blood on his clothing.

“Well, Master Burghart, what do you have to say for yourself?”

“My friend Gerhart and me were out walking last night when this man attacked us with a knife.”

“And what were you doing abroad late at night?”

“Naught, sir, we were returning from an alehouse.”

“And you say this man attacked you for no reason?”

“He set upon poor Gerhart, slit his throat like a pig, he did.”

“What did you do?”

“I ran off.”

“So you didn’t stop to help your friend?”

“Nay, sir, I was too frightened.”

The magistrate looked at him, searching for a lie. “How can you be sure it was this man? It was dark as pitch; there was no moon.”

Burghart looked at Wolfe who was instinctively pulling at his bonds trying to loosen them. He was still being restrained by two militiamen. The anger on his face was very evident.

“It <u>was</u> him, sir; I am certain.”

The magistrate turned to the militiaman.

“What other proof do you have?”

“Naught as yet, sir, but we want to search his dwelling.”

Wolfe interjected. "I have no dwelling here, sir; I'm a seaman from London. I sleep on the cog."

"But you speak German," said the magistrate.

"My mother was born here." He turned and looked at the young man. "This sot is clearly mistaken … Look, I have someone here who can speak for my character. Do you know Mathias Koch, the brewer?"

"But of course," said the magistrate.

"Sir, I am innocent of any crime, I am just a hard-working cog-man. Ask one of your men to visit Master Koch; he will speak for me."

"Very well. You will be kept here until we have word."

"Take him away," ordered the magistrate.

"What about this one?" asked the militiaman, indicating Burghart.

"Lock him up too. We may have more questions to put to him."

Wolfe was escorted along a corridor, lit by tar-torches, and then down another flight of stone steps, worn to the shape of a shallow crescent. As they reached the bottom, a further passageway stretched before them also illuminated by oil-lit torches at intervals along the wall. There were two doors on each side. Screams and shouts echoed across the dungeon. Wolfe was shepherded into the first vacant cell and the door locked. It was dark and cold, just a bare stone floor covered with a sprinkling of straw; the only furniture, an old bucket, the smell of which dominate the room.

Wolfe heard the footsteps recede and ascend the stairs.

Sometime later, Wolfe was seated on the floor against the wall in the corner of his cell, when he heard the footsteps return. He had no idea how long he had been incarcerated, several hours, certainly; he'd had no food or water in that time.

The heavy wooden door was unlocked.

The militiaman was stood at the doorway, his sword drawn.

"Out," he bellowed.

Wolfe raised himself; his legs were stiff. He left the dungeon and trundled up the stairs with the militiaman right behind him. He felt anxious not knowing what was going to happen. He was led back down the corridor to the magistrates room.

It was well into the evening and the room was lit with candles. Wolfe adjusted his eyes.

"Master Wolfe, what have they done to you?" asked a familiar voice.

He focused his eyes and then saw the man. He recognised him straight away, dressed in the finery of wealth with a particularly extravagant feathered hat. A top cloak was hung over his shoulders.

The magistrate was seated behind his desk.

"You know this man?"

"Aye, I do; I owe him my life; saved me from a cutpurse, he did."

"And you can speak for him?"

"Aye, most certainly, a man of utmost integrity. What crime is he supposed to have committed?"

"They say I murdered someone, Master Koch," interjected Wolfe.

"Quiet!" barked the magistrate, looking at Wolfe.

The brewer looked at the magistrate. "There has been a mistake; Master Wolfe is a hero and should not be treated like a common criminal. Release him at once."

"Into your custody, Master Koch."

"Aye."

"Very well, on your assurance, you can take him away."

Wolfe breathed a sigh of relief. The brewer walked towards him and placed a hand on his shoulder.

"Come, my dear friend, you do not belong here."

The pair headed out of the door without any acknowledgement to the magistrate. The militiamen looked at each other quizzically.

As they walked down the stairway to the exit, the brewer turned to Wolfe. "I have a carriage waiting, Herr Wolfe, you can stay with my family; we have plenty of room."

"Sir, I am, and always will be, forever in your debt."

"Nonsense, let's not talk of indebtedness; it's the least I could do."

Wolfe did have a problem. The two purses which he had taken the previous evening had been hidden in his room. He was confident they would not be discovered by any casual observer; he had paid the rent for two weeks, so the room was unlikely to be disturbed, but nevertheless, he would feel better with them being on his person. For the moment, his priority was to leave the prison grounds as soon as possible.

Outside the gates, a carriage was waiting, its two horses nickering, impatient at the delay. It was dark and still raining. Two glass lanterns containing lit candles were positioned either side of the waiting coachman. Seeing his passengers leave the building, he immediately got down from the driver's seat. He was soaking wet; rain ran down his cloak and onto the cobbles. He opened the door with a reverential bow. Koch got in; Wolfe followed.

The coachman returned to his seat, flicked the reins, and the horses took the strain at a gentle trot. Inside the carriage, Wolfe turned to his benefactor.

"For your intervention, sir; I am in your debt."

"Nay, nay, I can never repay you for saving my life …

Have you eaten, Herr Wolfe?"

"No, sir."

"Then I will ask the chef to cook something special. You are my guest."

Back in London, four weeks since Wolfe had gone to sea, Alice was cooped up in the house, only venturing out for food, and wool for her spinning. Her money, which Wolfe had left her, was almost gone, and she had no idea how long it would be before he returned from Cologne; she hoped it would be soon.

Today she would need to go to the market again. She checked her purse, then hid it inside her kirtle.

The market on Carter Street was busy as usual. She was at a stall when she saw one of the men-at-arms that had seized her and dragged her to Newgate. She ducked down and edged her way backwards into the crowd to avoid detection.

Suddenly, she felt pressure on her back, sharp pressure. She turned instinctively; it was another man-at-arms. He had a knife pressed against her back which would not have been visible in the crowded marketplace. He called out, and was quickly joined by his colleague.

Alice was roughly escorted a short distance to a narrow passageway, out of sight from the bustling stalls. They stood either side of her; the one still had his knife in his hand.

"What is this? Why have you dragged me here? Get your hands off me."

The first one spoke with a sneer.

"We've been on the lookout for you, Mistress Wolfe. Happen our sergeant was a blab-mouth after an ale or two, told us about how he would enjoy your favours."

She could smell his stale breath. "And you think I would pay the same attention to you?" said Alice, indignantly.

"Aye, happen we thought you might be favourable to such an idea. It would keep you safe from those that say you had cause to kill the sergeant."

"Ha, you haven't coin enough."

"Coin?"

"Aye, the sergeant did not get my favours for free."

The two men looked at each other. "We have coin sufficient for your favours." He took out his purse and took out two groats.

"Two groats? You couldn't find a dog who'd do it for two groats, or, if so, she'd be pox riddled."

The men looked at each other.

"It will cost you half a crown … each," countered Alice.

The pair looked at each other; it represented two weeks' wages.

"Half a crown? Happen, I could sard Anne Boleyn for less."

"You should go find her then," reposted Alice.

"Half a crown for both," offered the man-at-arms. "And thou'll not have any reason to concern yourself with any hue and cry."

The man-at-arms carrying the knife, put it back in its sheath. Alice leant against the wall and began to relax, considering the offer.

"Aye, but my husband returns any day."

"Today then."

"Aye, you know my dwelling, after the none bells have struck. Now let me finish my purchases."

Chapter Ten

In Cologne, the coachman guided the carriage up the long drive to the brewer's mansion. The rain continued falling. It had taken a great deal of concentration by the coachman to navigate the route in the dark. Wolfe was reflecting on his fortunate escape, but his next challenge would be to retrieve the purses from his lodgings. For now, though, his priority was to satiate his thirst and hunger, which his benefactor had promised he would do.

The carriage pulled up outside the grand entrance, and the coachman once again dropped down to open the door to help the passengers alight. He was soaking wet but would make no complaint. The brewer walked to the heavy wooden door to the house and opened it, then ushered Wolfe inside like a favoured son, with his arm around his shoulders.

"Heldin, we have a visitor," he called, as he entered the grand hall.

His wife joined them from an adjacent room.

"Herr Wolfe, what a pleasure to see you again."

"Frau Koche, it is indeed my pleasure, although the circumstances have been less than fortunate."

The brewer's wife expressed curiosity. "Why, pray?"

"Some villain accused him of murder, found him in Frankenturm, locked away like some common criminal," interjected the brewer.

"Oh, dear Lord! You are not hurt, I trust, Herr Wolfe? You hear terrible things about those places."

"Nay, your husband's intervention spared me any of that."

"Oh, I am so pleased … Come in, come in, make yourself comfortable. I will ask Emilinda to fetch some ale and food."

The three walked through into the luxurious sitting room, where they had enjoyed a convivial evening on his last visit. There was a burning fire, complete with chimney, the privilege of the wealthy in English houses.

They made themselves comfortable on the large couch.

"I have said Herr Wolfe can stay with us until his ship sails. He will be safe here from any problems with the militiamen."

"Nay, please call me John," said Wolfe.

"Yes, John, and you must call me Mathias, and this is Heldin."

Just then, a striking young woman entered the room. At first Wolfe thought it was the servant girl, but quickly revised his opinion.

"Ah, John, this is Inga, our daughter, recently returned from school in Lubek."

Wolfe stood up and bowed his head. "Frauline Koche."

"Herr Wolfe, please call me Inga. My father has spoken warmly of you, many times. We are grateful for saving his life."

"Nay, it is I who is in debt to him … Inga, and you must call me John."

Inga sat opposite Wolfe who was finding it difficult to avert his gaze. Germanic features, blonde, with deep blue eyes, she moved with a grace and confidence that came from education. She was dressed warmly on this winter's evening with an open-fronted gown, laced over a kirtle. There was a wide band of rich fabric heavily embroidered across her chest. She was also wearing a white barett - headgear popular in Germany at that time.

They were soon joined by Emilinda, the waif-like serving girl that Wolfe had met on his last visit. She was carrying two tankards of ale and handed one to the brewer and the other to Wolfe.

"Would you like some food, John?" asked Heldin.

"Aye, I would welcome such; if it's no trouble."

Emilinda was instructed to prepare a meal for Wolfe.

"I will help," said Inga, and she followed the domestic out of the room.

Earlier, back in London, the none bells had rung and Alice was waiting for her guests, considering her good fortune. Not only was she making money, but would be protecting her and Wolfe from any future hue and cry relating to the death of the sergeant. Not that there was much activity; the man was universally disliked, and there appeared little appetite to look for any possible perpetrator. The general gossip on the street was, that he had fallen into the river in a drunken state.

There was a knock on the door, a reserved, uncertain knock. Alice opened it and the two men-at-arms were stood there dressed in their normal peasant gear but without the armoury of their day jobs. They looked different, nervous even.

Alice invited the pair in; they removed their caps. She had lit a fire to warm the room and the layer of smoke hung in the air just below the ceiling like a blanket.

"Do you have the coin?" she asked, without any formality.

The first one handed over a half crown which she placed in a purse.

"Are you wanting to watch?" she said to the second.

"Nay, nay, Mistress Alice," he said sheepishly.

"Then wait outside."

He replaced his cap, then left the dwelling.

Alice turned to the first man. "Come on, we don't want to keep your friend waiting," she said, and led the man upstairs.

There was no ceremony. Alice just lay on the bed and raised her skirts, then stared at the ceiling.

It was over in two minutes. Alice sat up, and straightened

her kirtle. Then, she got up off the bed, and led the man down the stairs.

"You best tell your friend, and be quick; I don't want to light a candle yet."

The second man fared no better than the first, and, within five minutes, Alice was leading him down the stairs.

"If you want to return for favours, I will be at the alehouse. You can arrange it there," she announced as they walked away.

Wolfe had slept the sleep of a baby, particularly having consumed three tankards of the brewer's finest ale. After weeks of sleeping on straw and bare boards, the feel of a wool-filled mattress and bedding was a welcome change.

He washed his face in the porcelain wash basin placed at his disposal, then descended the stairs. He was warmly welcomed by his host.

"John, I hope you slept well," said the avuncular brewer. "Come, join us for breakfast; we're through here."

Wolfe remembered the dining room. The brewer's wife and daughter were eating. Wolfe was approached by the servant, Emelinda. Koche ordered a full breakfast for Wolfe.

"I hope you slept well, John," said Heldin, as Wolfe sat down.

Inga looked at him, then dropped her eyes, as if she had been caught doing something inappropriate.

"Aye, like a baby." John looked at his hosts and smiled. the first time in a while.

The brewer sat down opposite. "Do you have plans today, John?"

"Aye, I need to return to the cog to find out when they need me to prepare for sailing."

Wolfe had an ulterior motive; he needed to retrieve the

purses from the boarding house.

"Hmm, I think it is too dangerous for you to be walking about at the moment; it seems there is a murderer is at large. I happen to have a meeting in the city this morning. You can share the carriage with me; then we can meet you after I have conducted my business. How does that fare with you?"

"Aye, that fares well enough, sir." Wolfe was finding it difficult to call the brewer by his given name.

Mid-morning, the terce bells had sounded over two hours ago, and Wolfe and the brewer were riding in the carriage to the wharf. The brewer was explaining to Wolfe the trading conditions and the complexities of shipping barrels to Denmark and Holland; Wolfe was trying to understand.

It had taken over twenty-five minutes for the pair to reach the quayside, the cobbles making carriage-riding not the most comfortable of travel. Wolfe alighted and the brewer promised a return in about an hour. Wolfe watched the carriage turn and head into the city. Two of the crewmen and the captain were on deck and saw Wolfe arrive in style, but instead of heading up the gangplank, Wolfe walked quickly along the quay. He had another place to be.

It was only a ten-minute swift stride to his lodgings; there was no sign of militiamen; in fact, the quayside was quiet.

He entered the lodgings and headed up to his room. There had been no shortage of hiding places under the floorboards, and within minutes, Wolfe had retrieved the bounty and was walking back to the cog with the two purses safely secured under his doublet. It was a dull morning but without the rain from the previous day. Wolfe felt good and his stride was strong and purposeful. He reached the gangplank where the captain was talking to one of the crewmen.

"Ah, Master Wolfe, what brings you here today? You

were not required to work."

"Nay, Captain, came to enquire about sailing. Have you a thought on the matter?"

"Aye, I was going to pass the news around today. I'll need you back here in three days to start loading, we leave the morrow after … I saw you arrived in a carriage?"

"Aye, tis right."

The captain looked inquisitively, but Wolfe decided not to elaborate. Just then the sound of horses' hooves could be heard and the carriage appeared.

"See you in three days," said Wolfe, as he walked back down the gangplank to meet the approaching carriage. The captain was watching with interest. He couldn't see the other passenger in the carriage; the brewer was seated on the far side, allowing Wolfe to enter. Wolfe closed the door and the coachman tapped the horse with his long whip.

The brewer turned to Wolfe. "Has a decision been made on your departure?"

"Aye, in three days I will need to help load the cog."

"Then you must stay as my guest until you set sail; unless, of course you have other arrangements."

"Nay, sir, I'll gladly take up your generous offer."

They reached the mansion and the coachman pulled up in front of the front door.

Inside, lunch had been prepared and, again, Wolfe was invited to join them; he was now one of the family. As he was eating, he couldn't help noticing Inga occasionally glancing in his direction, followed by a coy lowering of the eyes.

Wolfe was relaxing in the sitting room when he noticed Inga walking towards the gazebo at the bottom of the large garden. It was a cool afternoon but bright, and Inga had a woollen shawl wrapped around her. Wolfe watched as she started reading a book. Occasionally she would look up in the direction of the house.

Wolfe decided to go for a walk, and headed out into the garden. Inga noticed him approaching and waved.

"Master Wolfe, tis a grand afternoon, if you're wrapped warmly."

"Aye Frauline Koche, so it is."

"I am Inga, please call me Inga."

"Aye, so I will; I'm John."

"Aye, I know … Tell me John, do you read?"

He looked down, embarrassed at his lack of education.

"Nay, reading and writing is something that has passed me by."

"In that case I will teach you. Come, sit down next to me."

"But happen, I've only got three days."

"We better start without delay, then. I will fetch charcoal and paper."

Inga went into the house and collected her writing materials, then returned to the gazebo and sat beside Wolfe.

For two hours Inga explained how letters were written and their sound, then how to recognise simple words. Wolfe was a keen learner; there was no doubt such skills would enhance his ambition.

The brewer gazed out of the window, noticing the pair together; he smiled to himself and wondered about the possibility of Wolfe joining the family firm. He would fit in well.

The tuition continued for the rest of the afternoon until the light began to fade.

"We should retire to the house, John, dinner will be ready," said Inga, as it became too dark to read. The bells would toll vespers in an hour.

The living room was bedecked with candelabras, a roaring fire burned in the hearth; the house had four chimneys to accommodate the respective fireplaces - the living room, kitchen, dining room, and the master bedroom.

Emilinda served a game pie which she had prepared that afternoon. Inga was seated next to her mother opposite John, who was beside the brewer. The room was bathed in the ethereal light of candles, the fire was burning logs in the grate, the atmosphere homely, something alien to Wolfe. In different circumstances he would have been eating in a dingy tavern somewhere; if they had food enough to sell.

After dinner, Inga suggested they continued the tuition by the light of a candle. Wolfe was only too pleased to agree. Although nowhere near literate yet, he was starting to recognise letters, but it was the allure of the brewer's daughter that was even more enticing. Her close proximity made concentration difficult.

The time flew by; in the distance, the last bells of the day – the compline, sounded across the city.

The brewer and his wife had retired to bed, leaving Inga and Wolfe together. Eventually, Inga called time.

"Aye," agreed John; it had been a lot to absorb.

"We can continue tomorrow," replied Inga, as she collected a candlestick.

She smiled a beguiling smile which had Wolfe's pulse racing. Emelinda was damping the fires and bolting the doors for the night, before retiring to her own quarters on the ground floor.

"I'll be to bed, John," said Inga, as she carried the candle-holder towards the stairs.

"Aye, it's been much to consider; my head is fare bursting, methinks. You're a good tutor, Mistress Inga."

"I've never had cause, till now."

Inga ascended the stairs, the candlelight causing glimmering shadows on the wall; Wolfe followed.

At the top of the stairs, Inga turned down the long corridor past her parents' room, until she reached her bedroom, opposite the guest room.

Inga pushed open the door; a single candle illuminated the room. She handed Wolfe the candlestick and walked inside. She half closed the door and whispered to Wolfe. "I'll have no cause to lock my door this night; happen you will protect me from harm."

"Aye, I'll always protect you," replied Wolfe, considering her words.

"That's pleasing to hear, indeed," replied Inga, and dropped her gaze, her face radiant in the flickering candle-glow. The door slowly closed but didn't click shut. Wolfe turned to his room with much on his mind; it was nothing to do with reading or writing.

Emelinda had considerately lit a candle, enabling him to see across the bedchamber; it was where he had slept on his previous visit. There was a large bed, a bucket, and the porcelain washbasin on a table which had been filled with water. There was even some sweet-smelling soap which Wolfe hadn't seen since London. He extinguished the candlestick he was holding.

Wolfe relieved himself, then stripped off and washed himself down. He was considering Inga's words. He put on his under garments and opened his bedroom door. He looked left and right; the corridor was in darkness. He could see the brewer's daughter's door opposite. His heartrate had increased significantly, partly anxiety, but mostly anticipation. He stepped across the narrow corridor and slowly pushed open Inga's door and peered inside. It was a large room dominated by a four-poster bed. There was a lighted candle on a small table next to it.

Wolfe entered, closed the door behind him, then crept towards the bed. He could see Inga lay on her back in the flickering candlelight, looking serene and beautiful; her blonde hair stretched across the pillow. She looked asleep. He watched her for a moment, then suddenly her eyes opened. She turned her head towards her visitor and smiled, then flipped back the coverlet; she was naked.

"I knew you would come to protect me," she whispered.

Wolfe removed his nightwear and climbed in beside her.

The pattern was repeated for the next two days with Inga continuing her tutelage and Wolfe providing close protection at night.

It was his final day before he had to return to the cog. During a break from his tuition, the brewer asked Wolfe into the sitting room. He couldn't fail to notice the closeness between his daughter and his guest.

Wolfe walked in and was invited to sit adjacent to the brewer.

"John, I wanted to discuss a proposition with you..." Wolfe listened in anticipation. "How would you like to work for me at the brewery?"

Wolfe was finding it difficult to take in. "The brewery? Well, I don't rightly know … I must say, sir, you've caught me by surprise."

The brewer continued. "I have in mind an important position; one in which I need someone I can trust. What do you say? I'm sure Inga would be agreeable, and I would provide you with a place to live. I own several dwellings in the city."

"That's a most generous offer, sir … In truth, I have no

words. I need to return to London; I have business there to attend and have signed for the voyage."

"Yes, I understand, but you could get the next cog back as a passenger. I'll pay for your passage after you have concluded your business."

"Let me think on it; there is a lot to consider."

"Yes, as you must, just let me know before you leave... I can make the carriage available for you in the morning to take you to the wharf."

"Aye, I'd welcome that, though I'm happy to walk. I don't want to put you to any trouble."

His last night with Inga had proved to be an emotional one. He was again required to give her close protection, which he was more than glad to provide. She knew about her father's offer of employment, and persuaded Wolfe to agree.

The following morning at breakfast, he announced his decision as he consumed his meal. He looked at his benefactor.

"Herr Koche, I have considered your kind offer to work for you and would be pleased to accept. I will return to Cologne at the earliest opportunity."

The brewer beamed a broad smile. "That is excellent news, John. I will make arrangements here." He stood up and placed a fatherly hand on his shoulder.

Inga looked across the table at Wolfe, her eyes wide; she too was smiling.

As he prepared to leave his hospitality, the carriage was duly summoned and Wolfe was given a parcel of food by Heldin which he stored in his trusty leather bag. He had transferred the coin from the purses into his money belt where it would be safe.

"Hurry back," implored Inga, as he boarded the carriage.

She walked away without a backward glance, fighting tears.

"I hope you will return soon, John. There's a position waiting for you," said the brewer.

"Aye, sir."

There was an emotional hug, then Wolfe alighted the carriage. The coachman flicked the reins on the horse's hind quarters and it slowly pulled away. The brewer and his wife were stood waving as it moved along the drive.

Half an hour later, Wolfe could see the river; the carriage was approaching the cog. He shouted to the coachman to stop. He had no intention of arriving at the wharf in a carriage; he would never live it down.

He thanked the coachman and watched as it turned full circle and retraced its journey.

Wolfe walked around the corner to the riverside where several cogs were berthed. He could see the London-bound vessel and walked to the gangplank. His two drinking companions were on deck helping loading. They spotted him and walked to the end of the wooden crossing to welcome him.

"John, lad, we've been concerned, Patrick and me. We didn't know if you would be here for the sailing or not. They said you had been arrested."

"Nay, it was a mistake; happen I had someone who spoke for me. I've been staying with him."

"It's good to have you back; the captain will be pleased. He thought we would be a man down."

Just then, Captain Harvey walked up on deck.

"Wolfe, they said you had been arrested."

"Aye, but happen, it were a mistake."

"Good, you can get about your duties."

It was a busy few hours as the cargo was loaded on board.

High tide was mid-afternoon and the captain was anxious not to miss it.

The none bells sounded across the city as horses' hooves could be heard approaching. At the head, Georg Giese was astride a white stallion, dressed in his merchant's finery.

They reached the cog and he dismounted. The horse behind was ladened with personal cargo. There was an attachment of six men-at-arms following Giese and they, too, dismounted and started transporting Giese's luggage onto the cog. The captain was quickly on deck.

"Master Giese, welcome, I have allocated my quarters for you as usual."

"I am grateful, Captain Harvey, my men-at-arms will be joining me for the journey. I assume you will have quarters and food enough for them."

"Aye, happen we can make room."

Within the hour, the cog was slowly easing away from the dock as the wind and tide carried it sea-ward.

An hour into the journey, there was a brisk wind and the cog was making good time. It was a dry, moonless night; clouds raced across the sky, and a myriad of stars sparkled in the firmament. Night vision allowed sufficient light to navigate the wide river. Knowledge of the terrain was important and, with an experienced crew, the captain was able to leave the steering compartment at the stern of the boat and join his esteemed passenger, keen for news of his investigation. It was his first opportunity since they had set sail.

He reached his quarters; he could see a candle burning on his desk. Giese was seated behind, studying some papers. He looked up seeing the approaching frame of the captain.

"Ah, Captain Harvey, set fair, I believe."

"Aye, Master Giese, making good headway … Pray, what

news of your investigation, I was anxious to hear."

"Ah, yes, it is good news, we have identified the culprit."

"You have!? Pray tell. Has he been arrested in Cologne?"

"Nay, nay, tis closer to home. Happen he's a crewman on this very cog."

The Captain looked at Giese with an incredulous expression.

"Nay, nay, that can't be so … On the cog?"

"Aye, tis so; it's why I have bought the militiamen with me."

"But what's to be done? Who is this man?"

"It's the one they call John Wolfe."

"Nay, nay, that can't be so. John Wolfe? Nay not possible."

"Aye, he was heard bragging about it in one of the alehouses."

"Bragging? Nay, that's not Wolfe's style; he keeps himself to himself. Not an easy person to get to know."

"Aye, well, one of the men came forward to claim the reward."

"Is that so? Well, varlets will say anything for sufficient coin."

"Nay, just enough for two tankards of ale."

"Is that the only witness?"

"Nay, it was Wolfe I saw among the cargo on the journey from London; I am certain of it. Looking for more pickings, I wouldn't wonder."

"But how could he have stolen it on the cog? It doesn't seem possible, and where is the coin?"

"Who knows? Maybe he has hidden it. We will find out when we question him."

The captain looked down for a moment taking in the information, then remembered Wolfe's visit to the cog in a carriage. How could he afford such transportation he suddenly wondered.

"What are your intensions? Do you want him arrested?" asked the captain.

"Nay, nay, he can continue the sailing, happen you'll need him."

"Aye, he's my best crewman."

"I'm minded we will wait until London Bridge, then arrest him and hand him over to the Lord Treasurer. He'll be taken to the Tower, methinks. In the meantime, my men will keep a careful watch on him."

"But what if he jumps ship?"

"And go where? He would not survive an hour in the water."

The captain was still considering this revelation; none of it made any sense, but knew better than to question the merchant.

Meanwhile, during a break on deck, Wolfe was seated with his two drinking companions who were keen to hear more of what had happened in Cologne and how he escaped the militiamen. They had not had chance since they left port. They spoke in English.

"Aye, it was some sot, too drunk to make reason. It was good fortune I had someone in the city who was prepared to speak for my character on my behalf. I owe my freedom to him. I was released when the truth was known. He invited me to stay as his guest."

"That is good fortune,, indeed, John," said Thomas. "Likely you would have hung."

"Aye, that's a fact."

He turned to Patrick. "So, what are your intentions when we return to London?"

Patrick was chewing on some bread. "Happen I'll look

for work until another cog returns."

"Will you return to Ireland?" said Thomas.

"I've not thought on't, but if there's no work to be had, happen I might. Sure I miss my family, so I do."

The men were called back to duty. For a moment, Wolfe thought about Inga and her soft body bringing that special comfort that only a woman can provide, but, for tonight, it would be straw bedding on a moving deck.

It was almost a week before the cog reached the inner reaches of the Thames. River traffic was busy as the vessel slowly eased its way to its destination on the morning tide. The voyage had been uneventful; the weather, overall, kind, although fog had slowed the journey. A further few hours would see them at the berth.

As the outline of London Bridge appeared on the horizon, Giese was on deck and summoned his six militiamen.

He gave orders to the sergeant. Wolfe was at the side of the boat checking the clearance when suddenly he was grabbed by two men. Before he could move, his wrists were pulled behind him and tied with twine. He was taken completely by surprise.

"Take him below, and secure him," ordered Giese.

"Release me, release me," protested Wolfe. "Why have you treated me this way?"

He was struggling with his ties but they held firm. He was quickly taken below deck.

Giese followed. "Search him," he ordered, and the sergeant roughly frisked Wolfe. He soon found the knife in its sheath, then discovered his money belt which contained the contents of the two purses. The sergeant showed them to Giese.

"What have we here, Master Wolfe? Is this part of the

hoard you stole from me?"

"Nay, I have earned that coin, every mark."

"I doubt that."

Giese tipped some of the contents into his hand. There were several gold crowns as well as German Marks and English coin.

"This is more than a seaman's wage for a good year or two." He examined the coin closely. "You have some explaining to do, Master Wolfe; but you can save it for His Majesty's Treasurer. He'll be very interested in your explanation."

Giese tipped the coin back into the money belt and tucked it into his tunic.

Wolfe was wild with rage and, if he could free himself, he would tear Giese limb from limb.

Back on deck, Thomas looked at Patrick, then walked to the captain.

"What's happening with John?" exclaimed Thomas. "Why has he been treated this way?"

"I can't discuss it with you, but they say he has been involved with a robbery."

"A robbery? Nay, that can't be right."

"Aye, we'll have to see what the magistrate has to say about it."

Thomas went back to Patrick. Other crewmen were quickly to him wanting to know why Wolfe had been taken into custody. Thomas recounted the explanation from the captain. There were looks of surprise from one or two, but others who knew Wolfe for a long time were not so surprised.

"Happen, justice has caught up with Master Wolfe and not before time," was one comment.

Mid-morning, a blustery, cold day, and London Bridge was raised, allowing the cog passage to the Steelyard berth. The crewmen secured the vessel and the gangplank put in place. Giese was waiting to cross, and ordered his men to bring Wolfe. He had been held below deck with his hands bound, and guarded by two armed militiamen; he was still protesting his innocence.

Giese walked up to the captain. “I am grateful for your co-operation, Captain Harvey; it will not go unrecognised. I’ll be keeping this man at the Steelyard until we can hand him over to the Lord Treasurer.

The captain watched as Wolfe was dragged, protesting vehemently, down the gangplank surrounded by the six armed guards. Two had their swords drawn; Georg Giese followed.

Chapter Eleven

Alice awoke to a new day. Her arrangement with the men-at-arms had proved to be a shrewd move, not only had she been handsomely recompensed, three times the rate for a prostitute; she was now safe from any enquiry concerning the dead sergeant. The accepted verdict was that he had fallen into the river while drunk, and drowned.

She had an errand today; she needed to find out if there was any information regarding Wolfe. He was long overdue.

She dressed warmly for what was a cold mid-winter's day, and set off an hour or so after the terce bells had rung. She cut through the passages, avoiding the main thoroughfares, not for any other reason than it was quicker; she had no concern for her security.

She entered Thames Street, walked along the wall of the Kontor until she reached the gate and was greeted by an armed guard.

"What's your business, Mistress?"

"I want to see the Supervisor. I'm enquiring the whereabouts of John Wolfe. His cog is long overdue."

The guard's attention was drawn to the request.

"John Wolfe?"

"Aye."

"You better come with me." The guard stood to one side and let her into the compound. "Follow me," he ordered.

As she walked behind the guard, Alice looked around at the splendid architecture and the fine clothes worn by the merchants going about their business. She was soon the centre of attention; women were not ordinarily allowed in the Steelyard.

The building which housed the supervisor's office was

above the passageway which led directly to the dock; Alice could see the river through the archway.

The guard opened a door to the right, under the arch, and Alice was ushered up some stone steps to a landing. To the left, was a grand room that stretched probably sixty feet from wall to wall. It overlooked the Thames with spectacular views, although not fully at its best on this rather dreary day. Several cogs could be seen berthed along the riverside. The windows were typically diamond shaped with lead surrounds which gave the office natural light.

There was a large desk at the back of the room where a man was seated, dressed in the manner of a merchant. The guard approached the supervisor with due reverence. He was clearly a man of some importance. They spoke in German.

"Sir, I have this woman here making enquiries of John Wolfe."

The supervisor looked at Alice with narrow, dark eyes; his full beard glistened as if recently dampened.

"John Wolfe, you say. What is your business with Herr Wolfe?" He spoke in a strong accent which Alice could just make out.

"I am his wife, sir."

"Wife? I see." He paused and thought for a moment. "We were not aware he had a wife; he had said naught."

Alice looked at the man with an expression of some concern. She spoke with impatience. "Do you know where he is? What say you?"

"Nay, not exactly. He was arrested on board the cog."

"Arrested!? For what reason?"

"Theft, they say he has committed a robbery … King's coin, serious charges."

"Nay, nay, that's not possible."

"That's up to the magistrate to decide."

"Magistrate?"

"Aye, he was handed over to the King's Lord Treasurer after the cog arrived. He's probably been taken to the Tower by now."

"Oh, dear Lord, no."

"That's my belief, but you should go to Westminster Hall; someone there will know."

Two days earlier, after the cog had docked, John Wolfe was taken to one of the secure buildings in the Steelyard next to the Winter Hall. An armed guard was placed outside. He continued to protest his innocence, shouting loudly from his cell to anyone who would listen.

Giese summoned a messenger to ride to Westminster Hall with a note advising William Fitzwilliam of their arrival and the apprehension of a suspect, awaiting collection. He then reported to the Chancellor, Hermann Wedigh, in his office. The elder seemed pleased to see Giese's return and welcomed him warmly.

"Please be seated, Master Georg; I have some refreshment to celebrate your safe return."

He produced a flagon of wine and two pewter tankards from an adjacent table. "From our wine-store," he confirmed, as he began filling the two vessels. He handed Giese his drink and sat back in his chair.

"So, Master Georg, you have found a suitable thief, I understand."

"Aye, sir, a well-known cutpurse and murderer, according to rumours. He will be no loss to this world."

"Hmm, but we must not underestimate the King's Treasurer, or Lord Shrewsbury, they are no fools. The man is, after all, innocent."

"We have the testimony of the crewman."

"Ha, the hearsay of a drunken sot anxious for coin. They would say anything for recompense."

"We do have the coin he had on his person, over fifteen crowns; more than a seaman's wage for five years. Wolfe said he had earned it, but that's not possible; I believe it was from a robbery. It will certainly add value to our cause."

"Aye, tis the truth, but I urge caution. If we are caught in a lie then the trumpery will be discovered, and then … " He stroked his chin. "I would not like to consider the consequences."

Giese took a sip of wine. "If he's sent to the Tower, he could well be tortured into a confession."

The Chancellor considered this. "Aye, that's a possibility, but for now, let's see what the Lord Treasurer has to say."

"I accept your council, sir, and will proceed as you suggest." He turned to leave before adding. "I have sent message to Master Fitzwilliam to say we have apprehended the thief; I'm awaiting a reply."

It was two hours before the sound of horses could be heard outside the wall of the Kontor approaching the Thames Street gate. The none bells had sounded an hour since, and the light was gradually fading.

William Fitzwilliam was at the head of a column of ten men-at-arms, carrying pikestaffs, and a carriage driven by a coachman. They reached the entrance of the Steelyard and were confronted by the duty guard.

The Lord Treasurer announced his arrival and requested that Georg Giese be summoned.

The guard went to collect the Deputy Alderman. Fitzwilliam dismounted and waited Giese's presence.

Giese had changed into his merchant's clothing to meet the Lord Treasurer. He walked the short distance to the gate with the guard and greeted his guest.

"Master Fitzwilliam, it is good to see you again." There was mutual bowing and removal of hats.

"Some time has passed, Master Giese, but I thank the Lord for your safe return … and with the culprit, I understand," said Fitzwilliam.

"Aye, but he doth protest his innocence … too loudly, methinks. Would you care to join me for some refreshment before you take him away?"

"Very well, Master Giese, for a short while. The light is fading and I have a distance to travel, but I would like to know how the thief was captured."

Fitzwilliam left his horse with one of the men-at-arms and followed Giese into the Steelyard complex. They headed to the Chancellor's office in the Winter Hall, and after a few minutes, entered the lavish room. Weidig was seated at his desk with quill in hand. A candle was burning close by, providing light for his endeavours. The Chancellor looked up.

Giese turned to his guest. "You recall, the Kontor Chancellor, Master Fitzwilliam?"

"Aye, of course."

Weidig got up and walked around to the other side of his desk. There was another mutual bowing. Fitzwilliam was invited to sit while Weidig poured a tankard of wine for their guest.

"I've been telling the Chancellor about the culprit, John Wolfe," said Giese, as Fitzwilliam took a drink.

Giese related the story that Wolfe had been heard bragging in an alehouse that he had committed the daring robbery. "And no-one was going to catch him, he said," expanded Giese. The story was already taking on its own momentum.

Giese presented The Treasurer with the money belt.

"When he was apprehended, he was wearing this."

Fitzwilliam weighed it in his hands. "There's a fair sum in there."

"Aye, profits from some strudung or such, methinks," said Giese.

There was a short conversation, but the room was getting dark, and the candlelighter was due any moment.

Fitzwilliam stood up. "I'll take my prisoner, if I may … and the evidence you have acquired. I have a journey to return to Westminster Hall, and my men will be thirsty."

Giese looked at Weidig, who nodded in a sagely way, then handed over the purse. Fitzwilliam secured it inside his tunic.

Two guards were summoned and sent to get Wolfe from the make-shift gaol.

Fitzwilliam waited by the entrance to the Winter Hall, and a few minutes later, Wolfe was being dragged towards him by two guards. His hands had been secured behind him.

The Treasurer looked at the prisoner, "So you're the caitiff that stole my money."

"Nay, nay, my lord, this is all wrong. I'm innocent. It's a mistake. I keep saying but no-one will listen."

"Well, you can tell that to the magistrate on the morrow."

Fitzwilliam thanked Giese and the squad left.

Wolfe was wrestling violently with his handlers, but eventually, with the encouragement of the point of a sword, they dragged Wolfe out of the Steelyard and into the awaiting open cart. Two men-at-arms joined him, and sat opposite, swords drawn.

There were more armed guards waiting for the arrival of Fitzwilliam and the entourage, as they returned from the Steelyard with the prisoner.

Fitzwilliam dismounted and supervised the opening of the carriage. Wolfe was bundled out and marched roughly towards the entrance of Westminster Hall.

"Take him to the cells," ordered the Treasurer, and he walked inside to report to Lord Shrewsbury.

Wolfe was escorted inside, then down the steps to the dungeons, still protesting his innocence. The way was lit by tar-torches. The cells were empty and deathly quiet.

A gaoler opened the first cell and Wolfe was pushed inside by two men-at-arms. His ties were cut, and he massaged the circulation back to his wrists where the twine had cut into his flesh. There was no light and the stone floor was covered by straw. The gaoler deposited a bucket, then locked the door.

Upstairs, The Treasurer was in conference with Lord Shrewsbury. It was dark and the room was illuminated by candles.

"You've seen the prisoner, Master Fitzwilliam?"

"Aye, my lord."

"And your impressions?"

"Protesting his innocence, most vigorously, my Lord. We will see what he has to say after a night in the cells. He's certainly a rough-looking type."

"What of the crowns? Have they been found?"

"Nay, my Lord, no sign, although the caitiff was carrying this money-belt; it's filled with coin."

He placed the money-belt on the desk. Lord Salisbury picked it up and examined it.

"You think it could be from the robbery?"

"Certainly from some robbery, methinks. It was more than any seaman could earn in a lifetime."

"Hmm … We need to think what to do with him; I will visit Cromwell on the morrow and get his words on the matter, but I believe justice would best be served with a visit to The Tower."

"Aye, my Lord."

In the cells below Westminster Hall, conditions were dire. Wolfe had no additional clothing; it was bitterly cold, and he had not eaten since his meagre rations on the cog. There was no window to give any indication of time, and he was becoming disorientated. He still had no knowledge of why he had been incarcerated. His only method of sleeping was to sit against one of the walls and wait for fatigue to take over.

The following morning, Lord Shrewsbury was taken by carriage to Austin Friars, the home of Thomas Cromwell. He travelled mid-morning and the streets of London were alive with people going about their business. The weather was, for the moment, dry, but rain threatened, and it was cold.

On his arrival, he was ushered into one of the annexes to await his audience. It was almost an hour before a clerk collected him and led him to Cromwell's impressive chambers.

"My Lord Shrewsbury," greeted Cromwell from behind his desk. He had been writing, and the feather quill was still in his hand as he looked up at the visitor.

"My Lord Cromwell, I come bearing news."

"I should hope so, else you would be wasting both our time." A feigned smile passed his face.

Shrewsbury was more relaxed in Cromwell's company now, and was not drawn to the comment.

"We have apprehended a suspect in the case of the missing gold."

Cromwell looked up and replaced his quill in the inkpot,

then sat back in his seat.

"Pray continue; you have my mind."

"Aye, my Lord, a seaman, he was aboard the cog that was carrying the cargo."

Cromwell squinted. "And where is this miscreant?"

"We have him in the cells at Westminster Hall, awaiting a magistrate."

"Nay, nay, we don't want a magistrate; he should be taken to The Tower. We do not want this incident to be known by one and all. Arrange for him to be taken there forthwith on my authority."

"Very well, my Lord."

"What about the gold? Has that been recovered?"

"Nay, the man protests his innocence, and says he has no knowledge of any gold, although he was found with significant coin on his person."

"And who caught this thief?"

"Master Giese delivered him. The man was heard in an alehouse in Cologne, bragging he was the thief, according to an eye-witness."

"An alehouse?"

"Aye, my Lord."

"And he was apprehended by the Hanseatic League merchant?"

"Aye."

"My Lord Shrewsbury, you know my thoughts on the League. It seems you have only the word of a sot, and this man's money belt. I smell a rat."

Shrewsbury looked down. "Aye, tis true."

"Have him sent to The Tower; they have means there of extracting the truth."

"Aye, my Lord."

It was early afternoon when Alice completed the three-mile journey to Westminster Hall. The threatened rain had arrived, and she was soaked; her clothes stuck to her, her wimple bedraggled, her hair lay lank beneath.

She looked up at the imposing structure, the domicile of merchants, clerks, and knights of the shires, not a usual place for a spinner of wool.

Undaunted, she reached the portico and walked inside the dark entrance chamber. She was immediately confronted by a master-at-arms.

"What be your business, Mistress?" asked the man, with one hand on his sword.

"I am seeking news of my husband; I have been told he has been brought here."

"What name does your husband go by?"

"Wolfe, John Wolfe."

"Stay here, Mistress Wolfe."

As she waited for news, Alice could see inside the grand hall, bustling with clerks going about their duties. After several minutes, she could see two men approaching, the guard and another man, dressed in an attire befitting a man of wealth.

"Mistress Wolfe? I am William Fitzwilliam. You ask of your husband, I believe."

"Aye, my Lord," replied Alice; she curtsied.

"What do you know about his recent whereabouts?"

"I have no knowledge, my Lord. Happen, he's been at sea for some weeks. They said at the Steelyard he has been sent here; someone has called him a thief."

"Aye, he has been arrested as such."

"Nay, that cannot be true; he's a God-fearing and honest man."

"It seems not, Mistress Wolfe. He's been sent to the

Tower, where his crime will be investigated."

"But what crime, my Lord? There has surely been a mistake."

"I cannot discuss it with you; it's no longer in my hands. I bid you good day."

Fitzwilliam turned and walked away.

Alice started to amble away from the Hall, trying to take in this news. It would mean another long walk on the morrow.

She trudged back to her dwelling. The temperature had dropped significantly, the sky now heavy and grey; daylight was fast receding. As she made her return journey, Alice was deep in thought at Wolfe's incarceration; there must be an explanation. She didn't know what she could do and felt disheartened.

It was early January 1532, and, overnight, the threatened winter snows had cast their grip on London. For anyone walking a distance, it was a bleak prospect.

Alice left the dwelling just after the terce bells had rung. Daylight cast a vision of white across the city; water dripped off the roofs of houses as the snow surrendered to the slightly above-freezing temperature. She had dressed warmly, complete with a cloak that would protect her from the worst of the cold. One of her many purchases during Wolfe's absence was a pair of leather booties. Her well-worn footwear would add some protection from the vile slush that would frequent her journey.

She headed towards St Pauls Church and through the Carter Street market. There were few people venturing out, and less than half the normal stalls were open, their proprietors desperately trying to clear a path to their wares using make-shift shovels, or even their bare hands. Walking was treacherous, the snow lay several inches deep and had yet to be trodden down.

For Alice, it was heavy going, and it was over an hour before she arrived at Tower Street, the road leading to Tower Hill and the magnificent fortress. She gazed at the sight stretched out in front of her to the left, with its four towers dominating the scene. Fifteen-feet thick walls surrounded the castle.

She turned south towards the river where she could access the main gate. Her boots were sodden from the snow, nearly a foot deep in places, where it hadn't been trodden down by footfall.

Everyone knew The Tower by reputation, magnificent and foreboding, the palace of Kings through the ages, and the keeper of traitors. It was still regarded as a royal palace, despite having been vacated by Henry V111 in 1509. A token guard of twelve Tower Warders remained, responsible for the security of the castle and guarding any prisoners being held there. The warders bore arms but were not liveried in traditional outfits.

Alice felt anxious as she approached the drawbridge at Middle Tower. She crossed the moat and passed the imposing Bywater Tower, then further until she reached the aptly named 'Bloody Tower'. Here, the snow had compacted making walking easier.

A warder was on guard, stood with a long pike, his sword was sheathed. He lowered the pike to forty-five degrees and challenged Alice.

"What's your business, Mistress?"

"I am Alice Wolfe; I have come to see my husband. I am told he was brought here yesterday."

"He'll be in the White Tower, Mistress. What's his name?"

"Wolfe … John Wolfe."

"And you're his wife?"

"Aye, sir."

Seeing she posed no threat, he raised his pike and directed Alice to the Coldharbour Gate which protected the main building. It was an open area from the guard to the White Tower. The snow was over a foot deep in the surrounds, but the footpath had been trodden down; this was a regular thoroughfare. Her boots squelched with every tread. She became more and more anxious approaching the entrance, aware of the impregnable walls and imposing towers that surrounded her. It's reputation as a place of evil and suffering was well deserved.

She reached Coldharbour Gate and was again confronted by a warder, dressed as the first, in a breastplate over his tunic and a metal helmet. He drew his sword.

"Who goes there?"

Alice froze. "I am Alice Wolfe; I am looking for my husband."

The warder approached, still holding his sword.

"What's his name?"

"John … John Wolfe."

"Aye, he's here."

"Then, can I visit him?"

"Wait here; I will enquire."

Alice tried to keep warm, rubbing her hands and pulling her cloak around her. The snow lay pristine and deep in the area between the White Tower and the Walls; the only footprints had been made by birds. The sky looked grey, and further showers threatened.

It seemed a long time before the warder returned. He was accompanied by another man, similarly dressed,

"You are Mistress Wolfe, wife of John Wolfe?" said the

new arrival.

"Aye, sir."

"I am William Denys, Yeoman Gaoler; follow me."

The man escorted Alice through a huge wooden door into a bleak chamber with stone floor and walls; open windows allowed some natural light. It was bitterly cold. Wide stairs descended to the right; Alice followed the man down several more stone steps, lit by tar-torches. At the end of a long corridor, they came to a locked door. The gaoler stopped.

"You have coin mistress?"

"Aye, sir."

"Your husband's condition can be improved by a suitable endowment."

"Endowment, sir?"

"Aye, a man's got to live."

"Aye, tis true, sir."

She retrieved her purse, took out a shilling and handed it to him. He looked at the coin and smiled.

"I can speak to the Lieutenant for you; he is in charge of prisoner benefits. I'm sure with more endowments, we can make your husband's stay more comfortable."

"Aye … aye, I will be most grateful."

He looked her up and down; his eyes narrowed. A lascivious smile prompted a remark.

"Perchance you might be able to show your gratitude in a more, ahem, physical way, Mistress?"

"Aye, if it will help John."

The gaoler produced a set of large keys and opened the heavy wooden doors to a cell and indicated for Alice to enter with a move of his head.

"Knock when you're ready to leave, Mistress Wolfe."

Alice entered the cell. It was dark, the occupant no more than a shadowy figure at the far wall. Alice squinted.

"John? Is that you?"

"Alice! ... Alice?"

"Aye, John. Tis me."

He moved towards her and they embraced.

"Wait, I cannot see you."

She turned and rapped on the cell door. It opened.

"Gaoler, I need light for my husband's cell." She went to her purse again and passed him two groats which Denys examined.

"Aye; I'll return in haste," he replied, and closed the door.

A few minutes later, the door opened and the gaoler entered with a lighted candle and two unlighted ones. Alice took the candles and Denys left the cell. Alice lifted the candle and Wolfe's face was illuminated in the dim light.

"Now I can see you, John."

She looked around the dungeon. The room was sparce. There was no bed, just a sprinkling of straw, a bucket, chair and a small table. She placed the candles down on the table."

Alice held John for a moment, then relaxed the embrace.

"Why are you here, John? They say you are a thief."

"Nay, Alice, tis a lie. They say I have stolen gold crowns from the King, but it is a falsehood. I know nothing about missing crowns. I need to convince them I am innocent."

"How can you do that?"

"I do not know. I was brought here, and locked in this cell, but I have seen no one since."

"Let me look at you."

She raised the candle closely and examined his face. She almost gasped in horror; he looked different. His visage was lined with pock marks and lesions, and there were bags under his eyes through lack of sleep. His beard and hair were long and unkempt, his tunic soiled and stained.

"Have you eaten, John?"

"Not since yesterday, happen my belly complains much."

"Then I will arrange food and water for you; I have coin."

"There is more coin at the dwelling."

"Aye, I knows; I found it."

"Is it still intact?"

"Nay, not all, happen I had to pay Master Thornton."

Wolfe looked down. "Aye, the rent was due; it had passed my mind."

"Do not concern yourself; I have seen to it."

The time passed quickly as Alice and John continued to reconnect. Whilst still physically in a poor condition, Wolfe's mental state improved following Alice's appearance. The door opened; it was the gaoler, William Denys.

"Mistress Wolfe; the light is fading; you will need to make haste."

"Aye, I will."

She said farewell to Wolfe with the promise of an early return.

The door closed. Outside the dungeon, the tar-torches flickered in the passageway. Alice produced a crown from her purse.

"Will you see that his Lordship, the Lieutenant, receives this and ensures my husband is properly fed and watered, and is provided with a bed?"

The gaoler looked at the coin.

"Aye, Mistress Wolfe."

"And will you see that he is not abused?"

"Aye, Mistress Wolfe, and how will you reward me?"

"We will have to see, Master goaler."

"Nay, Mistress Wolfe; it is William, William Denys."

"William, it is, then. I will return on the morrow."

The journey back to the dwelling, took over an hour. The weather had turned, and it was snowing heavily again; it was miserable. Very few people were about; which pleased Alice, just a small party of watchmen, who viewed her with some suspicion but did not detain her.

She breathed a sigh of relief as she opened the door to the cottage. She needed to build a fire and find something to eat.

Later, she had changed into more warm clothing and ate some dried meat and bread by the fireside – her boots were drying next to the hearth. She thought about Wolfe and wondered how long he would be detained. She believed him when he said he had no involvement in the robbery; she just hoped that those who had charged him would do the same.

Back in the Steelyard, Georg Gies was enjoying a tankard of wine with the Chancellor.

"Well, Master Giese, it seems you have got away with your, ahem, trumpery. I see little point in continuing with any investigation."

"No, sir, that would give a lie to our culprit."

"In the Tower, I understand."

"Aye, sir."

"I wonder what they will do with him."

"Try to get him to confess, most likely; they have some very persuasive methods," said Giese."

"Aye, I understand so."

"I can't see them believing his innocence; they will want to know the whereabouts of the booty."

"Which he won't be able to tell them."

"Aye, true enough. More wine, sir?"

Chapter Twelve

The following morning, the King's Treasurer and Lord Steward were waiting outside the entrance to Westminster Hall for the carriage that would take them to the Tower; their aim, to question Wolfe. They were dressed warmly to ward off the wintery chill. Snow was still lying on the ground making the cobbles slippery and dangerous for horses. The fetid slush of human and horse's excrement, together with rotting vegetation of all kinds made pedestrian travel even worse. There were few people about.

They had sent a messenger the previous afternoon to advise the Lieutenant of The Tower of their proposed visit. A small contingent of men-at-arms would accompany them. William Fitzwilliam looked up at the sky.

"Happen, the weather seems free from more snow, my Lord."

"Aye, God willing," replied Lord Shrewsbury.

As expected, given the slippery conditions, it was not a comfortable journey, and it had taken almost ninety-minutes to travel the three and a half miles to Tower Hill. The coachman steadied the horses for the slow descent to the river and the Middle Tower entrance with the fortress in full view to the left. Houses lined the right hand side, and water dripped steadily from the eves, as a wintery sun made its presence felt, suggesting the beginning of a thaw. The cobbles were already clear; puddles of melted snow and the foul detritus of the gutters were everywhere, causing hazards for the unwary.

The carriage drew to a halt as they reached their destination; the men-at-arms dismounted. Fitzwilliam and Lord Shrewsbury alighted the carriage and made their way across the drawbridge.

The duty Yeoman Warder was aware of their expected arrival, and escorted the party to the White Tower. The path had been compacted by the footfall of the warders, and was treacherous underfoot. The Inner Ward was still white with pristine snow.

The warder led the party to the Coldharbour Tower and into the main building. The escorting soldiers were required to wait outside while Fitzwilliam and Lord Shrewsbury conducted their business.

The ground floor of the White Tower was the domain of the Lieutenant of The Tower, and included his offices and private suite; he also had a house within the walls of the complex. He was in overall control of The Tower and its varying functions; he wielded a great deal of power as a result.

The warder ushered the guests into an outer room and asked them to wait.

Sir Edmund Walsingham had had a distinguished military career and had seen action at the Battle of Flodden. He had also accompanied Henry V111 to France for a meeting with the French King, Charles V. He was rewarded with his present post, Lord Lieutenant of the Tower, which he had held since 1520, on a stipend of a hundred pounds a year.

He had dressed for the occasion; it had been some while since he had received such distinguished visitors.

He came out to greet the guests, and welcomed them with the traditional extravagant bowing and doffing of hat, which was reciprocated.

"Come, come, my friends, we can go to my private chambers; it will be more comfortable."

Walsingham led the pair through a grand hall into an anti-chamber. It reflected the taste of a man with wealth.

Magnificent furnishings, a writing desk with the usual accessories, tapestries and paintings on the wall, and rugs on the floor. There was also a roaring fire, connected to a chimney. The room was warm and the guests removed their cloaks.

"Please be seated," invited the Lieutenant.

There were two leather-backed chairs in front of the writing desk, and his guests sat down.

Sir Edmund got straight to the point. "So, I understand from your message, you are here to interrogate one of my prisoners."

Lord Shrewsbury answered. "Aye, Sir Edmund, he is a suspect in a serious crime against His Majesty's Exchequer."

"I see, and that is the reason why he has been sent here, and not dealt with at Newgate?"

"Aye, sir, on Lord Cromwell's direction," interjected Fitzwilliam.

"Thomas Cromwell … Hmm, I see." Sir Edmund was deep in thought. "Oh, where are my manners? Would you like some refreshment after your journey? I have some hot mulled wine, freshly made, which will take away the chill of the day."

The pair looked at each other. "Aye, Sir Edmund, that would be most acceptable," replied Shrewsbury.

Fitzwilliam nodded.

A warder was summoned, and returned a few minutes later with a steaming jug of red liquid and three tankards.

"So, what's the story of John Wolfe?" enquired the Lieutenant as he took his first sip.

"A consignment of coin destined for His Majesty has gone missing and we have it on good authority he was the miscreant."

"I see, and do you know what has happened to this coin?"

"No, sir, we are hoping that we can find out that information," replied Fitzwilliam.

"Well, we do have facilities and equipment here that might aid you in your endeavours."

"Aye, I have heard such," said Fitzwilliam. He looked at Shrewsbury.

"There does seem to be money about, My Lord Shrewsbury. His wife visited yesterday," said the Lieutenant.

"His wife? He was allowed such comfort?"

"Aye, if they have money. She generously proffered a crown for his comfort."

A crown, you say?" said Shrewsbury.

"Aye."

"And where did she get such wealth, I wonder," said Fitzwilliam.

"Who's to say?" replied Sir Edmund.

They finished their drinks, and Lord Shrewsbury stood up.

"We should attend to our business, Sir Edmund. I am grateful for your hospitality. Can you arrange for my men to be made comfortable? We maybe some time."

"Aye, My Lord, I will get one of my warders to ensure they are given refreshment. I have allocated a room which will serve your purpose; I will get the prisoner brought to you."

Sir Edmund led the pair from his private office into an adjacent room, which was sparsely furnished, and cold. Two chairs had been placed behind a desk and a further one in front.

The guests made themselves comfortable while they waited for the prisoner.

A few minutes later, Wolfe was brought to them. He was

shackled by the wrists and legs and escorted by two armed warders.

The interrogators looked at him. His hair and beard were unkempt, his tunic torn and soiled. He was tied to the chair; two warders stood either side.

Lord Shrewsbury started the inquisition.

"Do you know why you have been brought here?"

Wolfe lifted his head; his face appeared gaunt, his eyes hardly focusing.

"Nay, my Lord. They say I have stolen coin that belonged to the King. I have no knowledge of such a crime; I am innocent."

"But you were on the cog which was carrying the coin."

"Aye, my Lord, all the crew knew about it. I saw the chest; it was sealed and chained to the deck, and it was guarded day and night. How was I supposed to carry out such a task?"

"Who knows the cunning of a thief?" said Fitzwilliam. "Someone could have broken the seal, removed the coin and sealed it again."

"Nay, sir." Wolfe coughed, a hacking rasp. He continued; his voice, wheezy. "How could that have happened? No-one carries such tools; and it was under guard … I tell you; I am innocent."

Fitzwilliam looked at Shrewsbury with a frown.

"What about your confession?

"What confession; why would I confess to such a crime?"

"You were heard bragging about it," said Fitzwilliam.

"Where was this?"

"In Cologne, an alehouse."

"Nay, that is not possible. Aye, I visited an alehouse with three friends, and they will stand by my side. I can give you their names. Happen, someone was after the reward; I hear it was a tidy sum."

Again, Fitzwilliam looked at His Lordship.

Wolfe looked up at the pair, his face one of realisation. "Wait, there is someone else who will speak for me, the brewer, Herr Koche. I stayed with him as his guest for the last few days."

"Herr Koche?" said Fitzwilliam.

"Aye, he owns the brewery in Cologne. He has even offered me a position when I return."

There were more looks between the inquisitors; it was not going the way they expected.

Fitzwilliam tried another tack. "What about the money belt you were carrying? It was more than a seaman's earnings for many years."

"Aye, I won it on the dice."

"The dice?!" exclaimed Fitzwilliam.

"Aye, sir, happen there's not much to keep a sailor occupied in Cologne once they've finished with the whores. There's gambling."

There was the briefest of smiles passing between the inquisitors.

"That was my money to buy a new house for my wife and me, to start raising children." There was a pause; Wolfe looked at the men in turn. "On my mother's grave, I did not do this thing."

Lord Shrewsbury looked at Wolfe with piercing eyes, searching out any sign of falsehood.

"You know they have means here to make you confess?"

"Aye, I knows that, but it changes naught; happen I cannot confess to something I have not done."

Lord Shrewsbury looked at Fitzwilliam, then one of the warders. "Right, you can take him back to the cells."

He looked at Wolfe, "We're not done here yet."

Wolfe was released from his shackles and dragged back to the cells, still protesting his innocence. "Speak to Herr Koche … Speak to Herr Koche," he shouted repeatedly, as he was being led away.

Seeing the prisoner being taken back to his cell, Sir Edmund returned.

"So, what's to be done with him?" he asked his guests.

Lord Shrewsbury answered. "We need to make further enquiries; he will remain under your control until we have completed our deliberations."

"Very well. What about his wife?"

Shrewsbury thought for a moment. "Aye, he can have visitations."

The pair thanked their host for the hospitality and headed back to the carriage with their men-at-arms. There was much to consider.

Shrewsbury turned to Fitzwilliam. "I think I should speak to Lord Cromwell. I will ask the coachman to detour there. It's not out of the way."

The coachman was given his instructions to head north.

Alice was also making the long trek to The Tower, but without the luxury of a carriage. Her booties had hardened by the fire, but at least it provided protection from the compacted snow.

It was another tortuous journey, but she eventually arrived at the gates carrying a basket. She was recognised by the duty warden, and, with visiting rights secured, was taken to the cells, where the gaoler, William Denys, took over. He unlocked the cell. Wolfe got up hearing the lock turn.

"Alice, you have journeyed here again; I was not expecting you so soon."

She was pleased to see a lighted candle and a straw

mattress.

"Aye, John, and I've brought you some food. I did not know if they had fed you adequately."

"I have been looked-after under the circumstances."

They embraced briefly. "I have also brought you this."

Under her cloak was a woollen shawl. She passed it to him. "Happen this will see you more comfortable at night."

Wolfe took it. "Aye, it will." He could see her eyes in the flickering candlelight. "I was questioned this morning by two men about the robbery I have been accused of."

"Oh, and what, pray, was their purpose?"

"They said I had stolen some money that belongs to the King. I explained it was impossible. I hope they believed me."

"But you are innocent John."

"Aye, but they say they have a witness saying that I had done it, but it is not true. They lie to collect the bounty, methinks."

"What is going to happen to you?"

"I don't know. They said they would return, but not when."

"I have paid the Lieutenant to make sure you are looked after. If you need anything you must tell me."

"Aye, I would like some writing paper and some ink."

Alice looked at him in surprise. "Paper and ink, but you can't write."

"Aye, but I can. I learned while I was in Cologne. I must practice."

"Aye, I will see to it."

"Have you enough coin?"

"Aye, do not trouble yourself, John."

They continued chatting for over an hour until the goaler opened the door and ordered Alice to leave.

They said farewell. The gaoler locked the cell, and led her up the stairs towards the exit.

"Would you care for some refreshment before you leave? I have some mulled wine which will warm your journey."

Alice looked at him, and realised the power he had. He could make Wolfe's life miserable.

"Aye, sir, happen I would welcome that."

The goaler's quarters were basic, the walls just the bare heavy stone of the building, but there was a hearth with a fire blazing. There was a straw mattress bed, two chairs. There were two candles providing limited illumination. It was comfortable enough for someone spending most of their time in residence.

Denys ushered her into the room and closed the door. "We won't be disturbed, Mistress Alice. It is all right to call you Alice … ?" He didn't wait for an answer. "Take a seat if you will. I will soon have something to warm you."

Alice complied, while the gaoler attended a small pot hanging over the flames. A few minutes later, seeing the contents were sufficiently warm, he removed the pot and poured measures into two wooden beakers. He passed one to Alice,

"The monks from the nearby monastery provide the mulled wine for the Tower," he commented.

Alice took a sip, but made no comment.

"You have a distance to travel, Mistress Alice?"

"Aye, sir, the other side of Bishopsgate, an hour or more."

"I wish I could find someone with your dedication," said Denys, and looked down.

Alice could see his reflection in the flickering of the flames. He was not a pleasing sight, dressed in peasants' clothing, with a beard, his hair protruding from his helmet. His face was pock-marked and lined. He was armed with a sword.

Denys took a long sip of mulled wine and wiped his beard with the back of his hand.

"So Mistress Alice, I understand your husband will be detained here for a while longer, following his questioning today."

Alice looked at him with a look of anticipation. "You know the outcome?"

"Nay, Mistress Alice, happen they will be making further enquiries, but at least they didn't order any torture."

Alice gasped. "Torture? Nay, my husband is innocent of any crime; he is s a God-fearing man."

"I hope you're right, Mistress Alice, but while he's here I can make his life more comfortable … or not."

"Aye, I know. What would you have me do to see he is well cared for? I have coin."

"It's not coin I need, Mistress Alice. Happen, you can provide comfort no coin can buy. You're a fine looking woman."

He was expecting some protest, but instead, Alice stood up from her seat and started raising her skirts.

Having secured assurances of Wolfe's favourable treatment from the gaoler, Alice left the Tower and made the long and treacherous trek back to the dwelling. It was starting to get dark by the time she reached the marketplace just a few minutes away from her dwelling. There was a shop she needed to visit.

Opposite the church, there was an apothecary. It sold all measure of potions; it also sold ink and pens.

She entered the shop which was now decked in candles. There was a smell, not unpleasant compared with the street smells, but certainly different.

There was a man bent low, the other side of a counter, behind him were rows of glass bottles containing numerous potions and cures. He looked old and frail. Alice had visited here before but was not a regular customer.

She looked at him in the low light; his hair was white and in thin whisps.

"Sir, I am wanting to purchase some paper and ink."

He looked at her with some surprise; such requests would normally come from his wealthy customers who would call in their carriages.

"What sort of ink will you be wanting?"

"I don't know, sir, what would you recommend?"

"Well, the best is this one." He produced a small bottle from the shelf containing black liquid. "It's made from oak galls, copper sulphate, wine, and gum Arabic. It is dear, but it is indelible; it won't run or fade. Just don't get it on your hands."

The description of the contents was lost on Alice. He handed her the bottle. "If that's what you recommend, I will take it, and I need a quill."

The apothecary produced two quills from a supply. "I can let you have two, considering you have bought the ink."

"That is most generous, sir."

"You mentioned paper."

"Aye, sir, what is your thoughts?"

"What is it for?... Important documents?"

"Ha, nay sir. Just to keep my husband amused."

The proprietor turned, opened a drawer and produced a few sheets.

"Will this be sufficient?"

"Aye, sir, it will."

Alice paid and left the shop carrying her purchases.

Light was fading quickly now, with the resultant drop in temperature. The snow was starting to harden as the frost descended. There were very few people about now.

Earlier, William Fitzwilliam and Lord Shrewsbury had made their detour and were in the residence of Thomas Cromwell, seated in a corridor awaiting an audience.

Eventually, Cromwell came out of his chambers and approached his guests.

The pair rose to their feet; Lord Shrewsbury spoke. "I am grateful, my Lord, for your time; my apologies for calling unannounced, I mean no discourtesy,"

"It's no matter, come through, gentlemen; the room is warm this cold day," replied Cromwell.

He turned quickly; here was a man of purpose. The pair followed Cromwell to his office and were invited to the two seats in front of his desk. Cromwell took up his usual position and started writing, then put down his quill and looked at the pair.

"Is this about the so-called theft, Lord Shrewsbury?"

"Aye, my Lord, we have just come from The Tower having interrogated the culprit."

"Alleged culprit," Cromwell interjected; his eyes narrowed. "Well, what were your impressions?"

"He gave a good account of himself," replied Fitzwilliam. He looked at Shrewsbury. "To be frank, my Lord, I cannot see how he could be the culprit. It appears it would have been impossible to steal the coin while onboard; it was guarded the whole journey. Even Master Giese admitted that. He claims he was accompanied on his visits to the alehouse, and has given the names of his two companions who will vouch for his behaviour. We can interview them at the Steelyard."

Cromwell appeared dismissive in expression.

Fitzwilliam looked at Shrewsbury and continued. "There is further alibi he has offered... He claims he was the guest of a Herr Koche, a brewer, whilst in Cologne, who, he says, has offered Wolfe employment."

"Hmm, the League are taking us as fools. I had my doubts from the start; this Wolfe fellow is a culprit of convenience to my mind. We have no proof that there ever was any coin; or, if there was, it was taken before it was shipped."

"What do you advise, Lord Cromwell?" asked Shrewsbury.

"Well, it certainly can't go to trial; we would be laughed out of court … His Majesty knows nothing about this, and I would prefer it if it stays that way; he has enough on his mind at the moment." He paused and stroked his chin, turning his attention to Fitzwilliam. "Truth be told, Master Treasurer, this is no longer of import. His Majesty is turning his attention to the monasteries and his financial position will greatly improve in due time."

"What do you want us to do?"

"Release the man," said Cromwell firmly.

"If I may make a suggestion, my Lord," said Shrewsbury. "We have discussed this in the carriage, and we would like someone to go to Cologne and speak with this brewer. If he confirms Wolfe's version of events, then we will release him."

"That is up to you, but methinks you're wasting time. What will you do with this man in the meantime?"

"He can stay in The Tower," replied Shrewsbury.

"Very well, I'll leave it in your hands. I have more important matters to attend. Now, if you will excuse me."

Cromwell stood up, indicating the audience was over. Fitzwilliam and Lord Shrewsbury both bowed and made their exits.

Back in the carriage, the pair continued their discussion as they travelled back to Westminster Hall. The compacted snow continued to make the journey hazardous.

"I fear Lord Cromwell is right," said Lord Shrewsbury. "The League has tricked us."

"Aye, and I took Master Giese to be a man of integrity."

"It seems not, Master Fitzwilliam."

"I would still like to go to Cologne and make contact with this brewer."

"Nay, I need you here; you can send a trusted emissary if you're still insisting on pursuing this cause. Do you have someone in mind?"

Fitzwilliam thought for a moment. "Aye, I will instruct my deputy; it will be a good experience for him."

"You will need to brief him thoroughly."

"Aye, my Lord."

The following day, Matthew Arnold was summoned to Fitzwilliam's office and given instructions. There would be some delay, however, in making the journey; the next cog would not sail until later the following month when weather conditions would be more amenable.

March 1st 1532.

The worst of the winter storms were over, and the trade traffic to Cologne had resumed. Arriving at the port, Matthew Arnold, deputy to the Lord Treasurer and his emissary, stood waiting to disembark. The gangplank was attached to the cog, and he walked off the boat. It had been a lengthy journey with winds not favourable. Today, though, was a bright, early spring day. The none bells sounded from a nearby monastery.

Given his status, Arnold was given leave to share the

captain's cabin as Georg Giese had done. Captain Harvey, who was again in charge of the vessel, was also able to provide Arnold with recommendations for accommodation. His mission would not be lengthy; he would return on the next sailing to London. He had disclosed nothing of the purpose of his visit, and the captain was unaware of his connection with the missing coin.

Arnold was dressed in the style of a merchant, complete with appropriate headgear, for the mission, and started walking along the dock area following the directions indicated by the captain. After a mile or so, he found the lodgings; nothing grand, but would be comfortable for his short visit.

With only German being spoken, Arnold had difficulty in making himself understood, but on mentioning the name Koche to the owner of the boarding house, his eyes lit up. "Ja, ja," he said animatedly.

With twilight fast approaching, it was not the time to take his enquiries further. Tomorrow he would order a carriage to take him to the brewer's mansion.

After a restful night and a hearty breakfast, Arnold waited outside for the carriage which would take him to his destination. The sky was cloudy but without the threat of rain.

He had been waiting for a few minutes, when a horse and trap approached. It was not what he was expecting, but it would serve his purpose. Arnold explained his destination to the coachman who nodded vigorously.

It took over forty minutes to reach Matthias Koche's mansion. The carriage pulled up outside the front door, and Arnold instructed the driver to wait; again, more nodding.

Arnold looked up at the magnificent building before

rapping on the door. There was no reply, he rapped louder.

A butler in full livery opened the door and spoke in German. Arnold replied in English.

"Herr Koche, bitte, I want to discuss John Wolfe."

The name seemed to register and the butler invited Arnold into the entrance hall, and was told to wait, with appropriate hand gestures.

A few more minutes passed before the distinguished brewer approached.

Arnold took off his hat and bowed reverentially.

"Herr Koche, I am sorry to impose on you, but I have a matter of some import I need to discuss concerning John Wolfe."

Koche spoke some English and understood.

"Very well … please you come."

Arnold followed the brewer into another room. He was having difficulty in taking in the grandeur.

Herr Koche indicated for Arnold to sit on an adjacent chair.

Arnold announced the purpose of his visit. He talked slowly. "My apologies for calling unannounced, Herr Koche, but I represent His Majesty's Treasurer, William Fitzwilliam. I have papers of introduction." He produced a parchment from his tunic and handed it to the brewer. "I come from England and it concerns a seaman called John Wolfe."

Koche's expression suggested he hadn't understood, but, on hearing the name, a girl of about seventeen appeared, her face etched with excitement.

"John Wolfe? You have news of John Wolfe." Her eyes were wide.

"You speak English?" asked Arnold.

"Aye, I was taught it at school, sir … You have news of John?" she repeated.

Herr Koche spoke slowly, considering every word. "Er … this is my daughter, Inga, her English, er, is far better than mine; she can speak for me."

He looked at the brewer.

"I am grateful for your time, sir."

Before he could continue Inga interrupted. "How is he? How is he? I have been waiting for his return."

"He is in prison, Frauline Koche, He has been accused of stealing a large sum of money which belonged to His Majesty, the King."

Inga put her hand up to her mouth in horror. "Nay, nay, he is a good man; he saved my father's life."

Inga translated for her father. He replied in German, Inga translated.

"My father says, he is not a thief, but he can no longer speak for his … er … trust." She looked down at her belly. "Whilst he stayed here, er, he took advantage of me … I am with child." She started to cry, but was comforted by her father. "I hoped he would return and we could wed."

Arnold considered this news. "How long did he stay on his last visit?"

"About three days, er, or four, I tought him to read and write; he learned very quickly," replied Inga.

"During his time here, did you notice if he was carrying a large sum of money?"

"Nay, nay," said Inga. "He was here the whole time; he had very little, er, what is the word? Er, possessions, just a … er … a bag … small." She indicated with more hand signals.

Arnold considered the account; it seemed to confirm the information he had been given. He needed to return to England and report to Fitzwilliam.

Chapter Thirteen

While matters were unfolding elsewhere, Alice continued her regular visits to the dungeons; she was becoming well-known among the warders, and was able to walk freely around The Tower. Wolfe was comfortable, or as comfortable as was possible being locked up in a cell. He had had no contact with anyone in authority, including the Lieutenant of The Tower, since his interrogation and, despite enquiries, learned nothing of his possible fate.

Alice was continuing her liaison with William Denys, albeit reluctantly, ensuring preferential treatment for Wolfe.

It had been six weeks since Wolfe's incarceration. In that time, she had moved from the dwelling that she had shared with Wolfe to be closer to The Tower, and had taken up a small lodging house just off Thames Street, less than ten minutes' walk away. She had told Wolfe of her new circumstances. It also meant she was free of the clutches of George Thornton, the landlord, who insisted on the rent being paid 'in kind'.

Alice was making one of her regular visits. She was greeted warmly by the Yeoman guard, who made a point of enquiring about her welfare. Word had also got out about her 'arrangement' with the gaoler.

As she arrived at the dungeon, carrying her usual bag, a new face appeared, younger than the previous warder, and more pleasing on the eye. The corridor containing the cells was dark, but in the flickering torchlight, Alice could make out his features, a strong jawline and sparkling eyes.

"Oh, you fare gave me a start," said Alice, as he approached her. "Where's Master William?"

"Happen, he's been moved duties … You are John

Wolfe's wife?"

"Aye … Alice."

"Well, Mistress Alice, my name is Bawd … John Bawd, and you won't be seeing the gaoler again; I have been assigned to guard your husband. It seems one or two warders were saying Master Denys was getting favours; bragging about it in the tavern, he was."

"Favours? ... From me? ... Nay, not so, Master? Been on the tickle brain methinks."

The gaoler would not have detected her expression of guilt in the shadowy light. He led Alice along the corridor to Wolfe's cell and opened it. "I'll see you are not disturbed."

His voice was deep and confident, not with the harsh menace of his predecessor. He was probably aged mid-twenties, but no more. Alice wondered about the new arrival and whether it would have any impact on Wolfe's treatment. She joined her husband.

"You have a new gaoler, John, I see," she said, turning and watching the door close behind her.

"Aye, this morning."

There was a fond greeting and Alice presented Wolfe with some food and a small flagon of wine.

"Happen he may want coin," said Wolfe.

"Aye, I have coin," replied Alice.

True to his word, the couple were left undisturbed and Alice was able to provide Wolfe with her full range of her favours. After an hour, there was the sound of a key in the lock and the door opened.

"You need to leave, Mistress Alice."

The couple embraced and said their farewells; the new gaoler led Alice back to the exit. As they reached the gaoler's quarters, Alice turned to the man.

"You will see my husband is well-treated, Master Bawd?"

"Aye, I can."

"Master Denys would offer me sustenance for my journey. Would you do the same?"

He looked at Alice; they were still on the stone steps. "Aye, do you knows where to go?"

"Aye, Master Bawd."

Alice waited for the gaoler to pass, and he led her to his quarters. Bawd opened the door to the room. Early spring, and it was warm enough not to need a fire; the grate was empty.

Alice sat on her usual chair and took off her cloak. She had dressed quite provocatively, assuming that the former gaoler would be on duty. She needed to please him.

"I have some wine, Mistress Alice," said Bawd, hardly able to take his eyes off the expanse of bosom.

"Wine would serve very well, Master Bawd."

"It's John, you can call me John."

"I can see me and you are going to fare well together, John," replied Alice.

He passed her a small wooden tankard. Alice took a sip.

"Are you wed, Master Bawd?"

"I were, but happen my wife was consumed by the plague and the Lord took her."

"Oh, it grieves me to hear of such tragedy, and you miss a woman's touch, methinks."

"Aye, verily tis so."

"Then perchance we can make that right." Alice leaned forward.

"Aye, Mistress Alice." His eyes were consumed by the delights in front of him.

"And you'll see that my husband is catered for favourably?"

"Aye, that I can."

"Then I think we have an arrangement that suits both our purpose." She dropped her dress from her shoulders.

The Vesper bells sounded around the city as she left the Tower, but there was still a good hour until sunset.

Alice made the short journey to her lodgings. It was just one room, with a straw mattress bed, a table and chair, dressing table, and the bucket. Quite different to what she had become accustomed, but it would serve her purpose until Wolfe was released.

Alice considered her most recent liaison, and was pleased with the new arrangement, which would ensure the continued comfort of her husband. She felt more inclined towards John Bawd. Different altogether from William Denys; Bawd was kind and considerate, easy prey for Alice Tankerville.

It was the end of March before the first cog from Cologne since December, docked at the Steelyard. On board, the emissary for the Lord Treasurer was pleased to be back, and relieved that the journey had passed without incident. He retrieved his luggage from the captain's quarters, dressed in his merchant's clothing, made his way on deck, and bade farewell to his host.

"I am grateful for the safe passage, Captain," he said, and doffed his hat.

"Thank the Lord, Master Arnold," said the captain and responded similarly.

Arnold nodded in acknowledgement and walked down the gangplank.

London was taking on the advent of Spring with renewed optimism, and bustled with activity. The Thames was alive with small rowing-boat ferries, flitting across the water delivering passengers to the various docking points along the river.

Arnold made his way to the Kantor's stables and hired a horse to speed his journey to Westminster Hall.

He reached his destination in under an hour, and sought out William Fitzwilliam. The Lord Treasurer was in his chambers and warmly welcomed the new arrival.

"Master Arnold, it is good to have you returned safely, May the Lord be praised."

"Amen, my Lord." Arnold bowed and removed his hat.

There was no more formality. "You have news from Cologne?"

"Aye, my Lord."

"Please, be seated. I will find some wine, and you can tell me all."

Having made himself comfortable, Arnold related his visit with the brewer. Fitzwilliam listened intently.

"It appears Wolfe is well-considered by the brewer. Happen, he saved his life from a robber, and, out of gratitude, Herr Koche has provided him with accommodation during his stay in Cologne."

"Hmm, so Wolfe's account would appear a truth."

"Aye, my Lord, although the brewer is less inclined towards him of late."

"Oh, and in what regard?"

"It appears Wolfe took advantage of his daughter during his stay, and she is with child."

"Ha, ha, the dog; it seems my impression of him was well met."

"Aye, my Lord, but I would say that he is no thief; that is the view of Herr Koche. According to him, it would not have been possible for Wolfe to have carried out the robbery and secreted the coin whilst in Cologne."

Arnold paused while Fitzwilliam absorbed the information. “Aye, and Captain Harvey is adamant the chest was not disturbed whilst on board,” said Fitzwilliam, more to himself. “It seems that Lord Cromwell was right.”

“Sir?” asked Arnold, not understanding the statement..

“Oh, nothing,” replied the Treasurer. “That will be all. I need speak to Lord Shrewsbury directly,” replied Fitzwilliam.

A little later, Fitzwilliam was in discussions with the Lord Steward apprising him of the latest news.

“Hmm, I think we have wasted enough time on this fruitless venture. I am with Lord Cromwell’s opinion that we have been played as fools. Either there was no coin, or it was stolen in Cologne before the chest was sealed. I favour the first … Did you speak to the two seamen at the Steelyard he mentioned?”

“Not personally, but one of my clerks did, and they confirmed Wolfe’s account,” replied Fitzwilliam.

Shrewsbury frowned. “Hmm, in which case, I will speak with Lord Cromwell and recommend the release of the prisoner. Unfortunately, I understand his Lordship has joined His Majesty at Hampton Court and I have no insight into his return.”

“I’m sure Master Wolfe will be content for a while longer; I understand he has been well catered for,” said Fitzwilliam. He paused for a moment. “What about The League?”

“What about the League? They have proved themselves to be racked with falsehoods, which will be forever etched on my mind. Perchance, we will have our day.” Lord Shrewsbury smiled.

It was early May before Lord Shrewsbury received news

of Cromwell's return, and arranged an audience.

He travelled alone for the meeting and was greeted courteously by the Chief Minister.

"How is His Majesty, My Lord Cromwell?" asked Lord Shrewsbury, as he accepted the chair.

"He fares well, my Lord Steward, presently occupied with tennis courts. At least it keeps his mind away from other issues of State." There was a hint of a smile on his jowly facade. "Down to business, what brings you to my offices?"

"The prisoner, John Wolfe, my Lord."

"John Wolfe? Why are you concerning me with this man; I though he was to be released, or have you found further evidence?"

Lord Shrewsbury looked down as if he had been reprimanded as a naughty schoolboy.

"Nay, my Lord; his account has been verified."

"Then release the man. See to it." Cromwell stood up indicating the matter was closed.

"I hope that's the last time I hear this man's name," said Cromwell, as he escorted Lord Shrewsbury from his chambers.

Meanwhile, the relationship between Alice and the new gaoler was developing in a way that she wasn't expecting. She had met many men during her time with John Wolfe, but John Bawd was different. So much so, she was beginning to have real feelings for him. In fact, she looked forward to her encounters with the gaoler more so than with her husband. More recently, she had not even bothered to visit Wolfe but had spent the whole time in Bawd's quarters. Her proximity to The Tower meant she was able to attend more frequently.

It was the end of June 1532 when Sir Edmund Walsingham received a messenger from Westminster Hall. He handed the Lieutenant a sealed letter, signed by Lord Shrewsbury, requesting the release of the prisoner, John Wolfe, from custody as a free man.

He ordered one of the warders to advise the gaoler of the decision.

John Bawd was given the message and trudged down the well-trodden steps to the dungeon. He unlocked the cell door.

"Master Wolfe, you are free to go." He held the door while Wolfe collected his meagre belongings, trying to take in this unexpected course of events.

"Follow me," said Bawd, as they climbed the stone steps.

They reached the outer door.

Wolfe turned to the gaoler. "Master Bawd, you have treated me well. I can have no complaints."

"I wish you good fortune, Master Wolfe."

The sunlight made Wolfe blink as he reached the outer door; he suddenly had a thought. He turned to Bawd.

"Master Bawd, I need my money belt that was taken from me; do you know of it?"

"Nay, Master Wolfe, let me enquire."

Wolfe was stood at the entrance and breathed deeply in the fresh air.

It was over ten minutes before the gaoler returned. "Sir Edmund says you must go to Westminster Hall, happens, it will be in the custody of the Lord Treasurer."

Wolfe was deep in thought, angry at the imposition.

"Aye, very well; I will go there directly." He was about to walk away but stopped. "Before I take my leave, Master Bawd, I need to beg your favour … My wife, I believe, has a fancy for you, and speaks fondly of your company. Given the turn of events, I have made up my mind to leave England for a while; it is not a safe place. Can I trust you to see to Alice and keep her safe for me, until I return?"

"Aye, Master Wolfe, if it is your wish; I will be pleased to offer such service."

"Aye, it is. I know will treat her well."

Alice had no knowledge of Wolfe's release, and made the regular short walk to The Tower. She was welcomed as usual by the duty warder.

"Mistress Wolfe … Verily, I am surprised to see you here this morn."

"Why say such, sir?" asked Alice.

"It seems your husband has been released."

"Released … ?" Alice tried to take in this information.

"Aye, not two hours since."

"But where did he go?"

"I cannot say, mistress; I have no ken."

Alice was deep in thought, considering the news. "I must speak with Master Bawd; he may know something. Can I see him?"

"Aye, allow me to accompany you."

"I know my way, sir."

The guard stood aside, his pikestaff in his left hand.

Alice made her way to the gaoler's quarters, and knocked on the door. Bawd opened it.

"Alice … ! I wasn't expecting to see you."

"Aye, I have just heard the news; it seems my husband has been released."

"Aye, tis so."

"Where did he go, do you know?"

"Nay, Alice, but he did say he would leave England."

"Leave? And go where?"

"He did not say. But there is something else."

Alice was not concentrating.

"He has asked me to look after you."

She refocused. "Er … Look after me?"

"Aye, Alice, he wants me to see you safe."

Alice looked surprised, and was trying to make sense of everything. "I must search for him; he does not know where I live."

"But you have told him that you have left the dwelling."

"Aye, but he has no knowledge of the whereabouts of my new lodgings."

The gaoler looked at Alice. "I know you must, but I've been giving it much thought. You can stay with me … I have room and I can look after you."

"Truth be, John, I can't think on't at this time. Let me find my husband and seek his mind. I will return again."

Bawd looked down in disappointment. "Aye, I'll wait for you."

Alice left The Tower in deep thought, considering possible places Wolfe would go. There was one destination that came to mind. Just outside the Steelyard there was an alehouse frequented by many of the crewman that worked there. It was a typical sailors' tavern, not one that would be patronised by the merchants. It would also be frequented by harlots; there was a healthy demand for their services. Alice couldn't remember the name but had an idea of its whereabouts.

She walked the length of Thames Street over a mile or so until she reached the walls of the Steelyard. She thought about asking the duty guard, but felt uneasy with any encounter in case it would jeopardise Wolfe in some way.

She spent over half an hour walking the streets

surrounding the Kantor, then came across an alleyway, and, just inside, she could hear the rumble of conversation. There was a wooden sign suspended from what looked like the top of a gallows protruding from the wall. A picture of a white anchor was painted on it – an alehouse.

The heavy entrance door was wedged open, and Alice walked in. There were three stone steps down which would prove a hazard for anyone not looking where they were going. Alice descended, sure-footed, into the tavern.

It was dark and dingy inside, and, with no natural light, heavy candles provided the only illumination. In mid-summer, the temperature created a foul smell of sweat, which overpowered the aroma of the ale being consumed. There were benches with high tables around the room and very little spare spaces, as men from the nearby docks were lubricating their throats either before a voyage, or to celebrate the successful conclusion of one. There were squeals and piercing voices from a group of women in one corner.

Alice squinted in the gloom to see if she could see Wolfe, but it was difficult to make out faces clearly. Just inside the door, the landlord was serving tankards of ale to thirsty seamen from three hogsheads. Alice was walking down the rows of benches creating many unwanted comments. One grabbed her and sat her on his lap to huge approval. Alice slapped his face hard.

"Unhand me, you dalcop, and pox on your tail," Alice exclaimed, as she stood up and tried to maintain her composure.

Then, a man approached her. He remonstrated with the miscreant and pulled Alice aside.

"You're Alice, methinks."

"Aye, how do you know?"

"I am Thomas Drake, a friend of John Wolfe."

"Aye, John has oft mentioned you; I am seeking him. They have released him from The Tower this morn."

"I thank the Lord for his deliverance."

"Have you an idea where he could be?"

"Nay, Mistress Alice, but, happen, he would call here. It is where we favoured before a voyage."

"Can you give a message to him."

"Aye, that I can; if I see him."

"Tell him the whereabouts of my dwelling." Alice gave Thomas the address, which he repeated to ensure understanding. "It's next to a candlemaker," she added.

"Would you like to take some wine, Mistress Alice?" asked the seaman.

"Nay, I will continue my search."

Alice had walked back and forth along the adjoining streets, but to no avail. The none bells sounded – mid-afternoon, and she was hot, thirsty, and very weary from her efforts to find Wolfe; she decided to return to her lodgings. Her garments were sticking to her.

Light was failing as she woke up from taking a nap. Something had disturbed her, a knock on the door. She got off the bed and went to open it.

"John!" she exclaimed seeing Wolfe stood in the doorway.

"Aye, Alice, Thomas said you have been seeking me."

"Come in, come in." Wolfe looked around at the meagre dwelling.

"Is this the best you can find?"

Alice looked at him. "Aye, John, it suits. At least I'm not asked to pay Master Thornton in kind anymore." Wolfe tried to reconcile the comment. Alice saw his countenance and continued. "Aye, not content with coin, he wanted favours from me."

John was beginning to get angry; Alice knew the signs. "Do you want me to kill him?" he asked,

"Nay, John, time has gone for that." The pair sat down. "So what be your plans? The gaoler said you are leaving England."

"Aye, happen I must, for a while. I have asked the gaoler to see you well."

"Aye, he said as such. He's asked me to stay at his dwelling."

"Then you should, until I can return; it will see you safe."

"What about coin?"

"Hmm, I have just returned from Westminster Hall; they have taken my money belt with enough coin to last many a year, but, happen, they say the money belongs to the Crown," said Wolfe.

"I have three crowns from the coin you had at the dwelling; you can have that," replied Alice.

"Aye, I'll take two, you will need some."

"Would you stay tonight?"

"Aye, Alice, then I will leave on the morrow."

"Where wouldst you go?"

"I have a mind to go to Ireland."

"Ireland? Why there? I hear it's naught but bogs."

"I know a crewman that comes from there; he speaks of work."

"Then you must do what is right, John."

"I had considered returning to Germany, but I think my presence would not be so welcomed."

"Why sayest that?"

"Naught for you to consider; just something I was told today while I was at Westminster."

The prime bells had just rung; it was an early start, and

John Wolfe said goodbye to Alice. There was a promise of a return but no indication of when that might be. Alice felt empty as she closed the door.

It was a fine summer's day as he headed west to the Steelyard in the hope of meeting one of his acquaintances. He was carrying his leather bag containing his worldly goods.

His first port of call was the Anchor Inn; it was where his fellow crewmen would meet before starting their toil for the day. He ordered a drink and some food, then found the corner of one of the bench seats to wait. The alehouse was less than half full.

He'd been waiting for an hour when Thomas Drake entered. He spotted Wolfe and joined him at the table. There was a warm greeting.

"It is good to see you, John; happen not so many leave The Tower alive."

Wolfe took a drink from his tankard. "Aye, true enough, Thomas, but happened it was a falsehood. It is with good fortune that I was released."

"Was it as bad as they say?"

"Aye, and more, but if you have coin, then you are treated fairly; I have no complaints."

"So, what are your plans. Alice was looking for you and said you were intent on leaving London."

"Aye, time to try my skills elsewhere."

"Have you a place in mind?"

"Aye, I wanted to see Patrick about going to Ireland."

"That is interesting to hear; he's been talking about such a return. He'll be here directly."

A few minutes later, the Irishman entered and immediately saw Drake and Wolfe in conversation and went to join them.

"Patrick, my friend," said Wolfe and they embraced warmly.

"Well, it is good to see you, so it is. We thought we had seen the last," replied Patrick.

"Aye, it had crossed my thoughts."

"Are you returning to The Yard?" asked Patrick.

"Nay, Patrick. I need to leave England, and I was seeking your council on such a matter. I'm thinking of trying my hand in Ireland."

"Ireland you say?"

"Aye."

"Pray why would you countenance such a journey?"

"It is not safe for me here, Patrick, and I think I have skills that would be of use."

"Aye, that you have, John … well, that is good fortune indeed. It is a trip I have been considering for a time … Sure, I miss my family."

"Then what say we go together? I have no knowledge of such a journey."

"Aye, we will need a pair of good horses. Have you coin for such?"

"Not sufficient, methinks, but by the end of the day, per chance. When can you leave?"

"I'll need to return to my lodgings. What say? After the none bells?"

"Aye, do you knowest a horse fair?" said Patrick.

"Aye, and they'll sell us a good horse; it'll cost though. A good sumpter will be ten shillings or more."

"And you can get such coin?"

"Aye, I think I can."

Wolfe arranged to meet Patrick McGowan at The Anchor, mid-afternoon, which Wolfe believed would be enough time for him to acquire the money he needed. In the meantime, Patrick would not be signing in to work at the Steelyard. They said their farewells to Thomas and went their separate ways.

There was only one way Wolfe knew to raise sufficient money for his journey, and it was potentially dangerous. Men-at-arms patrolled regularly, and merchants and the gentry were more wary of travelling with money unguarded.

He knew where the likely opportunities were, and he walked to the location of his earlier robbery where merchants were regularly seen.

The sext bells rang; it was gone midday, and the sun was beating down overhead; Wolfe had yet to find a suitable victim. He was sweating profusely. Then, coming out of an alehouse, he spotted a man dressed in the finery of wealth. He was clearly worse for ale.

Wolfe watched as he staggered across the road; it was busy with people going about their business. A group of children started to mock him; he slurred expletives at them, and they ran off. He turned into an alleyway. Wolfe was cautious; it was not an area frequented by the gentry, certainly unaccompanied. Then realised where he was heading; it was a brothel. The alleyway led to a small courtyard, similar to many in the area. The house of ill repute was in the corner.

Wolfe moved swiftly across the road, on the heels of the man. He looked behind him; no-one in sight. With his back to the wall of the alleyway, he approached the man from behind like a stalking panther. He grabbed him by the head and pulled it back, almost breaking the man's neck. Wolfe had his knife to the man's throat.

"Your purse, or I'll slit your throat like a pig." His voice was full of menace.

The man was taken by complete surprise, but, in his drunken state, instinctively started to hit out at Wolfe. In the struggle the knife penetrated the man's neck, and blood started to spurt in all directions as the man struggled, before slowly dropping to the floor.

Wolfe, searched for his money belt. There was a purse inside the man's tunic, which Wolfe grabbed. The man was holding his neck but still the blood spurted. A small puddle was forming.

Suddenly, there was a shout. Two men were exiting the brothel, and could see the man on the floor with Wolfe hovering over him.

"Stop, thief!" shouted one, and they started running after Wolfe.

With the purse secured, Wolfe turned and headed back up the alleyway. He ran across the road, past the alehouse and into another passageway. The following men continued shouting, and, as they reached the road opposite the alehouse, more people joined in. There was pointing in all directions as one of the pursuers started directing the search.

Wolfe, meanwhile, had made some ground and headed for the Steelyard; he would be safe there. He slowed down to make his appearance less-obvious, and employed a brisk walk. No one ran unless they were being pursued. Rubbish and rotting vegetables tangled around his legs as he quickly made his getaway. He was trying to think clearly; his body reacting to the threat had caused him to hyper-vent.

He reached Cosins Lane and the west wall of the Kantor, and, keeping in the shadows, he headed north into Thames Street, then followed the wall to the main gate. The duty guard was alerted. He spoke in German.

"John Wolfe, what brings you to the Steelyard? I heard you were leaving."

"Aye, tis so." Wolfe looked anxiously along the street, but couldn't see anyone. "I just need to see the superintendent; he owes me coin for recent labours."

"He's in his quarters, methinks," said the guard. He looked at Wolfe. "You're covered in blood. Are you hurt?"

"Nay, I was set upon by vagabonds; by the grace of God I was able to escape. I need to enter and retrieve my coin."

The guard moved to one side. Wolfe pushed past him and strode down the passageway which led to the Winter Hall. He stopped for a moment to gain his breath. As the guard had observed, the front of his tunic was bright red. He needed to change before more questions were asked.

Chapter Fourteen

Wolfe walked further into the compound past the Wine House until he came to the Winter Hall. He stopped and peered around the wall of the building. Sweat trickled down his forehead and into his eyes. He wiped the moisture away with the back of his sleeve.

There were several merchants moving between the Winter Hall and the Council Chamber; it was a busy part of the Kontor. Wolfe ducked back into the cover of the passageway. Behind him, there were some of the apartments of the administrative staff on the righthand side opposite the Hall wall. He had an idea.

Early afternoon, the merchants would be working. He walked back towards the gate and reached the entrance to the residences; he went inside. He did not know which apartment would be empty; it's possible the occupants could be resting. He thought of a cover story if he was disturbed. He took the stairs to the first floor where there was a corridor with doors on either side, and walked to the first room. He tried the doorhandle. There were no locks; security, such as it was, was by way of a bolt, but from the inside.

The handle turned and he pushed it open. The room was empty. It was very basic with just a bed, table and a chair. He quickly checked around looking for clothing. There was a large chest next to the bed. He tried to open it, but it was locked. He took his bloodstained knife, and wrenched at the lock. It succumbed, and Wolfe lifted the lid.

Sure enough, there were two shirts and a tunic on top. Below that a doublet and hose. He continued to rummage further … some papers, and then a purse. He didn't have time to count its contents, but, quickly, he took off his shirt, tunic and doublet, and replaced the blood-stained clothes with fresh ones from the trunk. He pocketed the purse and dropped the lid down on the chest.

He rolled up his soiled garments and secured them in his leather bag, then walked to the door. He stopped. He could hear footsteps coming up the stairs; voices in discussion. He hid behind the door, and waited. He could hear his own breathing. Someone was stood the other side of the door discussing some transaction with another merchant. He saw the door move; they were still in conversation. Then the door fully opened.

The occupant walked into the room. At first he saw nothing amiss, but Wolfe wasn't taking any chances. He crept up behind him and slammed his fist down on the back of the merchant's skull, sending him sprawling on the floor. Before he could move, Wolfe rained punches on the man's head. The merchant groaned; then closed his eyes.

Wolfe needed to get out. Crime in the Steelyard was extremely rare, and one such as this, unheard of. The hue and cry would be relentless; the consequences of getting caught within the walls of the Kantor, severe.

He left the apartment and hurried down the stairs, carrying his leather bag. It was less than a hundred yards to the gate, but it would be manned by an armed guard; the one he had seen when he arrived.

The guard moved across the exit, blocking Wolfe's way.

"You were quick, Master Wolfe; did you find the superintendent?"

"Aye."

"And, you have changed, I see."

"Aye, happen, I must haste; I have an appointment, and I have already been delayed."

"Aye, stay safe Master Wolfe, God speed."

Wolfe was in a quandary. He had people looking for him everywhere. He needed to reach The Anchor and meet up with Patrick, but he would need to be extremely vigilant.

The victim who had been on the receiving end of Wolfe's fists, was slowly recovering. The merchant checked around; his head was still fuzzy, and saw the trunk had been opened. He checked the contents, and his worst fears were recognised. His life savings had gone, taken, presumably, by his attacker. He staggered to the door and raised the alarm.

On hearing his cries, several merchants gathered in the alleyway next to the residencies and set up a hue and cry. A group reached the gate and enquired if anyone had passed through recently. The guard was able to confirm Wolfe's departure. It was clear he was the number one suspect. They would need to look outside the Steelyard. The master-at-arms was summoned, and a mounted search party organised.

Wolfe, meanwhile, was edging his way, towards the alehouse, dodging from alleyway to alleyway. He realised there now would be two different parties searching for him; those seeking the murderer of the drunken merchant, which was witnessed. He would also be implicated in the robbery at the Kantor, with unknown consequences if he were caught. The likelihood was, he would face justice within the Kantor under Hanseatic League jurisdiction and be hanged.

His senses were on high alert, his eyes darting this way and that. Eventually, he could see the alleyway in which the alehouse was located. He stopped and observed from the opposite side of the street. The none bells started ringing, mid-afternoon. He could see a lot of activity surrounding the entrance of The Anchor. Wolfe stayed in the shadows and watched.

A group of armed men appeared to be interrogating two

or three men; it was difficult to tell from the distance. He saw one of the men-at-arms draw a sword and place it under the chin of a man in custody. There was much waving of arms, and the sword was put back in its scabbard.

The men-at-arms, appeared satisfied, and walked to the street, then separated into three groups of two. One pair went north, the other south; the third group crossed the road and was heading towards the alleyway where Wolfe was standing. He quickly backtracked until he was again in Cosins Lane; the walls of the Steelyard were in front of him. Men on horseback were approaching from Thames Street, having just left the Kantor.

He looked one way, then the other; his life was in danger, but then a thought crossed his mind. He turned and walked briskly south towards the Thames, looking over his shoulder the whole time. At the bottom of Cosins Lane, where it reached the river, there was a small dock frequented by several wherries. Wolfe reached the first available boat and ordered the ferryman to row upstream. He continued looking back from the rowing boat as it moved away from the berth, and suddenly could see soldiers on horseback approaching the dock. Wolfe quickly averted his gaze and hunkered down lower in the boat. The ferryman noticed the strange behaviour, but said nothing and kept rowing. Wolfe waited a few minutes and checked again; the men had gone.

After twenty minutes, Wolfe ordered the ferryman to the nearest dock – Broken Wharfe, about a further two hundred yards up stream. He took a groat from his money-belt and gave it to the rower, then disembarked. Crossing the landing stage onto dry land, Wolfe was still in the proximity of the alehouse, just the opposite side. He started walking north along the cobbled road away from the river which would take him in the direction of his destination.

Then he had a stroke of luck. On the other side of the street, he noticed someone come out of one of the alleyways and cross the cobbles heading towards the alehouse. Wolfe recognised him straightaway. The area was still busy with people going about their business. He quickened his stride and caught up with the man.

"Patrick!" he called in a whisper.

The man turned. "John, my friend, I was beginning to worry. I hear there's a hue and cry, something about a murder."

"Aye, Patrick. I need to make haste; we can use the river. There'll be horses we can buy around Westminster, methinks."

"Aye, that's a fact, sure it is. I have connections there."

Wolfe and Patrick headed back towards the river at Broken Wharfe; the ferryman that had recently transported Wolfe was still waiting for custom.

It had taken over forty-five minutes for the boatman to row the wherry the three miles or so to the seat of Parliament. It was hot and thirsty work, and his sweat-stained shirt was sticking to him by the time they had arrived at Westminster dock. The ferryman held the boat steady as the pair alighted. Wolfe looked around; the area was heaving with river traffic, transporting clerks, merchants, and dignitaries back and forth along the Thames. No one appeared to take any notice of the arrivals.

Wolfe paid the rower a shilling; his eyes lit up as he received the coin. They left the boat and headed into the Parliamentary complex.

Behind the main building, there was a large paddock where a blacksmith plied his trade. He maintained and serviced the horses for the employees of Westminster, including the knights of the shires and the wealthier clerks. The farrier also rented horses to those having longer journeys, and, being Irish, he knew Patrick.

Wolfe and Patrick approached the stables where, maybe twenty, horses were tethered. Patrick walked towards the farrier who was attending a large black stallion.

"What about yer, Cormac," greeted Patrick.

The smithy turned around; he was holding the horse's back leg in one hand and a straight pein hammer in the other. He was wearing a thick leather apron.

"Patrick? What brings you to the big house."

"We need two horses, good stock; we have a distance to cover."

"Aye, my friend, let me finish here."

The farrier continued shoeing the horse, then led it to the tethering post ready for collection.

"Come this way; Patrick, I'll show you what I have."

Wolfe and Patrick followed the man to the stables and he pointed out two suitable mares.

"The best ones here; they'll see you to your destination, sure enough, if you don't run them too hard. Forty mile a day, I warrant. You want saddle and harness?"

"Aye," said Patrick, and they negotiated a price.

"A guinea should cover it," stated the smithy.

Wolfe had yet to open the purse he had stolen from the merchant; it was under his tunic, but his money belt was at hand. "A guinea for the pair?" queried Wolfe.

"Aye, they'll not let you down; it's a fair price."

Anxious to leave the London environs as quickly as possible, Wolfe was in no place to haggle, and agreed the price. A groom was called who proceeded to prepare the horses for travel.

With the horses tacked and ready, Wolfe and the Irishman headed out of the Westminster complex and the open road, with a long journey ahead of them. It was a brisk pace, a steady trot, with the pair side-by-side, and able to make conversation.

"We won't make Oxford until the morrow," said Patrick. "We'll need to find somewhere to stop the night."

"Aye, you know the way, Patrick. Where are we to catch the boat?"

"Chester, there are many ferries from there. Tonight, we might make Uxbridge, if we haste, five hours I would think. We can make most in daylight."

They headed away from Westminster, along King's Street, then reached Charing Cross where the bridleway turned north.

The sun had set and dusk was turning to night as the pair reached Uxbridge. The road was well-travelled, a busy route with commercial traffic, carts pulled by horses or, occasionally, oxen, distributing goods around the country. Coaching inns were springing up in most towns along the way, catering for the passing traffic, providing sustenance for the traveller and stables for the horses. A groom would be on hand to feed and water them. Tonight would be a brief stop.

Wolfe paid for their accommodation in one of the newer inns. Once settled in his room, Wolfe retrieved his soiled clothing and the purse he had taken from the merchant in the Steelyard, from his leather bag. It had been his first opportunity. He opened the purse and, seeing the contents, his eyes lit up. With the money he had taken from the unfortunate drunken gentry man, he had enough coin to last several months including paying his expenses for the journey to Ireland.

The following morning, Wolfe was up early; there were no bells to provide a measure of time, but the arrival of daylight had awoken him. It was a warm, sunny day, the temperature was already climbing with the appearance of the sun. He left the coaching house; he needed to dispose of his old clothes and buy replacements before they started their journey northward. He stood for a moment in the doorway and looked both ways. As one of the main routes between London and the north, the highway followed an old Roman Road, some cobbles, but mainly compacted earth, worn by centuries of foot and horse traffic.

People were already travelling. A horse and cart, with unidentifiable cargo, went past, being led by a man in peasant's clothing, his world-weary countenance suggesting a life of hardship.

To the right, in the distance, Wolfe noticed what looked like tradesmen setting up their wares for the day - a market of some kind. He headed in the direction of the activity and could see the temporary emporia taking shape. He walked among the stalls. Food was in plentiful supply for those that had money and he bought some bread and cooked veal for the journey which he would share with his companion. He eventually found what he was looking for – a fabric merchant and tailor. Here, he was able to buy two new shirts and a doublet. Rather than waste his bloodied clothes, he offered them to the stall holder. The vendor smiled; no questions were asked. He seemed pleased with the acquisition.

A week later, it was approaching dusk when Wolfe and Patrick entered the port city of Chester. It was the largest town on the journey and the final destination. After Uxbridge, the road had taken them through Oxford, Warwick, Lichfield,

Stoke, and Nantwich; towns where they had found shelter at various hostelries. Fortunately, there had been no rain for the entire journey, but the road had become dusty. The pair were desperate to find an alehouse and somewhere to stay.

There were no shortages of suitable inns, and, having secured a room for the night, and appropriate accommodation for the horses, they made their way to an alehouse.

It was much the same as any other alehouse, and was busy with the noise of conversation as Wolfe and Patrick entered. There was the familiar unpleasant smell of sweat and beer.

During the course of the journey the pair had become friends and, as they quenched their thirst they started a conversation.

"Patrick, have you thought on a suitable job when you get to Ireland?" asked Wolfe.

"Aye, to be sure, I'll stay with my mother for a while and see about a ploughman's job. There's always plenty about," replied the Irishman. "Are you still wanting to work for His Lordship?"

"Aye, if they'll take me on," replied Wolfe.

"Ha, you'll have no issue on that score, John, mark my words; you have skills much in demand."

Wolfe considered this remark and smiled briefly. "Aye."

The following morning there was work to do. Having made enquiries at the tavern, they had found a horse fair and sold the horses; they had served their purpose. Wolfe and Patrick would keep the money and buy new ones in Dublin.

The next task was to secure a berth to Ireland.

Chester at this time was a major port, with the River Dee navigable inland to the city. It handled the majority of sea traffic between England and Ireland with a wide range of produce leaving and arriving daily at the docks. As a result, it had become very wealthy from the revenues charged from the excise duties.

As the pair reached the port area, there was a change in the weather as some much-needed rain descended on the town, and people were making the most of the refreshing shower.

The most common ships sailing from Chester were two-masted luggers. They were ideal for navigating the Dee estuary which was too shallow for larger vessels. The ships had a crew of ten and would carry cargo as well as passengers. Wolfe and Patrick secured passage on a vessel leaving at six-thirty the following morning. With a fair wind, they would arrive in Dublin in a day.

The two men were on deck as the ship approached the quay in Dublin. Wolfe watched the unfamiliar skyline. In 1532, Dublin was a small, walled city with a population of between five and ten thousand people. It was the main port for traffic to England and, like Chester, attracted revenues from goods that passed through the town.

With dusk fast approaching, their first priority was to find somewhere to stay for the night, before resuming their journey the following day. They walked from the port into the town.

"God's teeth, Patrick, what dreadful stink is that?" exclaimed Wolfe, as they entered the narrow streets. "It seems the place smells like a turd."

"Ha, well met, John. I forgotten about the terrible smell, so I did, and don't be drinking any of the water either; it tastes the same as the stench, and will have yer stomach up in an hour, so it will."

"I'll take your words to heart, Patrick."

Dublin had no effective sewage system, and was renowned for its smell; human and animal waste littered the street.

Wolfe and Patrick secured lodgings and a tavern for the evening where the pair were able to share a tankard or two, their only means of quenching their thirst. The following morning, Wolfe was up early; he needed to acquire a change of clothing. Having been in the saddle for a week, his present attire would not make a favourable impression on his prospective employers. Patrick had directed him to a local market not ten minutes' walk away. Wolfe returned to the lodgings with his purchases, and joined Patrick for breakfast.

"Good den, John," welcomed Patrick, as Wolfe took a seat opposite. "I see you have made an early start."

"Aye, I needed to rid myself of the stink of horses. Happen, my tunic and breeches were only fit for fire kindle."

Patrick eyed his companion up and down. "Ha, yes. Methinks his lordship will look favourably. You have the look of a man of action."

Having eaten, their next port of call was a local stables where they purchased a pair of horses before setting off for Maynooth, a small settlement some twenty miles to the west. It would be the start of a new adventure for John Wolfe.

It was an uneventful journey from the port, and the pair arrived in the village by mid-afternoon. Patrick escorted Wolfe to the walls of Maynooth Castle, the ancestral home of the Fitzgerald family. Wolfe had changed into his recently-purchased apparel and looked the part of a merchant, complete with feathered hat, a far cry from his previous varlet-looking appearance.

There was a parting of the ways as Patrick left Wolfe to return to his mother's house some ten miles onward. Wolfe looked up at the imposing edifice, dismounted, and walked towards the portcullis that guarded the castle.

Maynooth Castle had dominated the community for over four centuries. It was a substantial fortress, built in Norman times, and, surrounded by the Lyreen River, made it easy to defend.

A man-at-arms approached Wolfe.

"What be your business?" he challenged.

"My name is John Wolfe, recently arrived from London. I am enquiring of work; I believe I have skills useful to his Lordship."

"My Lord is presently in London, although we do expect him to return within the month. Master Thomas is in charge in his absence."

"Aye, happen I can see Master Thomas, if you will be so pleased. I can attend to my horse while I wait."

Wolfe was led to the middle of the courtyard in front of the forebuilding, where there was a horse trough. His mount quickly made the most of the facilities; it had been a long journey. Wolfe was also thirsty, but he would have to wait.

Wolfe looked around at the magnificent fortress, high ramparts, thick stone walls; it was no surprise it had stood for all these years.

Time passed, and he was beginning to wonder if his request had been taken seriously, but then he saw the man-at-arms exit the main keep and approach him.

"Follow me," instructed the man.

Wolfe left the horse and took the stone steps to the entrance to the castle keep. There was an enormous oak door, with studs and metalwork further strengthening it. It would provide considerable protection for those inside.

Some of the features reminded Wolfe of The Tower, as he was led through the great hall, with its high open windows. It was a warm afternoon and the atmosphere was stuffy. Dust particles, highlighted by the sun, streamed through the openings. He was led to an antechamber where a young man greeted him, no more than nineteen-years-old, dressed in fine robes and sporting a developing beard. There was another man standing just behind him, armed with a sword.

He addressed Wolfe. "I am Thomas Fitzgerald, my father is Lord Kildare, presently in London, I am told you are offering your services."

"Aye, my Lord, John Wolfe, at your service." Wolfe removed his hat with an extravagant bow.

"Pray, tell me what skills you possess that would be of interest to my family."

Despite his relative youth, Thomas Fitzgerald had an aura about him that Wolfe had detected before in men of power.

"I am a man of action; I can handle a sword if threatened. I am strong-limbed and fearless. I can also make gunpowder."

"Gunpowder?"

"Aye, my Lord."

Thomas moved closer, interested in his response. "And where did you learn this skill?"

"In Cologne, my Lord."

"Cologne?" Thomas's eyes reflected surprise, but he did not pursue it further.

Thomas looked at his companion, whose relationship had not yet been established, and smiled.

"Aye, Master Wolfe, it seems we do have a need for someone of your … shall we say? Capabilities."

"I will not let you down, my Lord."

"Let me introduce you to Andrew O'Connor, my master-at-arms... Have you eaten, Master Wolfe?"

"Nay, my Lord."

"Andrew will take you to the kitchens and find you some quarters; we have spare. You arrived on horseback, I understand."

"Aye, my Lord."

"We have stables here which are at your disposal, and you can dine with me tonight. I will be interested to get to know you better. Return at nightfall and we can talk further."

"My Lord." Wolfe again made a show of respect. The master-at-arms joined Wolfe and led him out of Thomas's quarters.

Wolfe was given a guided tour of the castle and allocated a room in the domestic quarters. It was similar to others he had stayed in, better than some, worse than others. There was no window, just a stone wall, which made it feel more like a prison, but at least it would be warm. The man-at-arms had provided Wolfe with a candle.

He made himself comfortable on the straw bed. It was raised on legs which would keep it free from vermin. He was soon asleep, wearied by his journey.

Wolfe woke with a start. He had no idea how long he had been asleep; he had lost the concept of time. The candle had burnt out and the room was pitch dark. Remembering his dinner invitation from Thomas Fitzgerald, he slowly raised himself from the bed and found his way to the door by touch. Fortunately, the corridor outside was lit by torches. Wolfe left his room and retraced his steps to the main hall. As he walked down a long corridor, he could see through the open windows it was dusk. The glow from the dying embers of the day was just visible to the west. The sun had disappeared below the ramparts, but it was still a warm summer evening.

He reached the room where he had met the lord presumptive earlier, and knocked on the door. A servant, dressed in the style of a common serf, answered.

"Master Wolfe, I presume, come in; Master Thomas is expecting you."

They entered. Wolfe looked around the impressive room, decked with tapestries and works of art. A table had been placed in the centre of the room with two chairs, one either side. The chamber was illuminated by a number of large standing candelabra containing seven individual candles, providing a comfortable light.

Thomas had dressed formally in extravagant clothing, complete with an ermine stole. Wolfe was still in his merchant's clothing but had dispensed with the hat. Fitzgerald got up from his chair and welcomed his guest.

"Master Wolfe, please be seated. Some wine, perhaps."

"Aye, sir."

The host clicked his fingers, and the servant disappeared into an adjoining room, returning a few minutes later with a flagon.

The serf filled the two goblets on the table. Thomas raised his. "Here's to a fruitful union."

"Amen," replied Wolfe, and the pair touched vessels.

The serf returned with plates of beef, vegetables, and bread, and served the diners.

"So, Master Wolfe, what do you know about my family?"

"Naught my Lord, although I had heard of conflict. I travelled here with a companion who was employed here, heretofore."

"Oh, pray, what was his name?"

"Patrick, sir, Patrick McGowan."

"McGowen? Hmm, I don't recall the name."

"He told me he worked here. But it seems there was a disagreement or such, and he left to go to London. I have just returned with him."

"So, what did you learn from Master McGowen?"

"That you might be seeking someone with my skills."

Thomas took a drink, then looked at Wolfe.

"Aye, tis true, we have many enemies who would destroy us. What do you know about Piers Butler?"

"Naught, sir."

Thomas gave Wolfe an outline of his family's recent history.

The longstanding feud between the Butler family and the Fitzgeralds was marked by numerous conflicts. In 1485, Piers Butler entered into a strategic marriage with Lady Margaret FitzGerald, daughter of Gerald Maurice FitzGerald, 8th Earl of Kildare, in an effort to mend the rift between the two families.

Butler, a man of ambition, and his wife Margaret faced significant financial hardship in the early years of their marriage, largely due to the actions of James Dubh Butler, agent of the absentee 7th Earl, who resided in England. James Butler, Piers' nephew and heir to the Ormond earldom, was later ambushed and killed by Piers in 1497. Piers Butler was pardoned for this crime on 22 February 1498 and ascended to the title of 8th Earl of Ormond in 1515 following the death of the 7th Earl.

In an intriguing twist, one of the heirs to the Ormond inheritance was Thomas Boleyn, whose mother was Margaret Butler, the second daughter of the 7th Earl. Thomas Boleyn, father of Anne Boleyn, whose influence was growing at the court of King Henry V111, was granted the titles of Ormond and Wiltshire by the King. To facilitate this, Henry persuaded Piers Butler and his coheirs to relinquish their claims to the title on 17 February 1528. With the assistance of Cardinal Thomas Wolsey, Butler was subsequently created Earl of Ossory.

The tensions between these powerful families persisted. Both Kildare and Butler held the position of Lord Deputy of Ireland, the highest office in the province. However, accusations of malpractice against each other brought the feud to the attention of the King. In an attempt to resolve the conflict, Henry declared an entente, imposing a thousand mark penalty on the family that violated the agreement.

In 1524, Kildare was reappointed as Lord Deputy, succeeding Butler, but the hostilities continued. In 1526, Kildare was summoned to London and briefly imprisoned in the Tower of London by Thomas Wolsey, who had secured an order for Kildare's execution. This order was eventually revoked following Wolsey's death in 1530. Gerald Fitzgerald's safe return to his homeland and castle would be a great cause for celebration in Maynooth.

Wolfe listened with interest to Thomas's lengthy saga and quickly recognised this was a family of esteem with great power and influence. They continued talking over several goblets of wine, and the younger Kildare formed a good impression of his guest.

"And so, Master Wolfe, we eagerly await my father's return; within the month, I am informed."

News had reached Thomas that his father was returning to Ireland with Sir William Skeffington, the present Lord Deputy.

Eventually, the evening concluded with the promise of further meetings.

"Tomorrow, you can teach me the art of swordsmanship," said Thomas, as he escorted Wolfe from the room.

Chapter Fifteen

Meanwhile, back in London, Alice had left her dwelling and moved in with John Bawd, as Wolfe had suggested; she knew she would be safe with the gaoler.

His house was what you would expect from a humble prison guard, a living room with an open fire, where food was cooked, and a first floor bedroom. There were no glass windows, just wooden shutters which allowed in light and flies during the day, and cool drafts at night time. Like Alice's recent accommodation, it was also close to the Tower, but north of her location. After the excitement of being with Wolfe, she found the transition difficult. She was alone for much of the day while Bawd was on duty, and spent her time spinning thread. She was happy enough to continue providing Bawd with 'favours' but, somehow, it didn't feel the same as with Wolfe; there was something missing.

Bawd, on the other hand, couldn't have been happier. He was smitten with Alice, and would do anything for her. She had, however, made it clear that the arrangement was temporary until Wolfe returned. The gaoler had even asked Alice to marry him, but she refused. As far as she was concerned, she was married to Wolfe.

Financially, there were issues too; she had become used to having her own money for garments and entertainment. After buying material, the money she made from her clothing sideline wasn't enough to cover her day to day expenses.

Whilst spinning cloth one morning in late July, she thought of an idea that she hoped would solve the issue; something she had been considering for some time. That day, she started working on her plan, creating a false arm.

She made the shape from material she had bought in the

market and filled it with straw and off-cut cloth, then covered it with the same material as the other, real, arm and sowed it onto one of her dresses. She then draped a shawl around her shoulders and applied a glove to the false hand. She would carry a basket, which would further confuse any onlooker. So from the front, she would just look like any other woman in the marketplace carrying a basket.

She had constructed a slit in the side of the dress where her real hand could do its work. No one could see the sleight that would be needed to relieve someone of their purse. She practiced while Bawd was at work, placing an apple on a table and trying to pick it up with her hidden hand.

Satisfied she could make it work; she headed to the marketplace in the lee of St Paul's Church, where she used to be a regular shopper when living with Wolfe. At certain times of the day, the locale would be bustling with people, and her presence would not be remarkable; she could wander freely around the stalls without being noticed.

After a three-quarters of an hour's walk, she reached Carter Lane; the market was in full swing. Her first task was to find a likely candidate. Her heart was pounding with excitement, the adrenaline giving her a high. Suddenly, she had motivation and her saturnine disposition left her.

She spent a long time searching for someone who's purse was in plain sight. There were no shortage of merchants and well-to-do clerks, but lifting their purse was going to be more difficult than she had realised. Then she spotted a candidate. A man of mature years, dressed in the fashion of a clerk, quite frail, with a bow gait and using a blackthorn walking stick. She noticed him doddering about the stalls and moved closer. She watched as he paid for some rabbit for the pot, and saw where he placed his purse. She could see the top of it protruding beneath his tunic.

She moved closer, her heart pounding. He stopped again, and Alice edged next to him. Slowly she pushed her hand through the hole in her dress and her fingers could feel his tunic, a very light touch. The man was oblivious as he studied a possible purchase at another stall. Alice could feel the top of the purse and pulled.

The man turned quickly and the purse fell to the floor. Alice panicked for a moment, her heart raced, then calmed herself.

"Oh, sir, verily I have caught your tunic with my basket. Please forgive my clumsiness." She looked down. "Oh, you have dropped your purse; let me get it for you."

The man was momentarily confused. Alice picked up the purse in her free hand and gave it to him.

"My … that is so kind, young lady. Lifters are everywhere; it's good to meet someone with their honesty intact." He eyed Alice up and down; his wrinkled face transformed into the semblance of a smile. "And such a pretty young thing." He placed his arm around Alice's waist, as you would a friend; then moved it lower and squeezed Alice's backside. "I bet you could make an old man very happy."

"Aye, sir, happen I could, but I would not like to have your death on my conscience."

The man roared with laughter, then started coughing violently. He recovered and opened his purse.

He took out a groat and handed it to her.

"A reward for your honesty, and a token of my gratitude, mistress." He attempted a bow, but it was no more than a brief nod.

"You are most kind, sir," replied Alice, receiving the money and hastening away.

She breathed a sigh of relief. "A groat indeed," she said under her breath. She would need more than that. Undeterred, she continued her quest. She was thirsty, brought on by the adrenaline rush, and sought out an alehouse. Alice retraced her steps away from the market; there were no shortages of alehouses in the area, and stopped at the first one she came to, The Bell.

Like most of the taverns in the vicinity, while the market was open, it was busy, Alice walked down the stone steps to where the drinks were being dispensed and consumed, The combination of sweat and alcohol created an obnoxious cocktail, but no one seemed to notice. She ordered a tankard of ale from a stout-looking man with extensive whiskers. He eyed Alice up and down before serving her from the cask.

With her right hand concealed in her garments, she was ostensibly only using one hand, and Alice had to extract her purse and fumble for the coin. It was also her weaker, left hand, but eventually she manage to pay, much to the curiosity of the landlord. She found a bench and took a long sip of her drink, then eyed up her fellow customers. She was beginning to realise this was not as easy a mission as she had thought. Having learned from her previous attempt, she would need to be more careful. She had had a lucky escape.

There was no shortage of possible victims. The clientele was predominantly male and of the clerical class judging by their clothing. Most were young which did give Alice a problem; it was unlikely she would escape in the event of discovery.

She could see the different cliques engaged in conversation, some very animated. There was a copious amount of ale being consumed and one or two were becoming rowdy, succumbing to the alcohol. She sipped her ale and watched; she was in no hurry. There were three men on their own, not in a particular group, dressed in merchants' clothing, at the far end of the room. The alehouse, as with most, had no natural light and was illuminated by candle-lit chandeliers, which created shadows. She observed them, watching their every move. There was one who looked particularly worse for wear, and she saw him leave the group and head for the serving area. It was busy with customers and a small queue had formed which he joined. This was Alice's chance. She finished her ale and walked towards her target. He seemed to be swaying from side-to-side. She could see the top of a purse protruding from the side of his tunic. She moved up very close. Within a split second her hand had grabbed it. If he had felt anything, there was no indication.

Alice quickly hastened towards the exit with as much decorum as possible, not looking behind her. She ascended the stone steps and into the blinding daylight. She had to stop for a moment to clear her head from the miasma of the alehouse, then adjust her eyes to the bright sun.

She quickly turned left and headed east towards her dwelling, It was a long walk and she felt grimy by the time she reached John Bawd's house. He would be at work and she had the house to herself.

She retrieved the purse from her under garments and opened it on the table. Coin rolled out, a couple onto the floor. She bent down and picked them up. She counted her haul. Not a fortune, the meagre earnings of a clerk, but it would last her a week or so. Boyed by this success, she would try again soon.

She prepared a bowl of water and started undressing.

Back in Ireland, John Wolfe was making himself at home in his new surroundings. He had been there two weeks and made a favourable impression with his new master. Although only nineteen, Thomas Fitzgerald wielded a great deal of power by proxy of his father who had been in England for several years. Wolfe soon had the trust of the younger Fitzgerald, and set about building a fighting force together with the master-at-arms, Andrew O'Connor.

August 12th 1532 was a significant day in Maynooth and the wider community. Word had reached the younger Fitzgerald that his father had landed in Dublin. For all his disagreements with the King, Lord Kildare was well-loved locally, and was welcomed with great acclamation. Contemporaries praised him as wise, deep, far-reaching and well-spoken and, despite his failures, was a man of considerable intelligence, learning, and diplomatic skill. In private life, he was a devoted husband and father, a generous host, a connoisseur of art, and a great bibliophile.

His Lordship was accompanied by Sir William Skeffington, the elderly Lord Deputy of Ireland, but the crowds that had gathered to greet the arrivals were waiting to see Kildare to welcome him back to his homeland.

When news arrived of Lord Kildare's landing back in Ireland, Thomas arranged to meet his father and escort him to Maynooth. The castle was being prepared for the return. John Wolfe was summoned to join the younger Kildare as protector.

It was early morning, a bright summer's day, as the pair left the castle on horseback, both were armed with swords. Despite Thomas's reservations, Wolfe had insisted on a guard, and a small contingent of six soldiers would accompany them on the fifteen mile journey to the outskirts of Dublin.

They had no knowledge of when Lord Kildare would be leaving the city, and, as they approached the walls of Dublin, Wolfe noticed a small copse of trees close by a stream. It would protect them from the sun while they waited, and give them the opportunity of watering the horses. The group dismounted and the soldiers led the horses to the stream. Although Wolfe wasn't expecting any attack, the trees would also give them cover.

For over an hour they waited in sight of the city walls, then in the distance a small group of horsemen appeared, leaving the gate. As they got closer, Thomas recognised his father and ordered the group to remount.

Lord Kildare, with the Lord Deputy riding next to him, trotted slowly towards the welcoming committee, dressed in the finery of their position; two men-at-arms followed closely behind.

The reuniting of father and son was an emotional affair as they dismounted and embraced. Having greeted his father, the pair rode together at the head of the small party, with Skeffington and Wolfe following, the soldiers bringing up the rear. As they reached Maynooth, a large gathering cheered them into the castle.

A grand banquet had been prepared for the homecoming, and Wolfe was one of the invited guests. No expense was spared.

As with most wealthy households, there were clay ovens in the kitchen used for cooking. Joints of meat, bread, and pies were being prepared. There was also an array of vegetables - onions, parsnips, turnips, beans, and leeks.

A long table, covered by a linen cloth, had been set up in the banqueting hall, catering for twenty guests. An elaborately decorated marchpane cake was the centrepiece of the feasting table.

Wolfe felt on edge as he entered the grand room, dressed in the mode of a merchant; this was something he had never experienced before. He was not carrying his sword, but his dagger was safely concealed inside his tunic. Not that he was expecting any threat; it was just something he had always done.

It gave him piece of mind.

The wood panelling was decorated by large tapestries, and shields and swords, booty from previous battles. An array of candelabra was lit, bathing the room in a dim, but adequate, light.

Some guests were already mingling – men of influence, neighbouring landowners and gentry, as well as Lord Skeffington who had remained at the castle, and would return to Dublin the following day. A minstrel was playing a lute in the corner of the room. Wolfe looked around, feeling very uncomfortable in such company. Here were people he would normally consider potential victims for his cut-purse activities.

Lord Kildare and his son entered together to a great deal of bowing and hat-doffing, and the guests were invited to take their seats on long benches either side of the table. Serving wenches distributed tankards of wine as the diners settled. Wolfe was seated next to Thomas - at his insistence; he wanted to formally introduce Wolfe to his father. With the younger Fitzgerald continuing to sponsor Wolfe's employ, Lord Kildare took a great deal of interest in Wolfe's exploits. He was soon impressed by his character and skills, which, he was assured, would continue to be put to good use.

During the ensuing weeks, Wolfe was tasked with organising a small army of around seventy soldiers which he would train and equip, financed by his Lordship. In the meantime, Lord Kildare had wasted no time in settling old scores. He had already insulted Skeffington and degraded the Archbishop of Dublin. He was also hell-bent in continuing his feud with the Butlers. Wolfe was a loyal accomplice and, at his Lordships behest, occasionally led sorties into villages on the Butler land, returning with bounty.

The area around Maynooth was picturesque and on occasions, when opportunities allowed, Wolfe would exercise his horse along the riverbank, where a bridle path led to the next village about three miles away. It was a chance to clear his head.

Late September, he was making one of his usual trips. The bridlepath was muddy from recent rain, but a gentle trot would see him safe. The river to his left was flowing fast and coloured brown from the earlier precipitation; tomorrow it would be pristine again, home to trout and salmon, eagerly sought by scavenging villagers. He turned a bend, following the river, when he saw a young woman carrying two small wooden milk churns on a yoke, walking in the same direction about twenty yards ahead. Wolfe trotted alongside her; she looked up at him.

"Good morn, Mistress. Where are you heading?" Wolfe enquired.

Lost in her own thoughts as she walked, the greeting made her jump. She was suddenly anxious.

"Moyglare, sir, I deliver milk to the castle there," she replied hesitantly.

Wolfe dismounted. "Here, let me help you. This is much too heavy for a young lass to be carrying."

"It is of no concern, sir, I am used to it. I have been making this journey since I was fourteen years of age." She spoke in English but with a heavy local accent.

The girl stopped and, after some protests, she relented, and Wolfe lifted the yoke from her shoulders and placed it across the back of the horse, securing it with the reins.

The girl watched, still unnerved. Wolfe was dressed as a soldier, with hat, leather tunic, dark breeches, and carrying a sword. To a girl on her own, an imposing figure.

Wolfe sensed her unease.

"Pray, be of no concern: I will not hurt you. Let me escort

you to your destination."

"Nay, sir, it is a journey I make daily; do not disturb your riding."

"I insist; it will give me a chance to know you better. You're a fine looking woman."

"Ha, I am no such." She looked down and started blushing.

The girl was still not totally relaxed. She walked alongside Wolfe who was guiding the horse with the bridle. The milk-yoke secured across the horse's back; fortunately, each churn had a wooden top to prevent spillage.

"What's your name?" asked Wolfe, as they strolled on towards the village of Moyglare. The bottom of the girl's skirts were wet and stained brown from the mud; she skipped the occasional puddle.

"Aine O'Kelly, my friends call me Nan."

"In which case I shall call you Nan; if you wouldst consider me a friend," replied Wolfe.

She looked at him. "Aye, as you wish."

Wolfe eyed her up and down. She had all the hallmarks of a farmer's daughter; he had seen many. A white wimple with dark ringlets, simple dress, a ruddy complexion from being out in all weathers, green eyes.

"How old are you, Nan?"

"Almost seventeen, sir." She stopped walking for a moment and looked at Wolfe. "Are you John Wolfe?"

"Aye, what gives you that mind?"

"You have a reputation, sir."

"Oh, and what might that be?"

They continued walking. "That you are a man of action; some say a soldier of fortune."

"Ha, is that the truth of it? Aye, I can see why some might say as such."

"Some say you kill people." She looked at him, watching for a reaction.

"Only those who might do me harm."

Wolfe was looking at the girl. No-one had engaged him in this way, certainly since he had arrived in Ireland. In fact, this was the first conversation he had had with a girl. With access to women at a premium - he had refused to join others at the brothels in Dublin, renown for being a certain way of contracting the pox; he had led a monastic life.

After another twenty minutes, the outline of Moyglare Castle came into view. It was nothing like on the scale of Kildare, more a large mansion house with fortified walls; it was home to the Wentworth family. Being close neighbours, the clan was generally supportive of the Kildares, but distanced themselves from the conflict with the Butler's.

Wolfe carefully removed the yoke from the horse, trying not to dislodge the tops and spill any milk, and placed it around the girl's shoulders. He stood outside the walls, still holding his mare, while she delivered her milk to the gate-keeper. Mission completed, she turned and could see Wolfe waiting for her. She hesitated before returning to him. It had started to rain.

"Come, let me see you safely to your dwelling," said Wolfe, as she approached carrying the now-empty milk-churns.

"It is not necessary, sir; I am familiar with the path, so I am."

"I am returning to Kildare; it is not out of my way."

"What about your horse, sir? Won't she need her exercise?"

"It will exercise enough."

Unable to think of any further rejections for Wolfe's company, she walked beside him, the yoke preventing any close contact. Wolfe made conversation with the reluctant farm girl.

"You have a family, Mistress Nan?"

She looked at him. "Aye, me Mam, Da, and brother, Ryan."

"And how old is your brother?"

"He'll be coming up to twenty."

"He'll be ready for a fight then. I'm looking for strong lads for his Lordship's service."

"Aye, I had heard as such. He's too busy on the farm since me Da took sick."

"Hmm, maybe I should speak with him and persuade him where his allegiances lie."

She looked at him, her face reflecting horror.

"Nay, sir, I beg you. He is just a boy; he has nothing to do with the way of the sword," she pleaded.

"We must all fight for what we believe in, Mistress Nan."

Nan felt threatened. The loss of her brother to Wolfe's band of militia would have dire consequences for her family. It would leave just her and her mother to run the farm, and her mother was having to spend most of her day attending to her husband. She was desperate; the family's livelihood was at stake. She thought quickly.

"What can I do to persuade you to leave Ryan be, sir?" There was little conviction in her voice, knowing the possible implication of her question.

Wolfe looked at her and offered a smile, not a pleasant smile, more a salacious sneer.

"Aye, Mistress Nan, I am sure we can come to some agreement; you're a pretty enough lass. Happen you can bring some brightness to this drab day."

He looked up at the leaden skies; the rain continued to tumble from the skies. Just then, they approached a small copse which bordered the river; its relentless flow gave a background sound that would be pleasing and gentle in normal times, but deaf to the milkmaid's ears.

Wolfe pointed to the small wood. "In there … there'll be shade enough; we'll not be disturbed."

Nan was in no doubt of Wolfe's intentions; she was shaking with fear. "Aye, sir," she managed to acknowledge.

Wolfe tethered the horse which immediately bowed its head and started to chew the lush grass around it. Nan removed the yoke and placed it next to the horse, then followed Wolfe into the wood. The trees were starting to shed their foliage ahead of the autumn storms, and the floor was covered in dead leaves.

The canopy provided some respite from the rain which was confined to large droplets cascading from the leaves.

Wolfe walked Nan to a large oak and pressed her against the trunk. The ground was covered in old and decaying acorns, and leaf-litter. Her booties were caked with mud.

He lifted her skirts. "Hold this," he ordered, and she held the muddied hems, exposing her nakedness.

He removed his sword and placed it on the ground, then pushed down his breeches. Nan gasped as she saw his erection and braced herself for what was going to happen. Wolfe moved towards the luckless Nan. He moved her hips towards him to enable connection, then cradled her backside. Nan turned her head as Wolfe entered her. The pain was excruciating, and she gave out a scream, which seemed to just spur Wolfe further. It was less than two minutes when Wolfe let out a groan and Nan could feel the results of his passion trickling down her thighs. She was determined not to let him see the sobs she was holding back.

Wolfe started dressing.

"And you will keep your promise?" pleaded Nan, as she

dropped her skirts.

"Aye, you have my word; you'll have no visits from me. Your brother will not be troubled."

Nan bowed her head, unable to speak; still numb from her ordeal.

Wolfe walked to the bridle path, retrieved his horse and mounted. "Happen we'll meet again, Mistress Nan," he called as he galloped away.

She wiped away tears as she left the shelter of the oak. The back of her skirts were soiled from bark moss, and she was uncomfortable. She had another mile or so before the turning for her farm, and started walking, The rain continued to pour down; her wimple was soaked and her hair hung down her face. The empty yoke was draped across her shoulders.

The O'Kelly farm was just outside the Kildare estate, and had been in the family for a hundred years. It was a small-holding with four cows, chickens, and two pigs. There were two adjacent fields which had been planted with potatoes, recently harvested and stored.

The main daily income came from milk and eggs, but the potato crop was vital for the sustainability of the farm and the well-being of the O'Kelly's.

The family dwelling was a small, thatched cottage, and a few yards away, the cowshed-cum-barn where the cows would be milked and the potatoes stored.

Nan walked up the path towards the cottage from the bridleway, still trying to shake off the memory of her encounter with John Wolfe. She continued sobbing.

She reached the barn and went inside out of the rain; chickens scurried everywhere. She took off her sopping wimple, and shook her hair. Her brother had been collecting eggs and was holding a trug almost full. He saw his sister.

They spoke in the Irish language.

"Nan, you've been long, this morn."

He looked more closely and could see she had been crying.

"Pray, what troubles you, Nan?"

Nan started crying again and in between sobs outlined the course of events.

"So you gave away your honour to save me?" he summarised.

"Aye, it was all I could think of; I couldn't let him come for you. If you were called to the service of his Lordship, surely the farm would not survive. And what would happen to us all?"

He put an arm around his sister. "I cannot let this man Wolfe get away for what he has done. By the grace of God, I will have revenge on this blaggard."

"Nay, nay, Ryan, this man is strong; he has the devil at his shoulder."

"Aye, that's as may be, but my time will come. He will pay a high price for taking my sister's honour. Come let's see to you."

They walked across to the cottage and went inside.

On his return to the castle, Wolfe was called to his Lordship's chambers.

"Ah, Wolfe, I've received message that a cargo has arrived from England and I would like you to collect it. You will need to take a guard unit with you."

"Aye, My Lord, may I enquire as to the nature of the cargo?"

"Yes, two canons and shot, arrived from France. I will need your knowledge of gunpowder and to train some of the men. I take it you can do that."

"Aye, My Lord … What about transportation?"

"I have arranged for carts and horses; they just need to be brought here."

"Aye, sir. I can round up some men and leave first thing on the morrow."

"Very good … You will need to see the dock-master; he has been suitably recompensed for his discretion."

"Aye, sir."

"Then we can set about the Butlers once and for all."

The following day, just after sunrise, Wolfe rounded up a squad of ten men-at-arms to accompany him to the port to pick up the French munitions. On arrival at the docks, he reported to the dock-master and was directed to the goods. They had been stored on three wagons away from the regular cargo. Horses were attached to the heavy carts and, after a break for refreshments, the squad started the slow return journey.

It was late afternoon by the time the party had arrived back at Maynooth with the valuable freight. Unloading the heavy guns required the efforts of twelve men, using wooden ramps to lower them from the wagons. The cannons and one hundred cast-iron balls were hauled from the courtyard to the storeroom under the watchtower. Wolfe supervised the storage of the five barrels of gunpowder, ensuring it would be kept dry.

Over the next few weeks, Wolfe spent the time organising his militiamen into a fighting force. He had trained selected men to fire the canons and had made more barrels of gunpowder from ingredients purchased in Dublin to replenish the stocks used for practice. The private army were now well-prepared and ready for the next skirmish, or to defend the castle in the event of attack. Kildare valued Wolfe's dedication and ability; he was now firmly among his Lordship's inner circle.

The feud with the Butlers continued unabated, and, on Lord Kildare's orders, Wolfe continued to lead raids on their villages. He would be regularly accompanied by Thomas, the heir apparent.

The noise of the canon fire had not gone unnoticed at the O'Kelly's farm as the retorts echoed around the countryside. Since his sister's trauma, Ryan O'Kelly had spent much of his spare time in and around the castle, trying to locate John Wolfe, and had seen the activity. Nan had provided Wolfe's description but Ryan believed he would recognise him. He had not formed any specific plan; he would bide his time watching for a suitable opportunity.

The winter months passed and Ryan O'Kelly had been busy on the farm. Nan had stopped her milk run following her ordeal and her mother had taken over, leaving Nan to look after her father.

Mid-April, Mrs O'Kelly was returning from her latest milk delivery when she spotted a man on a horse trotting towards her. She stood to one side to let the horseman pass, but straightaway knew who it was. She hastened away, back to the farm, and called her son.

"Ryan, are you there?"

Ryan appeared from the barn, "Aye, Ma, what is it?"

"I've just seen John Wolfe, not ten minutes since."

"You have? Where?"

"On the bridlepath heading for Moyglare."

"Very well, leave it to me."

"Be careful, Ryan, be careful."

Ryan went into the barn and put on a leather tunic. He looked at his weapon, hung up on one of the rafters. He was a skilled shot with the crossbow, as many rabbits would testify. He lifted it from the nail that had secured it to the wooden beam and slung it around his shoulder by its leather strap. He chose three bolts; he would not need, or have the time, to load any more.

Placing the bolts inside his tunic, he left the barn and walked up the track to the bridleway.

Chapter Sixteen

Ryan reached the main thoroughfare, just over a cart-width; it was deserted. A bright spring morning, the trees were beginning to display their luxuriance; everywhere looked green from the regular April showers. He turned right in the direction of Moyglare, and eventually came across the same copse that had been the location of Nan's ordeal.

He hid behind a large beech tree next to the bridleway and removed the crossbow from his shoulders. It was a powerful weapon and loading it required a great deal of strength. He held the tiller, the shaft that would hold the bolt, and placed it on the ground using his feet to hold the bow, He pulled the string to the firing mechanism that would hold the bolt in place. He took out one of his bolts and loaded it, then he looked up into the canopy and offered a prayer to keep him safe. Now he would wait.

Wolfe was taking a break from his duties; the weather was pleasantly clement, and he decided to exercise his horse again. He had no business to attend in Moyglare; it was merely a recreational journey, and one he had done many times before. As he trotted along the bridlepath, he would often think about the milkmaid, hoping he would meet her again. He would enjoy a repeat performance.

He followed the track along the course of the river which was now clear, with trout and salmon visible from the path. It was a scene of tranquillity, far removed from his normal routine.

He reached the castle gates, turned, and headed back to Maynooth, just a gentle trot, with the occasional canter to exercise his mount.

Around twenty minutes into his return journey, he

approached the group of trees. His thoughts suddenly turned to his encounter with the milkmaid; the longing returned.

Ryan had seen the approaching horseman, and knew straightaway it was John Wolfe. He readied himself, his breathing deep and unsteady. Shooting rabbits was one thing, but another human being was a different proposition. He focussed on his mission and the reason he was there. The defilement of his sister fuelled his anger. He peered again from his vantage point, trying to work out the distance. Although the crossbow was powerful, it became less accurate the further away from the target. He wanted a close up shot; he couldn't afford to miss.

Wolfe was admiring the view to his right as the river meandered its way to the coast.

Suddenly, his horse reared up, disturbed by movement directly in front of it. Ryan had rushed from his hiding place with Wolfe less than twenty feet away, causing the mare to rise onto its hind quarters. Ryan took aim and fired. The unexpected change in direction had thrown Wolfe off balance, and he was in the process of falling to the ground. He felt a sharp pain in his left shoulder.

He hit the floor and was momentarily dazed.

As his senses returned, he saw the end of the crossbow bolt protruding from the top of his arm, then the sight of someone rushing towards him with a knife.

He rolled over, dodging the blade, which became embedded in the ground.

Ryan was no match for Wolfe, who was quickly on his feet and retrieving his own knife from its sheath.

The farm boy had managed to extract his knife from the turf, but in the split second it had taken, Wolfe was on top of him. In one movement, Wolfe had plunged his knife into Ryan's belly below the leather tunic and proceeded to pull the blade upwards with tremendous force until it reached his ribcage.

Wolfe pushed him over. Blood was oozing from the large gash in Ryan's abdomen; his entrails protruded from his stomach onto the dirt. Blood spluttered from his mouth, then his head slumped to one side.

Wolfe examined the crossbow bolt protruding from his arm. It was a handmade wooden arrow with a metal point and feathered flight. He gritted his teeth and gave it a sharp pull; the bolt came out. He stifled a scream. He reached over to the farm boy's prostate body, and tore the sleeve off his shirt. Wolfe used it to bind his wound.

He dragged Ryan's corpse the short distance to the riverbank and pushed him into the fast-flowing waters, then bent down and washed his hands and knife in the water. He watched as the current took the farm boy's body downstream.

Wolfe's horse had settled and was on the other side of the bridlepath merrily chewing grass. He remounted and headed back to Maynooth.

On his return to the castle, Wolfe went to his quarters and cleaned his wound. He had been lucky; the bolt had entered his arm just below his shoulder at an angle and, although painful, would heal in time.

When Ryan hadn't returned to the farm after an hour, his mother and Nan started a search until nightfall, but to no avail. The following morning, the pair enlisted the help of neighbours, but, despite a lengthy hunt, there was still no trace of him.

The next day, Nan and her mother had no option but to abandon the quest; the farm required their attention. It was around nine o'clock; Nan's mother had returned to the farm after delivering the milk to Moyglare. They were in the barn collecting eggs when they heard the sound of a horse and cart outside. Nan went to investigate.

Seamus O'Riordan, one of the neighbouring famers, was stood holding the bridle of a large work-horse. It was pulling a flat-bed trailer; there was the unmistakeable shape of a body onboard, covered by a sheet.

"Master Seamus, what brings you here?" greeted Nan. Then she noticed the cart, and put her hand to her mouth.

"Oh, no!" she cried.

Her mother came out from the barn and saw the sheeted figure; she knew straightaway it would be Ryan. Nan ran to her and they hugged.

Nan composed herself; she looked at the farmer.

He took off his cap. "One of the hands found him this morning in the river; snagged on a branch, so he was, a mile or more downstream. I thought it best to bring him home, so you can give him a decent burial."

"That is very considerate, Master Seamus. Do you know how he died?"

"Aye, belly's been slit open; reckon he's been murdered."

Nan looked at her mother, her eyes still watered. "That would be that John Wolfe, I warrant. I curse him with every part of my being," said Mother O'Kelly.

"Aye, but I know not what can be done. He has Kildare's protection," said Nan.

"Aye, true enough," replied the farmer. "But I'll put word out in case there's an opportunity. Happen, the Butlers might be interested. I'll make sure they get to know."

Wolfe returned to his duties, albeit restricted due to his shoulder injury. Two days later, he was summoned to his master's quarters before breakfast.

"You wanted to see me, sir?" said Wolfe, as he entered the Earl's chambers.

His Lordship was seated on a casual seat adjacent to a roaring fire, which had taken the early-morning chill off the room. He looked up at Wolfe who had not been invited to sit down.

"Yes, Wolfe, I'll get straight to the point; there's a rumour that has been brought to my attention concerning the murder of one of the O'Kelly's. It seems you are implicated. What say you? The truth mind."

Wolfe thought for a moment. He considered lying, but decide to tell the truth.

"Aye, sir, he fired a crossbow at me; then came at me with a knife." Wolfe pulled down the top of his tunic to reveal the angry wound in his shoulder.

"It was in self-defence, sir; I would never deliberately kill a farm boy."

The Earl thought for a moment. "And why would he fire a crossbow at you?"

"I have no mind, sir; in my job you create enemies. It's possible the Butlers have put a bounty on my head."

"Hmm, yes, now that could account for it… " His Lordship paused and stroked his beard in a sagely fashion, a familiar habit. The latest attention was something the family could do without; it could even drive allegiances into the Butler camp. He looked at Wolfe in a fatherly way. "I want you to know, Wolfe, how much I have valued your contribution to the Kildare family since you arrived in Ireland; both Thomas and I have appreciated your enterprise..." He paused. "It irks me to say this, but I believe, given the circumstances, you should leave Ireland and return to England. It will only be a matter of time until they try again. I also have to consider the reputation of the family name."

"Aye, My Lord, it is a consideration. Happen you could be right." Wolfe was deep in thought weighing up the implications.

His Lordship continued. "I'll pay for your transportation and you can choose a suitable horse from the stables to take you to Dublin. You might want to take a small contingent of men with you."

"Aye, sir, if that's your wish, I can leave directly."

His Lordship stood and approached Wolfe. He threw his arms around him in a manly hug. Wolfe winced as his shoulder reacted to the gesture.

"We are indebted to you, Wolfe; I will always be grateful."

Lord Kildare was true to his word, and, within the hour, Wolfe, with his worldly possessions in his leather bag, was on his way to Dublin, accompanied by six men-at-arms.

The contingent reached the docks by late morning and Wolfe dismounted. The smell of the city attacked his nostrils. He had no intention of staying any longer than was necessary. He said farewell to his guard unit with whom he had worked for several months; they would return his horse to the castle. He watched as the troop turned and headed back to Maynooth. Wolfe suddenly felt alone.

He checked his immediate locality for possible threats, but saw none, just the normal activity of the dockworkers. He thought for a moment about his work at the Steelyard. That was not going to be an option.

His first priority was to find suitable accommodation and a berth to Chester. His Lordship had provided sufficient coin for his journey including the hire of a horse to take him to London. Wolfe broke into a quickened stride.

There were no shortages of alehouses; most of which had

rooms to let, and he settled on the first one he reached, a short walk from the dockside where a two-masted lugger was being prepared for sail to England.

The tavern was busy; he could hear the buzz of conversation from outside. He entered and took a moment to adjust to the dim lighting. He was greeted by the usual smell of a tavern which was marginally better than the smell permeating the city.

He secured a room for one night, before settling down to some food and ale.

Having quenched his thirst and satiated his appetite, Wolfe returned to the dockside and was able to purchase a passage to cross the Irish Sea the following morning.

The sailing mercifully passed without incident. It was a fine day with a brisk wind, and the two-masted lugger made the crossing within the day, arriving in Chester in the late afternoon. After disembarking, Wolfe decided to stay the night before attempting the long journey south, and found suitable accommodation.

Feeling more refreshed after a welcome rest, Wolfe was up at dawn, and his first mission was to find a horse, a sturdy mount that would get him to London. He returned to the stables which he and Patrick had used previously, just a short walk away from his accommodation. There were several from which to choose, and he agreed a good price with the stable owner. A groom prepared the horse, a black mare.

The only luggage he had was his leather bag, which contained his clothes; his money belt was securely fastened around his waist. His dagger was inside his tunic.

He would use the same route as he had taken with the Irishman, only in reverse. It was a dry, cloudy morning as he set off. He would make Nantwich before nightfall.

As the main thoroughfare heading south, this well-worn road had been in use since Roman times when it was the route of cohorts heading to Deva Victrix, the fortress that eventually became known as Chester. It was the width of more than two carts, a mix of cobbles and compacted dirt, and was always busy. The range of travellers using the route was varied - merchants, messengers, soldiers and men-at-arms on horseback, even groups of nuns could be encountered. Then there were the nobles and gentry in their carriages, even tax collectors and travelling judges, all making journeys.

Wolfe, being on horseback, towered over the pushcarts and pedestrians on the road, occasionally trotting, but mostly, keeping the horse at walking pace. He was always on alert, either for his own security, or for any easy pickings that might come his way; coin was always needed.

Two days later, after leaving Stoke, among the usual beggars and vagrants, he encountered a travelling theatre, consisting of a covered wagon - presumably containing props and scenery, followed by the players on horseback. He passed the group with a gentle canter, and acknowledged them with a touch of his hat. As he rode on, he considered that lifestyle for a moment; what opportunities might that open for expanding his fortune. It was no more than a meandering thought, the kind which kept him occupied on his solitary journey.

He met other travellers on the way; some he had accompanied for a leg of the trek for company.

On reaching Warwick, Wolfe had chosen an inn which was a popular stop for travellers. It included substantial stables to cater for teams of horses from the various coaches that also used the facilities. It had accommodation and food.

A groom greeted Wolfe as he entered the stables; he dismounted and handed the reins to the lad who proceeded to lead the mare to a stall where it would be rested for the night. Wolfe gave him a groat. He was about to leave the stables and secure his accommodation, when he spotted a man tethering his horse. He removed a leather saddlebag and carried it under his arm. He was quickly greeted by the groom, who again led the man's mount to a stall. The new arrival was of advancing years, clearly someone with the trappings of wealth, judging by his dress.

Clothing was important in Tudor England; it was a symbol of position in society. As a result, it was easy to determine whether someone was a peasant, a merchant/clerk, or a member of the gentry, or aristocracy. Wolfe eyed the man, clearly of merchant class; the gentry/aristocracy tended to journey by carriage, usually accompanied by men-at-arms. These were aspects of life that Wolfe had learned during his travels.

Wolfe walked over to the man.

"Good den, sir," he proffered, and removed his hat in customary fashion.

The merchant looked around, still clutching his saddlebag. There was an anxiousness in his expression. Casual introductions weren't the norm; they posed a possible threat. He eyed the enquirer up and down. Wolfe was also dressed in the style of a clerk/merchant.

"Good den," he replied, but didn't respond with the hat removal.

"Travelled far?" enquired Wolfe.

The merchant was still hesitant. "Aye." He didn't elaborate.

"Heading for London?"

"Nay," replied the merchant.

Wolfe gave up. He nodded to the man, turned, and walked to the entrance. The inn was a substantial, black and white, stone-built building, purposely constructed to service the coaching traffic. The property was on three different levels, due to the slope of the road. It was less than ten years old, with a tiled roof and six chimney stacks. There was a heavy wooden entrance door, which had not yet warped, Wolfe pushed it open and went inside. It was busy with people milling about in the large entrance area. To the right, a man was seated behind a large desk. Wolfe approached him and paid for a bed for the night. He was directed to the first floor.

The room was basic and typical of those he had stayed in during the journey, a straw mattress-covered bed, table, and bucket. The windows were glass, which at least kept the room relatively free from flies. It felt stuffy this warm early summer evening.

Having settled in, Wolfe headed for the eating area and ordered food and a tankard of ale. The room was large with wood-panelled walls, but nothing in the way of decor. There was a buzz of conversation from the many travellers.

Dusk was moving into night and candles had been lit. Wolfe was eating his meal of pottage, vegetables, and bread, looking around the room, when he spotted the merchant from the stables. He was sure there was coin to be had. He finished his food, and decided to try again. The man was on his own and appeared to be staring into his tankard. Wolfe left his bench and walked over to the man.

"Hail fellow," said Wolfe, as he sat down opposite.

The man looked up from his ale. His eyes suggested this was not the first tankard of ale he had consumed, heavy and bloodshot. His head wobbled and he had momentarily lost the power of speech. He was still dressed in his clerk's clothing, but had dispensed with his hat.

"How met!" he managed to reply.

"What's your name, sir?" enquired Wolfe.

"John Murdock," replied the man.

"Would you care for another tankard, Master Murdock? I was about to fill mine."

The man looked at Wolfe and took some moments to consider the question.

"Aye, happen I have the devil of a thirst today," he managed to slur.

He lifted his tankard to his lips; ale dribbled down the side of his mouth and onto the table. He pushed the empty mug towards Wolfe. He took the tankards and went to the serving area for a refill, direct from one of the five hogsheads being used.

He returned to the bench and handed the tankard to the traveller. The man looked at Wolfe and nodded.

"Where are you headed, Master Murdock?" asked Wolfe.

"Oxford, a day's ride, no more."

"Aye, but I heard weather's on the turn. Rain tomorrow."

"Aye?" Murdock was trying to focus. "Happen road will be all the better for it. The dust gets in my throat." He coughed as if to exemplify the condition.

"You are a merchant, perchance?"

There was a long pause as Murdock took another drink. "Nay, sir … King's business."

Wolfe remembered the saddlebag; a tax-collector maybe? Now that would be a prize, make no mistake.

After an hour of limited discourse, Wolfe suggested that the merchant should retire. He was almost asleep.

"Let me escort you to your room, sir."

Murdock managed to stand and staggered to the stairway holding onto Wolfe's arm.

They ascended the stairs; Wolfe taking all the man's weight and reached the corridor which was lit by tar-torches. Murdock was trying to remember his room, but then stopped and opened the door to his right.

"Let me help you, Master Murdock."

Wolfe pushed open the door and helped the man inside. It was a similar room to his own, and there was a lighted candle on the table. Murdock flopped onto the bed and promptly fell into a drunken stupor.

Wolfe looked at the man; then spotted the saddlebag on the floor next to the table. He bent down and checked the contents. One side contained papers and writing material, quills and a bottle of ink; the other, six purses of coin. He wasted no time in transferring the bags into his tunic.

He stood up and looked at the clerk, still comatose. Wolfe was in a quandary, but this was no time for sentiment. He leaned over and placed his hand over the mouth of the unfortunate Murdock; then pinched his nose. There was only a token resistance. It was less than five minutes, his chest stopped moving up and down. Wolfe checked; there was no sign of breathing.

The corridor was deserted as Wolfe closed the door and hurried to his own room. It would be unlikely that Murdock's body would be found before daybreak, but he would take no chances. The further away from Warwick, the safer he would feel.

The room was dark, but there was enough ambient light from the window to see. He transferred the stolen purses into his leather bag, then secured his money belt around his waist. Finally, he checked around and left.

It was gone midnight and the entrance lobby, a hive of activity earlier, was deserted. Candlelight, shone from a room behind the proprietor's desk, providing a modicum of illumination. Wolfe kept in the shadows and made his way to the entrance door. He pulled it open and closed it behind him, hoping he hadn't disturbed anyone.

Wolfe was still on high alert; he was wide awake, driven by adrenaline. He walked the short distance to the stables and found the stall with his mare. The saddle and tack was lay in the straw next to the horse. The mare snorted and nickered at being disturbed; horses in neighbouring stalls followed. The noise seemed loud to Wolfe; he quickly resaddled his mount.

It took a few minutes, but eventually, Wolfe led the horse from the stables the short distance to the road by the reins. He remounted and broke into a trot, heading south; next stop Oxford. It had started to rain.

It was early June 1533, when Wolfe finally entered the city of London via Bishop's Gate. The remainder of the journey had been uneventful. His quest for coin, for the moment, had been satiated; the proceeds from the robbery of John Murdock was substantial, and would keep him in relative comfort for the foreseeable future.

After such a long time away, the peel of the none bells ringing out around the city was a welcome sound, much missed. It was mid-afternoon, and his immediate priority was to find somewhere to stay.

He found a stables near the gate and negotiated a sale of his mare. He would have no requirement of a horse in London. Then, as he walked the streets searching for suitable accommodation, he considered his options. He needed to work; however, he could not return to the Kontor; he was still a wanted man there. Moving back to Cologne had crossed his mind on several occasions during his journey; there was the offer from the brewer, but getting a berth from the Steelyard, again, was not an option. It would mean a trip to one of the other Hanseatic ports.

There were no shortages of boarding houses. He chose

one at random, one that merchants would use, and, having secured accommodation, he sought out an alehouse. He was thirsty from his journey. Tomorrow he would need to buy some new clothes and then search for Alice.

The following morning, Wolfe, worn out by his journey. was awoken, later than normal, by the terce bells. He lifted himself from his bed and groaned. Although his shoulder wound had healed, it still ached, and, after his long journey, the muscles had tightened. He rotated his arm several times to lessen the stiffness.

He made use of the piss-pot and mentally planned the day ahead. His first priority was to replace his clothes; his present attire would not be fit for vagabonds.

He was confident that any hue and cry that had been searching for him would have long since been disbanded, but he would take no chances.

It was with some caution, therefore, that he made his way towards Watling Street, the famous thoroughfare where the gentry would shop, renowned for its woollen cloth and fine tunics.

One thing that hadn't changed since his departure was the smell. The foul petrichor of excrement and rotting vegetables seemed to follow him as he walked the streets. The cobbled roadways were still wet from overnight showers, and dangerous for the many pedestrians that traversed them. He passed a water carrier; his cart laden with jugs. People were lined up with containers to buy their needs for the day.

Half an hour later, he had reached his destination. It was busy, and lined on both sides with tailors' shops and haberdashers. He walked along the street for a few minutes and decided on a more modest-looking emporium which would cater for his needs.

He entered the premises; it was dark and dingy. Stocks of clothes lay around the interior; a man of advancing years was seated in the corner, and quickly made Wolfe's acquaintance.

It took over an hour to replenish his entire wardrobe, with spare tunics, breeches and undergarments. He changed out of his old clothes, and left them with the tailor to dispose.

As he exited the shop he had a thought. Despite his newly acquired attire, he realised his appearance still resembled that of a scoundrel. He stroked his untidy full beard; he hadn't shaved or trimmed it since before leaving for Ireland. It suited his purpose to look fearsome, but now he needed to look the part of a successful merchant.

Barber-surgeons were a common presence; the ubiquitous red and white painted pole could be seen in most areas of London, not that Wolfe had used them frequently. He'd noticed such an establishment en route to the tailor. Armed with his purchases, he entered the nearest, towards the end of Watling Street.

Inside it was eerily quiet. The barber was stood at the back of the establishment sharpening a razor. He was dressed in a leather apron and resembled a smithy.

"Good den, sir," greeted the man.

Wolfe acknowledged and explained his requirements.

The barber indicated a chair, and produced a straight razor. With little formality, the man started trimming Wolfe's beard and locks. Wolfe was pleased with the result and tipped the man a groat on top of the charge, before bidding goodbye.

Buoyed by his new look and purchases, Wolfe headed out of Watling Street towards St Paul's church which dominated the distant skyline. He needed to buy food and wanted to make enquiries about Alice; the alehouses around Carter Street would be a good place to start.

He found the Bell, a tavern he had used before, but not for some time. He was able to get breakfast and a tankard of ale.

He was seated at one of the benches when a familiar face walked in. It was Henry Thornton, Wolfe's former landlord.

Thornton spotted him and joined the table.

"Well, John Wolfe, as I live and breathe, and I thought you would be locked away in a dungeon somewhere … I barely recognised you; you have clearly done well for yourself."

Wolfe stood to greet his friend and there was a semblance of a hug.

"Aye, Henry, happen I were for a while, but here I am, a free man."

Thornton retrieved a tankard of ale and rejoined Wolfe at the table.

"And where have you been since I saw you last?"

"I've been seeking my fortune in Ireland; returned less than a day ago."

"And, pray, it seems you have found your fortune, judging by your fine visage."

Thornton playfully stroked Wolfe's sleeve.

"Nay, the place is as poor as a church mouse." This did little to satisfy Thornton's curiosity.

Wolfe took a drink of his ale and change the subject. "Have you seen Mistress Alice, hereabouts, Henry?"

"Nay, John, not for some time. I heard she had taken church somewhere over east, by the Postern Gate. Been in trouble for lifting, so I heard."

"Ha, sounds like Alice, a most resourceful girl."

The Postern Gate was situated to the north of The Tower and the easternmost gate in the city. Having finished his discourse with Henry Thornton, Wolfe decided to explore that vicinity to see if he could locate Alice.

He had visited several churches without success, but, early afternoon, just after the sext bells, he reached the church of St Magnus the Martyr. It was a large building at the north end of London Bridge, conveniently close to the River Thames, and an important meeting place, where notices were exhibited, proclamations read out, and wrongdoers punished.

He walked up to the front door and went in. There was no service and the large church looked deserted; the alter at the far end was lit by two candles either side. Wolfe strode up the aisle, then noticed a man in the habit of a friar attending to some manuscripts. He approached the cleric.

"Pray, forgiveness for the intrusion, father, I am seeking the whereabouts of a girl who may have claimed sanctuary here, Alice Tankerville."

The priest stopped his labours and looked at Wolfe. He thought for a moment.

"Nay, sir, that name is not familiar to me … Wait, … we have an Alice Wolfe."

"Alice Wolfe? Aye, that will be her."

"She's here, under God's protection."

"Where? I need to find her."

"She's in one of the cottages within the precinct."

"Can you show me father? She'll not be harmed; I swear on the bible."

The priest eyed the visitor up and down, initially with some suspicion, but Wolfe's new appearance earned him a degree of respect. "Hmm, very well, follow me."

They walked back to the entrance, exited the church, and turned right. The friar pointed to a group of three small cottages in front of the boundary wall, adjacent to the graveyard.

"Father," said Wolfe, and gave a nod of his head in reverence.

He walked along the pathway that led to the dwellings.

The cottages were small, thatched, with just a single room on one floor. He reached the first one; the door was open. The inside was dark after the bright sunshine and Wolfe squinted to see inside. There were several straw mattresses scattered around the room. All were occupied.

"Hello, I'm looking for Alice," announced Wolfe from the doorway.

"Her be next door," came a woman's voice in reply.

Wolfe left and went to the next door. Again, it was open, undoubtedly, to provide some respite from the warmth of the sun.

Wolfe could see someone busy spinning. He recognised her straightaway.

"Alice?"

The girl stopped her labours and looked up.

"John!" she exclaimed and left her labours.

She went to Wolfe and immediately the pair embraced.

"I knew you would come; I knew you would find me," she said, trying to hold back tears of joy.

"Come, Alice, you don't belong in any church. You'll be safe with me."

"I will need to see Father Thomas to be released."

"Aye, let's get this done."

"What about my yarn?"

"Leave it for one of the other unfortunates; you won't need it anymore."

They walked back to the church entrance, and Wolfe waited outside while Alice went to secure her release.

She returned a few minutes later and walked side-by-side with Wolfe out of the church yard. There was a period of silence as Wolfe led Alice to his boarding house.

As they reached the lodgings Wolfe turned to her. "How long have you been in church?"

"Two months or thereabouts."

"But why did you seek such shelter?"

"I was accused of lifting by some old sot. He wanted to take me to the magistrate, but I managed to escape before the men-at-arms arrived, and came to the church to claim sanctuary."

"But why? I left you with coin enough."

"Happen Master Bawd had no money to keep me in my normal style."

"So you left him?"

"Aye, I was spinning yarn to earn some coin, but it wasn't enough."

"Well your spinning days are over, Alice. I'll look after you now, and tomorrow we can find somewhere to live; I have coin enough."

Mid-summer, the air was humid as they walked back to the lodgings. Wolfe looked up at the sky; the bright sunshine had been replaced by rolling clouds. "There's a storm due, methinks; we should make haste."

They increased their stride and reached the dwelling before any rain arrived. Wolfe led Alice to the room. It was comfortable enough compared to some Wolfe had stayed. It had wooden shutters as windows, which Wolfe had opened to keep the room cool. Unfortunately, as they entered they were met by swarms of flies. The pair set about clearing the room, splatting the insects as they landed on a surface. Wolfe closed the shutters just as the first clap of thunder echoed around the neighbouring houses.

The rain fell in torrents; the rubbish from the gutters

would be swept away to form fetid puddles where it could escape no further.

Early evening, the vespers bell rang out across the city. Mid-summer, and it was still broad daylight, The storm had abated, replaced by a welcome cool breeze. As a tavern, the accommodation also served food and ale, and, after freshening up, Wolfe and Alice left their room and headed to the alehouse on the ground floor.

There was little discussion about the intervening months, but Alice was keen to learn Wolfe's intentions.

"I have in mind leaving London."

"And go where?" enquired Alice.

"Oxford, maybe … away from the stench and the crowds."

"Why Oxford?"

"Seems a fair city."

"You'll need coin."

"Aye, happen I have coin, but will need more. Methinks a large house."

"Your stay in Ireland has tickled your brain, I fancy. Where will you get coin enough?"

"I'm in no hurry."

The following day, the pair left the temporary accommodation and went in search of a more permanent residence, one with windows, fireplace, and a chimney.

The street was awash with small pools of putrid water left by the storm making walking hazardous. Random piles of litter had formed, swept into the roadside by the rain; it had not improved the stench. After making enquiries in several alehouses, Wolfe and Alice were eventually directed to a property by a weaselly-faced man, Richard Denby, who, it transpired, owned several houses in the area. It was similar to others in the neighbourhood, typical wattle and daub, within a courtyard.

Denby and Wolfe agreed a price for a three-month tenure.

A few weeks passed; Alice had made the dwelling homely, but Wolfe was restless. He had not been able to secure any meaningful work and was not cut out for domesticity. As a result he spent much of his time in different alehouses, while Alice had taken up spinning again to pass the time. His booty from the Warwick theft was dwindling, and any thoughts of escaping London were fading. His mind turned once more, to his alternative means of securing money.

As chance would have it, he was in an alehouse, early afternoon, not far from his new home, frequented by merchants and clerks. Alice was back at the house, cooking. The tavern was busy with the buzz of conversation.

He was seated on a bench on his own, holding a tankard of ale, but in earshot of two men. They were clothed in the style of merchants, but, more elaborately, with dark cloaks. They were speaking in English but with strong accents, and were in dialogue with two other men seated opposite, more conventionally dressed and certainly English. Body language between the four suggested business was being discussed; there was not the jovial countenance as you might see among friends.

He cocked his ear to the exchange. It was not possible to hear all the conversation, but the 'foreign' pair were speaking slowly as if trying to make themselves understood, and Wolfe gleaned enough to make out what was happening. It became clear that there was some negotiation involving a substantial amount of money in payment for a consignment of wool and cloth destined to be shipped to Genoa. As the meeting concluded, the four stood up and bade farewell;

a further meeting had been arranged to finalise the deal in two days' time once the shipment had been examined. The Englishmen left and the two remaining merchants started talking in an unfamiliar tongue.

A few minutes later, a serving wench attended the table and started collecting the empty tankards. She looked at the merchants and addressed them in a jovial manner. "Hello, my lovelies, not seen you in here before."

The merchants looked at her and smiled. "Si, si, er … no … we... er, visit... er, business," said the younger of the two.

"Will we see you again in here?"

There was a pause. "Si, si, er … tomorrow we come, er … to eat … er, same time. We like … er … here, zee food."

"Pleased to hear it, my dears. Tomorrow we do pig roast."

There were looks of confusion. The girl made a snorting noise. The men laughed. "Ah, si we understand … We … er … like that." The merchants looked at each other and spoke in their language.

The girl smiled and took away the empty goblets.

After a few minutes, the pair finished their drinks, stood up, then walked to the exit. Wolfe decided to follow them and quickly tipped back his ale.

It was now dark, but the moon was full and visibility good. The lodgings were only a few streets away and he watched them enter the terraced property, still talking loudly. Wolfe turned and walked back to his dwelling. He was deep in thought. Two days until the money would change hands; he needed a plan.

On return to the house, Wolfe described his encounter to Alice and its potential, his face reflecting excitement. "This could be the chance we have waited for, but I will need your help."

He outlined his plan.

"You will do this, Alice?"

"If it means we can leave London, aye, of course."

The next morning, Wolfe rose just after the terce bells tolled. He had not slept well; his heart was still pounding with the weight of his mission. Timing was crucial for his plan to work.

Alice was still in bed and Wolfe nudged her. "I need to make arrangements; I'll return anon."

"Aye, I'll be ready," she replied.

Wolfe left the house and made his way to the dockside. This was no ordinary task—this was a special assignment that could change everything. As he headed for the river, the early morning sun cast a brilliant glow over the bustling streets, which buzzed with activity even at this hour. Wolfe felt an electric charge in the air as he considered the plan in his mind. A lot was depending on his next meeting.

He reached the dockside. There were numerous wherrymen busy ferrying passengers to and from the quay. He looked at the line of boats; he was searching for one in particular who frequented the same alehouse, and was always complaining about the lack of money. Wolfe had a proposition.

He spotted the boatman waiting for business beside a rather handsome boat which he had customised with decorative cushions and cloth to make it a more comfortable journey for customers. It was not unique; several wherrymen had done the same thing; anything to attract clients. It was quite large and would easily accommodate seven people. The man would be in his early-thirties, long hair, moustache and beard, with rugged features from working outdoors in all weathers. He was dressed in basic tunic and breeches, as most boatmen; it was a warm morning and would only get hotter.

"Good den, Robert, how fairest you?" said Wolfe as he approached.

The boatman looked around. "John Wolfe, verily it has been some time. I fair well. What brings you to the river this morn? Are you seeking passage?"

"Not just yet, Robert, but I have a proposition, for which you will be well-rewarded."

Wolfe outlined his plan. The boatman appeared uneasy.

"What if we are found out?"

"If we follow the plan, that won't happen."

Wolfe took out a purse and took out three crowns, at least three month's work. He handed the coin to the boatman. His eyes lit up.

"There will be more when the deed is done."

"I will need another rower with a full wherry."

"Do you know someone you can trust?"

"Aye, happen I do. Richard Croft, he'll do it."

"I don't know the man," said Wolfe.

"I'd trust him with my life," replied the boatman.

"Aye, very well." Wolfe handed Robert another crown.

"That's for him; tell him to keep his counsel. I will join you here, after the strike of the none bells, and then we will need to go to the Strand dock. Can you do that?"

"Aye, John, we'll be here."

The next part of the plan would involve a two mile journey to the Strand where rooms were available for hire. He decided to walk rather than take a ferry, which would have been quicker, but more expensive. Adjacent to Durham House, the London home of the Bishop of Durham, an episcopal palace where Anne Bolyn was in residence, was a large property known as the Durham rents. Wolfe was aware of it by reputation but had not visited it before. According to rumour, it was where the local harlots would entertain their wealthier clients.

Wolfe reached the building, situated at the back of the palace, a typical terraced property on three floors with a heavy wooden entrance. He pushed it open. There was another door to the left and stairs ascending in front of him. The door opened and a woman of advancing years in a white dress and wimple greeted him. He could hear giggling in the room behind the woman. Wolfe explained his requirements.

"Will you be wanting a girl, dearie? You can choose one of mine."

She pushed open the door and there were six or seven girls in revealing clothing looking at him.

"Just the room, Mistress, if you please."

He paid for a room for the afternoon, then returned to the dwelling to meet Alice.

At just turned midday, Wolfe and Alice walked to the alehouse. If the conversation with the serving wench proved correct, the merchants would be returning for food sometime in the early afternoon.

Alice had dressed alluringly, wearing a touch of makeup; not the garish paint of a common whore, but enough to highlight her natural features. They found a seat and waited. The tavern was busy. There were three glass windows along the left hand side of the drinking area, and the bright sunshine outside bathed the room in some natural light, a welcome change from the dingy candlelight normally associated with alehouses.

There was a fire burning, adding to the outside temperature. Customers were wiping sweat from their brow. Women were cooling themselves with homemade fans. The smell of roast pig permeated the tavern from a spit being turned in front of the fire by a buxom woman.

The sext bells rang. Wolfe looked at Alice, it was half an hour after midday.

"Perhaps they're not coming," said Alice.

"I'll order a tankard; there's no hurry."

Despite the attraction of roast pork, John didn't feel hungry. There were many elements to his plan, many of which could jeopardise the whole enterprise.

Wolfe returned to his bench with two tankards and handed one to Alice. She showed no sign of anxiety and calmly removed a fan from beneath her blouse and started wafting it.

Wolfe was starting to feel the pressure.

"I need a piss," he announced, and left Alice to relieve himself outside.

There were no toilet facilities as such. It was a question of using an area of the outside wall that had been reserved for this purpose.

It was another twenty-five minutes when two figures appeared in the doorway, merchants with extravagant hats, white ruffs, and black cloaks. Alice noticed them straightaway.

"Aye, that's them," said Wolfe, nodding in the direction of the new arrivals.

The pair watched as the men collected their ale and food, then found an empty bench in the corner. It was in shadow, and Wolfe couldn't see what they were doing.

Alice turned to Wolfe. "Leave it to me."

Alice picked up her tankard and walked over to the two men.

"Hello, kind sirs, may I sit with you? It seems room is

scarce," she said, and looked both of them in the eyes.

The men were both eating. They looked at each other. "Er … si … of course, Mistress," replied the younger merchant.

The accent was strong but understandable. Alice put her tankard on the table and sat opposite the men, bending forward to reveal more of her bosom than was normally acceptable.

"Your accent is different, where are you from?"

"We … er … from the … Republica di Genova," said the same man. He would be in his mid-to-late-twenties, olive-skinned and handsome, with a boyish look, his long dark hair falling down below his flamboyant cap.

"I'm Alice, what are your names?"

"Si, I am … Jerome, Jerome De George."

"I am Charles … er, Bench," said the other, older, probably in his thirties, with an impressive moustache.

The pair leaned forward, giving Alice their full attention.

"And what is your business in London, if I may be so bold to ask?"

The pair looked at each other and the elder man spoke.

"Si … we are, er … merchants from Genova; we buy here zee wool and clothing, and, er, we sell oil from the olives."

"Oh how interesting. It must get very lonely travelling."

"Ha, si, that is so," said Jerome. He looked at his colleague and smiled. "Would, er … you like to eat with us?"

"Nay, sir, I have eaten my fill." Alice picked up her tankard and took a sip.

The three continued chatting for some time while they drank their ale. At one point, the younger merchant refilled their tankards. Wolfe was observing the interchange from his bench.

They continued chatting with the conversation gradually becoming more ribald, although how much the merchants understood was debateable. Then, judging the time was appropriate, Alice made her move.

"I have quarters, not a mile hence, if you might prefer a woman's company. We won't be disturbed."

The men looked at each other and smiled. "Si … si," said the elder, and the more senior, of the two.

"Follow me … not twenty minutes," replied Alice.

Wolfe saw them get up and walk towards the exit. Alice turned and nodded to Wolfe and smiled.

Alice knew the whereabouts of the Durham rents, about a mile away from the alehouse, and proceeded to lead the men to The Strand and the room that Wolfe had rented. The sun was beating down and smell from the street was worse than ever, making it difficult to breathe comfortably.

They reached the building and Alice opened the door. Straightaway, the madame appeared. Alice confirmed the reservation, and the woman returned to the room. The merchants followed Alice upstairs to the first floor. There were numbers on the doors. Alice found number seven and opened it. It was basic, just a straw-mattressed bed, piss-pot, and washbasin on top of a chest of drawers.

As the men watched, Alice stood by the bed and started undressing.

It was over an hour since the none bells; Alice had spent the afternoon 'entertaining' the two merchants from Genoa. The men were lay on the bed, both spent.

"It is time we should go," said Alice, as she started dressing. She turned to the men who were also dressing. "I have a wherryman who will take you to your lodgings. It is not far; it is the quickest way," she explained.

The men looked at each other and shrugged their

shoulders, not understanding. Alice explained again using hand signals to aid their comprehension.

"Si, si, we, er … understand. We, er, go with you," said Jerome, and handed Alice a shilling for her services.

Alice thanked the man and placed the coin in her purse.

It was just a ten minute walk downhill to the riverside at the end of The Strand. Alice went ahead of the two men, turning every now and then to ensure they were following. "Nearly there," she encouraged.

The merchants were chatting enthusiastically with broad smiles, undoubtedly recounting their experiences and good fortune.

As they approached the dock, Wolfe was waiting for them. He was dressed as other boatmen, and standing next to a large wherry, holding an oar; two other men were alongside.

Alice gave Wolfe a coin and the wherrymen helped her into the middle of the rowing boat on one of the seats facing the rear. Wolfe then assisted the two merchants on board, and were directed opposite Alice facing forwards. Then, the two ferrymen boarded at the front and placed their oars in the oarlock, facing Alice and the merchants. Wolfe was behind the passengers at the rear holding a tiller.

They were rowing downstream towards London Bridge, some two miles away, at a gentle pace against the tidal flow of the river. To the left, the bank was leafy with willows dipping their boughs in the water. A kingfisher skimmed the water looking for a stickleback.

After a few minutes, the shoreline footpath, which ran parallel to the river, became obscured by a row of low-hanging willow trees. Wolfe looked around for any other wherries in close proximity, checking they were out of sight of any casual observer. The coast was clear; he left the tiller. The two ferrymen continued rowing as Wolfe crept behind the merchants with his dagger drawn. Within a split second he had dispatched the two merchantmen, slitting their throats in turn. Blood spurted in all directions. The two rowers stopped in complete shock and horror.

"What are you doing? I didn't agree to this," protested Croft, the younger oarsman He looked at his colleague who was still in shock.

"Nay, but it's done. Take these for your trouble," said Wolfe, handing them the merchants' purses.

Alice searched them for any keys, and, on one of the merchants, found a metal ring with three attached. She handed them to Wolfe who put them inside his tunic. The pair then trussed up the victims by tying the arms of their tunics together.

Wolfe looked at the oarsmen. "Quickly, we need to rid the boat of the bodies."

The boat rocked as the ferrymen stood up, shaken into action. Between them they managed to tip the men into the fast-flowing Thames without capsizing the boat. The coverlet and cushions were red with blood, having absorbed most of it. Wolfe and Alice continued to clean the surfaces before throwing the soiled cloth over the side.

"Take us back to the quay," ordered Wolfe.

Still in shock at the course of events, the wherrymen complied, turned the boat around, and headed back. As they approached the dock, Wolfe gave them a warning.

"If you know what's good for you, say naught of what you have witnessed today. If word gets out, we will all surely hang."

"Aye," said the pair.

After leaving the rowing boat, Wolfe and Alice found an

alehouse to relax after their exertions; both were high on adrenaline and needed the comfort of a tankard.

It was well after the vespers bell had sounded, dusk was heading into night, before Wolfe felt it was safe to continue their mission. The pair left the tavern and headed to Lambert Hill, and the merchants' dwelling.

It was a warm evening; the failing light meant careful steps, but, eventually, they found the lodgings and approached the front door. Wolfe checked around ensuring no-one was about; there was no-one in sight.

"Give me the keys," whispered Wolfe, and Alice handed him the key ring.

He was about to insert the key when he heard a rustling sound. Alice grabbed his arm. He stopped; his heart beat faster. A large rat scurried past and disappeared down an adjoining alleyway. He checked again, still all clear. He turned the key, opened the door, and they entered the dwelling. It was gloomy and stuffy with an unpleasant smell. There was just one room downstairs and another on the first floor. It was just possible to make out a flight of stairs on the far side of the room.

"There, the stairs," whispered Wolfe.

It was quite dark now, but, in the absence of a candle, they used their hands to guide them to the top of the stairs.

With their eyes adjusted to the light, they could see across the sparce room; there was a large bed, which the men had obviously shared, and, beside it, a trunk. Not bothering to fiddle with the keys, Wolfe opened it with his knife, as he had done with the Steelyard merchant's chest. He felt around, There were six moneybags, he counted, together with various papers, which he discarded. Wolfe collected the purses and handed them to Alice for carrying.

Quickly, the pair left the merchants' lodgings and headed

back to their dwelling. In the pale light of a candle, they opened the purses, enough and more to finance their move to Oxford.

At low tide along the Thames, scavengers would search the mud for anything of value that might have been discarded from a boat or washed up by the tide. Robert Breakshaft was a such a man, and with his son, David, would scour the beaches until the water returned. Two days after the murder, the pair were squelching through the sludge just downriver from London Bridge. The father noticed something being lapped by the river about twenty yards away. It looked like a bundle of rags.

"What be that?" said Robert.

"Let's take a look," replied his son.

They reached the object.

"It be a body. Quick, drag him to the bank."

The pair pulled the body to shore.

"His throat's been cut," observed David,

"Aye, a man of wealth by the looks of him. Here, help with his clothes; he won't be needing them no more."

They stripped the man down to his undergarments. "Come on, let's get home."

Carrying the bundle, father and son quickly left the scene.

It wasn't until later when a watchman passed and saw the body. He looked along the shoreline and could see another man being dragged from the water by two men. On seeing the watchman, they left the body and ran off.

The watchman called for help, and two men who were passing, waded in to assist. Between them they managed to drag the second body along the shoreline to the first body.

"Looks like a merchant," observed one of the men.

"Aye, happen they be those missing merchants from

Genoa we've been told to keep watch for. Wait here, we need a cart," ordered the watchman.

A cart was subsequently requisitioned and the three men loaded the two bodies on board.

The corpses were eventually identified and a hue and cry announced; it was unprecedented. A group from the Genoa and Venice delegations in London demanded to see Cromwell, strongly requesting that action was taken to find the perpetrators, threatening to withhold any transactions until the culprits were found and arrested.

Under pressure from the merchant groups, Cromwell ordered a full investigation and offered a substantial reward for the identification of the criminals.

Two days later, Richard Croft was in an alehouse, buying rounds of drinks and announcing his good fortune. It was just after the sext bells had sounded, early afternoon. Despite pressing from his fellow drinkers, he refused to disclose the source of his change of circumstances. However, it was soon clear the coin had not been earned honestly. With the substantial reward on offer for identity of the perpetrators of the merchants' murder, his name was soon given to the local constable. A squad of men at arms entered the alehouse late afternoon where Croft was still drinking.

He was initially taken to Newgate prison but, after being advised of Croft's capture, Cromwell ordered him to be taken to the Tower.

The following day, Croft was dragged from his cell by two gaolers into a special dungeon with all manner of tools hanging by hooks on the walls. He screamed his innocence as his shirt was ripped from his body. A rope descended from the ceiling. Croft's wrists were bound and the two gaolers pulled on the rope, suspending him until his feet just touched the floor.

A large, hooded man in a leather apron and tunic was stood next to a brazier where a poker was glowing red in its flames. Another man in the robes of a lawyer was stood next to him.

He spoke in harsh tones. "We know it was you who killed the merchants, Master Croft, but we know you did not act alone. Who were your accomplices?"

Croft continued to scream his innocence again.

The torturer pulled the poker from the fire and pressed it into Croft's back. A piercing scream echoed around the dungeon. Croft passed out. One of the gaolers retrieved a pale of water and threw it over the unfortunate boatman. As he came round, the torturer acted again, this time lower. There was a sizzling sound and the smell of burning flesh.

The lawyer moved closer. "I say again, who were your accomplices? We can continue this all day. I think the privates are next … Gaoler, remove his breeches."

The man pulled down Croft's breeches and undergarments. The torturer moved forward and pressed the poker into Croft's buttocks. The scream would be heard throughout the prison.

"Wait, wait … stop … " Croft was sobbing bitterly. "I will … tell you … everything."

The lawyer approached him. "Go on."

He listened as Croft explained, in faltering terms, the approach by Robert Hall, his fellow wherryman, an opportunity to earn coin. "I didn't know they were going to kill them, verily. Robert said they were just going to rob them."

"Who else was involved?"

"It was John Wolfe; he slit their throats like a pig... I was in fear for my life, sir; verily, I thought he was going to kill me as well. He was with a woman; they call her Alice."

Satisfied with the interrogation, the lawyer ordered the guards to drag Croft back to his cell. He was in a bad way. Left without food and very little water in the most unsanitary of conditions, the wounds from the torture would eventually turn sceptic leading to a slow and painful death.

Wolfe and Alice, in the meantime, continued planning for their departure. The haul from the merchants had amounted to over forty crowns which was more than enough to give them a new start.

They were returning from a visit to the market to buy supplies for their journey, and had reached the street which contained their dwelling, when Wolfe noticed a squad of armed soldiers walking ahead of them. His blood ran cold. He stopped and put his arm out to prevent Alice from moving forward.

"What is it?" asked Alice.

"Men-at-arms, must be twelve or more."

They watched from the shadows of the houses opposite as the men drew their swords and knocked aggressively on their front door. They forced it open and went inside.

Alice was in a state of shock. "What do we do?"

"We need to get to a church," replied Wolfe.

"What about our coin?"

"Too late, we need to get away from here."

"I am sure Father Thomas will grant us shelter; he was very kind to me," said Alice.

The couple turned and headed for St Magnus the Martyr, where Alice had been staying.

A search of Wolfe's cottage produced irrefutable evidence of their involvement in the robbery. Two money bags bearing the name of Jerome De George were dicovered hidden under the bed.

A manhunt was ordered.

Wolfe and Alice, meanwhile, had reached the church and presented themselves to Father Thomas. As was required, they confessed their acts of felony in the eyes of God, and were granted asylum.

The hue and cry continued, and a further reward was offered for information leading to the capture of Wolfe and Alice, which prompted many false leads.

Following Croft's confession, Robert Hall was arrested and taken to the Tower. He, too, was brutally tortured, but was unable to provide any further information on the Wolfes's possible whereabouts. In frustration, the torturer inserted the poker into Hall's rectum. The pain caused Hall's heart to give in. Death came as a welcome release.

Several weeks had passed, without success. It was the largest manhunt for many years. Notices were displayed in every alehouse, and nightly armed visits took place. Wolfe had been a familiar face in many alehouses, and known haunts were raided with many men taken in for questioning.

Having scoured the alehouses without any result, a routine search of the local churches was ordered by Cromwell, under pressure from the Genoan delegation.

Eventually, the men-at-arms arrived at St Magnus's Church.

The sergeant at arms approached the door and knocked with the handle of his sword. Father Thomas answered.

"We seek the whereabouts of John Wolfe and his harlot." He spoke aggressively.

"We are a place of sanctuary; I cannot disclose our guests."

"Guests!? The pair are vicious murderers. You would give them protection?"

"They are under the protection of The Lord, sir," replied the Friar.

"So, they are here?"

"As I said they are under God's protection. They cannot be harmed or taken."

"We'll see about that," said the sergeant.

He turned and led his squad away, but left a small contingent to guard the church,

The Master-at-arms returned to Westminster to report back to Cromwell. Wolfe and Alice's hiding place had been dicovered.

The lobbying of the Genoan merchants, important trading partners with London, to trace and punish the murderers, had reached the ears of the King, and Cromwell was sought to see how the matter could be brought to a speedy conclusion.

It was a private audience at Greenwich Palace in the King's lavish personal chamber. At the meeting, Henry was seated on his throne, while Cromwell outlined the issue with which they were faced.

"Sire, we have strong evidence that a known felon, John Wolfe and his mistress Alice Tankerville were responsible for the murder of the two Genoan merchants."

"I see, and what do we know of this man Wolfe, Crom?" asked the King.

Cromwell spoke in solemn tones, as he was often inclined to do, giving gravitas to his narrative.

"His name is known to me, sire. As I recall, he was imprisoned in the Tower some time ago, accused of the theft of gold coins, but was proved innocent. It seems, according to my sources, he was recently returned from Ireland. I understand he was working for Lord Kildare."

"Kildare? That treacherous snake." The King became animated. "So, what's to be done?"

"Sire, we have a dilemma. Wolfe and his mistress are in protection of the church."

"Sanctuary? But why can't you just arrest them; they are murderers. The church can't protect them, surely."

"It's not so straightforward, sire. You may recall the case of Bull and Roo last year."

The King looked at Cromwell inquisitively. "Remind me again, Crom."

"Two burglars, Maurice Bull and Nicholas Roo, you may recall, sire, yeomen … using the protection of the church while continuing to commit felonies." The King frowned. Cromwell continued. "They were caught in the act and brought before the court of King's Bench to answer for their crimes, but claimed their right to sanctuary."

"Ah yes." The King nodded in recollection.

"Yes, sire, two juries, no less, upheld the sanctity of the Church in protecting felons. It's a case etched in my mind."

"A felon's charter, no less," replied the King.

"Yes, sire. It gives leave to all manner of miscreants to escape justice."

"We can't allow this Wolfe to escape justice. What's to be done?"

"I have been giving it some thought, sire, and I do have a solution."

"Pray, tell."

"You will recall the case of Elizabeth Barton?"

"Ha, the Witch of Kent!"

"Indeed, sire, she, too, was claiming the protection of the church, but it was resolved by Parliamentary attainder. Parliament passed a law giving leave for the woman to be arrested."

The King's eyes indicated recall. "Ah yes, I remember such an instance."

"Then we will apply the same principle. Now there's a precedence; it will be passed by Parliament, of that, I am certain."

"So be it, Crom. Inform me of the outcome."

"Sire."

The Lord Privy Seal bowed reverentially and made his exit.

It was early January and the winter snows had appeared by the time the Act of Parliament condemning the Wolfes was passed. It specifically barred them from being able to claim either sanctuary or benefit of clergy. The pair were sentenced to death in their absence.

For Wolfe and Alice the last three months had proved difficult. Their modest accommodation within the church grounds was cold and damp. It was just one room, with straw for bedding and no washing facilities. Wolfe's shoulder injury from the crossbow bolt had long since healed, but the poor conditions caused his muscles to stiffen; he was in constant pain. They had fled with just the coin on their person which had long run out, so food had not been plentiful. However, the main problem was boredom. They were reluctant to attempt to leave the church, as discovery would mean certain arrest. So visits to alehouses were things of the past. Long days sat huddled around a fire trying to keep warm was not the future they had envisaged.

With the situation desperate, Wolfe made a decision. It was another evening, following a day of inactivity. Outside, the temperature was below freezing, making the humble dwelling unbearably cold. The pair were still clothed in the garments they were wearing when they sought sanctuary.

"I have been much in thought," said Wolfe, standing up to give his legs some movement.

"Aye, it seems so," replied Alice, with little energy. "Pray what's on your mind."

"Happen, we'll die here if we spend more days in this hovel. We're prisoners in all but name."

"You have a plan, John?"

"Aye, on the morrow we will take our chances. If we move swiftly, we can reach the Postern gate. With good fortune, we can find a purse to lift, and with coin, we can leave London."

It was the semblance of a plan formulated in desperation; they were unaware that the church was being guarded.

However, before they could action any escape plan, events overtook them. With the Act of Parliament now passed, the following day, a squad of armed men trudged through the lying snow to St Magnus church. The Master-at-arms led a contingent to the church door. A friar answered the urgent knock.

"I call on the King's business. I need the whereabouts of John Wolfe; he's under arrest."

"Wait," said the friar, and Father Thomas was called. Moments later he appeared at the door.

"I am Father Thomas," he introduced himself. "What's this I hear about an arrest. These people are under God's protection."

"Not anymore. I have an order here for their arrest, by the Grace of His Majesty, King Henry."

He was holding a parchment which he handed to the clergyman. Father Thomas read the dictum and looked up.

"Very well. You will find them in the first cottage." He pointed in the direction.

The squad marched to the indicated cottage with swords drawn with snow clinging to their boots. Before Wolfe and Alice could do anything, they were dragged from their quarters, protesting vehemently, and escorted off the church premises.

This time there would be no escape.

Chapter Seventeen

A horse and two-wheeled cart was waiting at the church gates, and the pair were lifted onto the back, their hands and feet tied. Two men-at-arms joined them on board. The pair remained standing as the cart slowly trundled its way towards the Tower. The pair shivered, not just because of the cold, icy air, but the apprehension of what lay ahead.

Late January 1534, and the road was pitted with compacted snow and ice, making the journey hazardous. Bystanders watched the sight; speculation mounted about who the couple were and what were their crimes. One or two threw rubbish and excrement at the cart. It was a common sight for felons to be paraded through the streets; public executions attracted large crowds.

They were taken directly to the Tower, where the pair were separated. Alice was taken to a dungeon and shackled to the walls by her hands and feet with iron manacles, with only a slither of light from the tiny, barred window of the heavy oak door. The flickering flame of the tar-torch outside the cell door provided the only illumination.

Word of the Wolfe's capture reached the ears of her former gaoler, John Bawd. On hearing the news, he set about having his duties reassigned to enable him to be closer to his former lover. Alice was being held in Coldharbour Tower, the inmost Tower ward, and not easily accessible. Built by Henry III, two centuries earlier, to protect his royal palace, the Coldharbour Gate was defended by huge cylindrical turrets. In order for anyone to get to Alice's cell, they would need to first pass through Middle Tower, Byward Tower, and Bloody Tower.

It was the early February by the time Bawd was able to

make his first visit. He reached Alice's dungeon and was horrified to see her shackled and chained. The cell was dark and cold; the smell took his breath away.

"Alice?" he said, as he reached her.

She appeared to be sleeping, hanging from the wall. Bawd hardly recognised her; her clothes were dirty and soiled, and hung from her frame from weight loss.

Her eyes opened and focussed. "John Bawd? Is that you?" she managed to whisper.

"Aye, Alice, let me remove your chains."

Bawd unlocked the shackles, and she dropped to the floor. Straw was scattered around the sparse cell scarcely sufficient to make a bed. Alice lay in a heap hardly able to move.

"Don't worry Alice, I will soon have you comfortable."

He left the cell and returned a few minutes later with some food and a cloak. As her gaoler, he had a certain amount of discretion on her incarceration. It was of little interest to his colleagues, and he set about making her life more comfortable.

Over the next two weeks, Alice's condition improved under the care of her former lover, and she gradually regained her strength. Bawd had managed to find fresh clothes and bedding, ensuring she had plenty of food. He spent most of his day, when not on his rounds, in her cell. He had lit candles to provide light.

In another part of the Tower, Wolfe had not fared so well. He, too, had been shackled in his cell with no sympathetic gaoler to attend him. Once news of his crimes was known, life became extremely hard. He had been regularly beaten with clubs; food was no more than subsistence level. He was allowed to use the bucket once a day. On several occasions it was tipped over his head once it had been used.

Early March, and Bawd opened the door to her cell and the pair embraced.

"Alice, I cannot bear to see you being in here any longer; it grieves me beyond all measure to see you locked away like this."

"But what can we do? They will have my head when it suits their cause." Alice put her hands to her face in despair.

"Fear not, Alice, I have been working on a way to relieve you of this hardship."

"What say you? Escape, you mean?"

"Aye, I have an idea. I have been sleepless considering this."

Bawd outlined the details of his plan.

"But will this work?"

"Aye, with God's grace and good fortune."

"When do you suggest?"

"The next moonless night. I will see everything is ready."

The afternoon of the twenty-third of March, Bawd arrived at Alice's cell with a heavy hessian bag over his shoulder. Alice greeted Bawd and straightway was intrigued by his accoutrement.

"Pray, what do we have here, John?"

"We go tonight; everything is ready."

He tipped out the contents of his bag, a thirty foot length of rope, a duplicate key, and an oiled stick, shaped as a wedge. There were also more clothes and a dark cloak.

"Now, listen well, Alice."

Bawd went to some lengths to explain the plan in detail, and made sure Alice understood what was to happen. He nervously repeated it again; the stakes were high. As she listened, her mood changed and her spirit returned as the possibility of escape appeared real.

"You must wait until the warder has made his final round and then leave. I have arranged horses, and a cottage beyond the city gates where we can wait until the search has stopped. Then I have a mind to escape to France."

"Oh, John, pray to God it can come true."

"Aye, I'll be waiting."

The next few hours seemed to pass as slowly as anytime Alice could remember. She was hunched up in the corner of her cell. She had changed into the new clothes that Bawd had provided, which were more in keeping with a merchant's wife. She wrapped the cloak around her to keep warm. Alice tried to sleep but it was illusive. Bawd had brought in more straw, but it was still insufficient to ensure a restful night. The noises of the Tower were intrusive and frequent; screams of the tortured echoed around the corridors. The shivers of anxiety returned.

The concept of time in a room with no daylight proved difficult. Each noise represented an alert that could signal the start of her attempt to escape. Then she heard the unmistakeable sounds of footsteps, coming closer, then disappearing after they had passed her door. This was it.

She tipped out the contents of Bawd's bag. She looked at the tools she would need and focussed. First, the wedge. Bawd had oiled it and she remembered the instructions. She went to the door of her cell and forced the piece of wood under the door, pushing it as hard as she could. Slowly, the heavy wooden door lifted off its hinges. She pushed again with her foot until the door gave way and hung to one side, giving Alice enough space to walk through.

She replaced the contents and picked up the bag, wrapped the cloak around her, and headed through the gap.

The corridor was dimly lit by tar-torches every twenty

yards or so, casting menacing shadows that seemed to dance and writhe. Alice crept along the wall, her breath shallow and fearful. She dragged the heavy bag, its weight slowing her progress. Within fifty yards, she had reached the Coldharbour Gate, an imposing iron barrier that loomed ominously, barring her escape.

She stopped for a moment, looked around, and listened; it was eerily quiet, just the ambient sounds of the Tower. She removed the duplicate key from the bag. Her hands were shaking so much she could hardly hold it, but after two tries, managed to guide it into the lock. She started to turn it, but it was stiff. She used both hands but still it wouldn't turn. She was beginning to panic; she could hear her own heart beating. Then, she took the end of her cloak to give her a better grip and tried again.

This time there was movement. Alice used all her strength to turn the key, then felt the lock drop and the handle turned. She quickly passed through the gate and closed it behind her. In front of her was a series of descending stone steps, which Bawd had described. She couldn't remember them from her journey to her cell; that was just a blur.

She reached the bottom and walked through the archway onto the outer wall close to Beauchamp Tower. Bawd was waiting. She dropped the bag and rushed to him.

"John, you are there."

"Aye, we must be quick before the watchmen return their rounds. Do you have the rope?" he whispered.

"Aye."

Alice handed Bawd the bag and he retrieved the rope. He coiled it around one of the stone balustrades and tied it off, then pulled hard to ensure it would take the weight. He threw the loose end over the side of the wall to the edge of the moat.

"I'll go first and wait for you below," he whispered.

Bawd scaled the parapet and gently lowered himself the thirty feet to the ground. There was less than a yard distance between the Tower wall and the water. He scanned the area, still no sign of guards. "Now Alice," shout-whispered Bawd.

Alice wrapped her cloak around her and anxiously peered over the top. It looked a long way down; she panicked momentarily. "Hurry, Alice, we have to go now," said Bawd, and gesticulated wildly with his hands. "Don't worry, I'll catch you."

She hitched up her skirts and climbed onto the parapet; her legs were shaking so much she could hardly stand. Her eyes adjusted to the available light. The dark moat shimmered below, just the stars reflecting on the surface. She could see a small rowing boat secured by a rock to the bank a short distance away. The heavy rope was rough, hessian, but offered a good grip.

Alice took the strain and nervously climbed over the parapet. She looked down and could see Bawd holding the rope. She started gently lowering herself down; hand over hand. Her descent was slow and ungainly; her skirts were proving a hazard, catching on the rope, but, using all her strength, she reached the ground. Bawd grabbed her before she lost balance and fell back into the icy water.

Leaving the rope, Bawd led Alice to the boat and steadied it so she could get in, then he stepped aboard and pushed it away from the bank. Quietly he pulled the oars, giving the boat some forward momentum, then stopped. The boat glided a few yards, then Bawd pulled again. Although the moat was not particularly wide, it was deep, designed to deter any invading army; it had successfully done that for several centuries.

Bawd slowly dipped and pulled his oars, gently easing

the boat along the dark waters below the walls towards the back of the Tower, where it was not guarded. He saw the spot he was looking for, and pulled into the bank on the opposite side. He scrambled out of the boat and helped Alice up the steep incline.

There was a dirt footpath leading away from the moat across East Smith Field ahead of them. It would take them to Hog Lane - a bridleway, and the route to their destination.

Bawd placed his arm around Alice, as lovers might do. Her cloak was wrapped around her shoulders and covered her head like a bonnet. In five minutes they had reached Hog Lane and walked briskly along the wide path away from The Tower. Bawd continued glancing over his shoulder to make sure they weren't being followed.

"Not far now, Alice," Bawd whispered after ten minutes.

The sense of relief was overwhelming; her anxiety had been replaced by determination.

They continued walking and reached a bend in the lane; it was lined with trees, their branches swayed in the night breeze.

Then Bawd stopped in his tracks. In front of them, a group of six armed watchmen approached them; their armour and swords rattled as they marched. The leading soldier was carrying a lantern to light the way. They had seen the couple. Bawd had no option but to continue. He avoided any eye contact as he passed the squad. Alice had her head covered by the cloak.

They had passed the group, when one of them stopped.

"Wait, that's Alice Tankerville," said the last watchman.

The troop quickly drew their swords and surrounded the couple. One of the men grabbed Alice's cloak and pulled it down from her face and lifted the lantern. "By God, so it is … and John Bawd, no less. You are both under arrest."

The pair were marched back to the Tower; both knew their fates were sealed.

Alice was returned to her cell, and, this time, the shackles were tightened and heavier. There would be no reprieve.

Sir Edmund Walsingham was informed of the escape, and he ordered a full investigation into the circumstances. He decreed that an example was to be made of Bawd to deter other possible collaborators.

John Bawd's punishment was severe. He was initially placed in an oubliette in Wakefield Tower, a small stone indent with a metal grill, known as 'Little Ease'. It was rightly named; the dimensions would not allow either standing or sitting, meaning his knees were bent at an angle, causing excruciating pain.

He was kept in that hole for three weeks with little in the way of food or water. He was eventually released and dragged from his confinement to the dungeon where special treatment would be administered. There would be no clemency.

He was in a pitiful state, painfully thin and unkempt. Without toilet facilities, his clothes were soiled. Two gaolers held him. In front of Bawd, the rack.

As a gaoler, Bawd was familiar with the apparatus and its potential for exacting pain. He screamed for mercy, but his cries were in vain.

The wooden frame was slightly raised a foot or so from the ground, and he was secured by his wrists to the top. Bawd's legs were splayed wide and his ankles chained to a roller at the foot of the device. One of his former gaoler colleagues turned a handle to the ratchet mechanism which gradually retracted the chains, slowly increasing the strain on Bawd's shoulders, hips, knees, and elbows. Bawd's screams echoed the corridors of the Tower, even reaching the Lord Lieutenant's ears.

They continued stretching Bawd's limbs until they burst out of their sockets; sinews snapped, muscles torn. Pain unimaginable, he lost unconsciousness.

They waited for him to come round. "Mercy, I beg you have mercy," he uttered weakly.

His shackles were removed but this was no reprieve. His tormentors tore what was left of his clothes from his body until he was naked.

Fear and abject misery etched his face, not knowing what was happening next. For a moment he thought he was being carried back to a cell, but, instead, they turned and dragged him to the high battlements. A chain was attached to one of the parapets. His arms were tethered together and attached to the other end of the chain. Two gaolers picked him up and dropped him over the side. His body jerked as the extent of the chain was reached, leaving him hanging in mid-air.

There was a final plea for help, but his cries were ignored. He would eventually die of exposure before the carrion would feast on his rotting corpse.

With Alice Tankerville and John Wolfe in custody, there was a discussion involving Sir Edward Walsingham on how their death sentences should be carried out.

On the thirty-first of March 1533, two men at arms opened Alice's dungeon. She was still chained and hung down, suspended by her arms. She was surrounded by bits of straw; it was bitterly cold; there was no bucket. Her shackles were release and she dropped to the floor. She was roughly bundled to her feet and dragged from the cell. In another part of the Tower, Wolfe was given the same treatment.

With scarcely any food or water, both were in deplorable condition; their clothes reduced to mere rags. Four guards, armed with swords, hauled the pair down the stone steps all the way to the Tower's base. Heavy clouds, with drizzle in the air, greeted the party as they reached bottom of the ramparts. The Thames' ominous grey waters lapped menacingly at the fortifications. It was low tide, the gaolers squelched through the thick clawing mud as they cruelly chained the pair to the stone foundations. Neither resisted; both were barely conscious, too feeble and drained of strength to fight back.

Wherrymen along the river, seeing the activity, lined up to watch what was happening. Word of the event soon circulated, and, with the rising tide, more ferries arrived carrying paying customers, lining up to watch the final moments of Alice Tankerville and John Wolfe, until the icy waters took their last breaths.

THE END

A Note From the Author

There are many interpretations of the story of Alice Tankerville and John Wolfe, however there is a great deal of inconsistency and many accounts are plainly inaccurate. Although this is a fictional story, I have tried to piece together a dramatised version of a likely timeline of events based on extensive research.

The incident relating to the gold crowns is of particular note; the money has never been discovered. But it begs the question, why would the Hanseatic League send Henry V111 such a large sum of money (around a million pounds in today's value), when they were embroiled in an expensive war with the Papal States, with towns in Eastern Pomerania under siege? I concluded that a ruse as described in the narrative was entirely plausible, if not, probable.

Finally, I have deliberately not used Olde English as the primary dialogue because it would not have been easily understood (or easy to read), but I have tried to create the appropriate ambience by using certain words and phrases of the period and avoiding modern day parlance.

Alan Reynolds, April 2025

Dramatis Personae

Gerald Fitzgerald – 9th Earl of Kildare. Was twice married and had eight children. He held two important positions in Ireland - Lord High Treasurer of Ireland (1504–1514) and Lord Deputy of Ireland (1515-1518; 1524-1529). In 1534 he was again summoned to court, and returned to London in poor health. On his arrival, he was arraigned on several charges and imprisoned in the Tower of London where he died on 12 December 1534 aged forty-six (or seven).

Thomas Fitzgerald – 10th Earl of Kildare. In October 1535, having renounced his allegiance to King Henry V111, he led a rebellion and stormed Dublin Castle. The uprising was eventually crushed and he surrendered to the new Lord Deputy of Ireland, Lord Grey, on assurance that he would not be executed. He was taken to London as a prisoner, to the Tower of London. Despite Lord Grey's guarantees, he was executed along with his five uncles at Tyburn, London, on 3 February 1537 aged just twenty-four.

William Fitzwilliam, First Earl of Southampton - he acted as "enforcer" for King Henry VIII in the fall of the King's wives, Anne Boleyn and Catherine Howard; the Pilgrimage of Grace, and the Exeter Conspiracy. In 1539, as Admiral, he conveyed King Henry's future fourth wife, Anne of Cleves, from Calais, and on first meeting her, wrote letters in her praise to the King. From 1540, William Fitzwilliam was a capable Lord Privy Seal until his death in 1542 in Newcastle.

George Talbot - 4th Earl of Shrewsbury - He supported the King's divorce and gave evidence at Catherine of Aragon's trial.

He signed the letter to the pope urging him to grant the divorce. He also signed the articles against Cardinal Thomas Wolsey in 1529 which eventually led to the Cardinal's execution. He died in 1538 at the age of seventy.

Georg Giese - After returning to his home city of Danzig, in 1535, he married Christine Krüger, daughter of a prominent Danzig merchant, Tiedemann Krüger, and grand-daughter of the Mayor of Torin. The couple had ten children. Giese died on 3 February 1562 in Danzig aged sixty-four.

Thomas Cromwell (c1485 – 28 July 1540) - He married Elizabeth Wyckes in 1515 and had three children with her before she died in 1529. He served as chief minister to King Henry VIII from 1534 to 1540 but fell from power in 1540, despite being created Earl of Essex that year, after arranging the King›s marriage to the German princess Anne of Cleves. The marriage was a disaster for Cromwell, ending in an annulment six months later. Cromwell was beheaded on orders of the king, in what was considered to be a plot by fellow Lords.

Sir Edmund Walsingham was appointed Lieutenant_of the Tower of London at a stipend of £100 a year in 1520, a position he held until Henry VIII's death in 1547. In the 1530s Walsingham acquired long-term leases of the manors of Tyting in Surrey and Stanground in Huntingdonshire, and in 1543 purchased the manors of Swanton Court, West Peckham and Yokes near Scadbury. In 1539, after the Dissolution of the Monasteries, the king granted him nine houses in London that were former monastic property. He was twice married and had eight children by his first wife, Katherine. He died in 1550 at the age of seventy.

Sir William Skeffington (c.1465 – 31 December 1535) He was appointed Lord Deputy of Ireland in 1529 at the age of sixty-four after a distinguished career serving both Henry V11 and Henry V111. He was married twice and had a number of children.

Alan Reynolds

After a successful banking career, award-winning author Alan Reynolds started a training company in 2002, managing projects across the UK, Europe, and the Middle East. His interest in psychology and human behaviour, along with his leadership training, influenced the strong characters in his books. Initially writing as a hobby, he completed his first novel, 'Flying with Kites', in just three weeks. Positive reviews led him to pursue writing full-time. Drawing inspiration from real-life events, Alan creates fast-paced, engaging fiction across various genres including adventure, romance, and historical drama.